Praise for

"This collection is fantastic! The characters and plot are fully developed, the pace is fast and the sex is hot."

— *RT Magazine*

"*Doms of Dark Haven* is an edgy, erotic anthology that is satisfying to read."

— Shayna, *Joyfully Reviewed*

A Recommended Read! "This anthology was nothing short of a masterpiece. I thoroughly enjoyed all three stories, enough to stay up past bedtime, unable to put the book down."

— Sin, *TwoLips Reviews*

5 Hearts! "Multi-talented authors Belinda McBride, Cherise Sinclair and Sierra Cartwright know how to please and set the tone creating sizzling hot stories that seduce the reader into a world of dark sensuality where domination and submission prevail."

— Shannon, *The Romance Studio*

5 Stars and a Top Pick! "Awesome book and a great way to spend a summer afternoon or a stormy night or just about any time."

— Terri, *Night Owl Romance Reviews*

"If you're in the market for some blistering hot erotic romance, *Doms of Dark Haven* is just the ticket."

— Fern, *Whipped Cream Reviews*

Loose Id®

ISBN 13: 978-1-61118-918-6
DOMS OF DARK HAVEN

Cover Art by April Martinez
Cover Layout and Design by April Martinez

Printed in the U.S.A. by
Lightning Source, Inc.
1246 Heil Quaker Blvd
La Vergne TN 37086
www.lightningsource.com

Contents

MET HER MATCH

(A Hawkeye Story)

Sierra Cartwright

Chapter One

Torin Carter snarled and pushed his way through the crowd.

Three weeks ago he'd been assigned a partner he didn't want: Mira Araceli.

Despite the fact he didn't want to be teamed with anyone, especially a female, Torin believed in rules, and he was inflexible in his adherence to them.

If Hawkeye, in his infinite wisdom, had decided Torin and the so-sexy-he-was-going-to combust Mira were stuck together, they were stuck together. And that meant he had to keep his legendary libido in check. He'd been doing okay, that was until Mira had shed her clothes and exposed her pretty little ass and freshly shaved pussy to him two nights ago.

He curled his right hand into a fist when he finally found her.

His partner was strapped over a spanking bench, her long, Victorian-style gown and a stupid number of layers of ruffled lace were tossed over her waist. Not only were her delectable, round butt cheeks completely exposed, but she was being flogged by Blake Miller.

Thank God she had on a very modern thong; otherwise he would have had no control of his fraying temper.

Torin had nothing personal against the puny man—well, besides the fact he was wielding a leather flogger that was turning Mira's butt pink.

He'd only seen Mira's naked rear once. Because her body aroused him so much, it had taken him less than thirty seconds to jack off after he'd tossed her out of his bedroom.

Blake caught her full on with the flogger, and her hips swayed from side to side. Little vixen obviously loved getting spanked.

His momentary relief at actually finding her faded and became a torch of anger directed as much at Blake as at her.

Right now Torin Carter was a dangerous man.

"Only five more, pet," Blake said. He drew back his arm again and soundly smacked Mira with the leather straps.

Mira rose up as much as the restraints allowed, and arched her back.

Even from a few feet away, Torin had heard the difference in the intensity of the stroke. Blake was taking Mira to more extreme pain levels. From her reaction, the blow had clearly stung as it was meant to.

Fury overcame reason.

Through the years, he'd played with dozens of women, most of them at this club. He'd enjoyed showing up and having a new woman kneel at his feet each time. But this was different. This was Mira.

Despite Dark Haven's rules, despite the fact his partner was obviously a willing participant, Torin acted.

He grabbed the smaller man's wrist. If Torin exerted a bit more downward pressure, the man would be on his knees. Still more and the bones in Miller's wrist would snap. Part of Torin wished the other man would give him the excuse. "Playtime's over, Blake."

Mira obviously recognized the sound of his voice, and she froze, becoming silent and still. Smartest thing she'd done today. Today? Make that in the past three weeks.

Torin glanced at the gathering crowd. There were plenty of doms and subs captivated by the scene he was creating. Waiters and waitresses continued on their rounds, too highly trained to stop and gawk. A dungeon monitor stopped nearby, his arms folded across his chest.

Everyone but Torin was dressed for the evening's Charles Dickens theme. In his fury, he'd stormed past Destiny at the door. Bad-mannered, ill-tempered bastard that he was, he'd ignored the club's theme night and Destiny's protests that he couldn't come inside. He'd cut the receptionist, in her revealing and attractive purple formal wear, a quick don't-fuck-with-me smile. She'd set her mouth in a frown that showed off her lip piercing perfectly.

Now, deep inside the caverns of Dark Haven, he realized he looked completely out of place. Instead of a fancy frock coat, he was wearing jeans, uncivilized boots, and a brown leather bomber jacket. Not that he cared.

His focus was totally on the immobile woman strapped to the spanking bench. "Move along, boys and girls," he said to the doms and the couple of dommes who were still staring.

"Trouble?"

Xavier, legendary owner of San Francisco's Dark Haven dungeon, calmly walked over; the crowd parted to let him through.

"Carter interrupted my scene." Blake all but sputtered the words as he struggled to pull away.

After flicking a nonexistent speck of dirt from his elegant black frock coat, Xavier studied Torin. "By 'Carter,' you mean Master Torin?" Xavier asked, maintaining decorum. Despite the tension, no matter what kind of tension, Xavier never raised his voice. Trouble in the club was handled professionally, defused by the power of the man's mystery and magnetism.

Torin struggled to maintain his own composure. He was accustomed to being in charge, alpha even in a pack of alphas. But here, Xavier was law. Torin met the more controlled man's eyes.

Blake—Torin wasn't one to extend the courtesy of addressing the man as Master Blake, no matter what Xavier insisted—had to tip back his head to look at them both.

"The woman Blake's beating—"

"Sub," Blake interrupted. "At Dark Haven, she's a sub."

"The *woman*," Torin corrected, tightening his grip inexorably, "is my partner. As such, she is under my care and protection." More than anyone, Xavier would understand what that meant.

"Fine job you're doing of taking care of her," Blake said.

Torin exerted a bit more pressure. The other man paled.

"No one, *no one*, but me touches her," Torin said.

Mira struggled against her bonds and made tiny mewing sounds. Since she wasn't shooting off her mouth, she was obviously gagged. At least that was one smart thing Blake had done. Gagging the unruly Ms. Araceli was a supremely good idea. Torin should have done it weeks ago.

With his left hand, Torin flipped the material of her dress back down, covering her ass. Even though she was wearing a scrap for panties, he could tell she was dripping with arousal. Dear God, he couldn't wait to get her alone.

"Maybe we should ask the sub what she wants," Blake said.

"Excellent idea," Xavier said.

Torin disagreed. Asking her anything was a bad idea. God only knew what she'd say when that gag came out of her mouth.

He hoped, for both their sakes, that she was as intelligent as he believed. If not, trouble was already on slow boil.

Xavier waved over the young blond dungeon monitor.

With a nod to acknowledge the order, the man moved toward Mira.

Torin struggled against the instinctive caveman act. He wanted to be the one to detach her from the bondage. He wanted to toss her over his shoulder, drag her back to the safety and seclusion of the Hawkeye house where they were training together then he would soundly beat her himself.

She'd been asking for it since they'd become partners.

Torin realized it was partially his fault she was here in the first place. But damn it, he'd had no idea how serious she was about getting her desires met.

Having no choice at this point but to follow Dark Haven's protocol, he watched as the dungeon monitor systematically unhooked the clips that held her firmly against the leather spanking bench.

“Master Torin, you can release Master Blake,” Xavier said. His tone brooked no disagreement.

Reluctantly Torin loosened his grip. “Drop the flogger,” he told Blake.

“I—”

“If you don't,” he said with a quick smile, “you're giving me a reason to break your wrist.”

Elegant, calm, in control, Xavier nodded toward another dungeon monitor. The man moved in and extended a hand toward Blake. The dom glared at Torin before turning over the flogger.

“Now release Master Blake,” Xavier said to Torin, his tone still not wavering.

Slowly Torin followed instructions.

Blake rubbed his bruised skin. Torin had a moment of regret that the man's wrist was still functional.

The dungeon monitor helped Mira from the bench and held on to her arm for a few seconds, obviously giving her time to catch her bearings and get her circulation back. Torin scowled. He'd meant it when he said he didn't want *anyone* touching her.

For a second she looked at Torin. Her brown eyes were wide, focused on him. She blinked, and then, seeming to recognize her error in staring at him, she dropped her gaze.

Jesus God.

What the hell had he been thinking in not making her submit?

The little sub had begged him to flog her. More than begged she'd also cajoled. And when that had failed, she'd, in her charming way, even demanded, trying to goad him.

He preferred to play with superbly trained subs he might or might not ever see again. He'd never had an exclusive relationship with a sub, had never collared a woman. In his line of work, being moved around the country or planet depending on Hawkeye's needs, it had never seemed prudent. He'd never even been tempted.

He'd never played with a colleague either.

He had rules. Rules were rigid. They kept the world in order.

Still, two nights ago, she'd gone as far as to crawl into his bedroom completely naked, his leather belt held delicately in her mouth. He'd drawn on his adherence to rules—well, rules and the mental reserves developed from a lifetime of studying martial arts—to send her away and lock his door.

The dungeon monitor secured her hands behind her back and then exerted pressure on her shoulders so that she knelt before them.

"Take out the gag," Xavier said.

Shit.

The dungeon monitor unbuckled the gag and slowly drew it away. She swallowed several times, and Torin couldn't take his gaze off her. Mira was as lovely as she was determined.

Her long black hair was pinned back in Victorian fashion, and a few tendrils had escaped their confines. The strands curved alluringly across her cheeks and at her nape.

Her gown was cut fairly low, in a way he was pretty damn sure would have been scandalous when Queen Victoria had sat on the British throne. The style of Mira's dress emphasized the alluring swell of her breasts. Her exposed skin had a lovely olive tone that spoke of her Spanish heritage.

On her knees, her head bowed, she was exquisite. And he was nearly undone.

"You are...?" Xavier asked, looking at Mira.

"Mira Araceli, Sir."

"My Liege," Torin corrected. "You will address Master Xavier as 'my Liege.'"

She looked up at him, then instantly back down. In front of everyone, he'd corrected her, and he knew she hadn't missed the fact he was establishing even more firmly his dominance over her.

"Yes, Sir," she said without a hint of her customary defiance.

"Now answer Master Xavier's question."

"My name's Mira Araceli, my Liege," she said softly, more softly than he'd ever heard her speak.

The complete contradiction to the Mira Araceli he knew stunned him. Even when she'd crawled into his bedroom, she'd taken the lead, and that's what he expected from her. Hawkeye didn't waste his time hiring women, or men, who weren't leaders, who weren't resourceful. In addition to providing personal security services to the rich and famous, Hawkeye, Inc. employees operated in the world's most hostile environments.

Mira had passed the Hawkeye screening process, and Torin had taken the time to read her personnel file along with every report she'd written. She'd been in the Middle East, and she and her client had been the only survivors of a gun battle. She knew how to remain levelheaded in stressful situations; she knew how to handle herself. So this...

And why the hell hadn't he recognized her true submissive nature?

He'd thought she was likely a masochist. That wouldn't have shocked him. In their line of work, raw, nasty, gritty hook-ups were common, a way to celebrate being alive, a way to remind themselves they were still human.

Most of the personal security agents he knew were adrenaline junkies. Some drove too fast or burned through the gears on a crotch rocket; others signed up for extended tours and crawled through jungles or endured a mouthful of one-hundred-ten-degree sand. A handful he knew enjoyed sadomasochism; it was another way to fuel the fire.

He'd heard that the infamous Ms. Inamorata, Hawkeye's right-hand woman, even dabbled in the world of BDSM. He wasn't sure he believed the rumor, and even if it were true, he had no idea which side she would be on. The woman was tough enough to chew nails. He could picture her as a domme with tall, spiky stiletto heels. He couldn't see her as a sub, but then again he'd never pictured Mira as a sub either.

Xavier spoke, cutting into Torin's thoughts. "I take it, Ms. Araceli, that you were willingly engaged in a scene with Master Blake?"

Torin snapped his back teeth together. Dark Haven might be Xavier's club, but Mira was Torin's partner. "Xavier—"

She interrupted Torin's protest, saying, "Yes, my Liege."

Fuck a goat, the woman had just given Torin another reason to punish her.

She continued either not recognizing or, more likely, ignoring Torin's clenched jaw.

"My Liege, I approached Master Blake when I arrived. He made certain to ask if I was alone."

"Goddamn it!"

Xavier raised a hand to silence him. "Master Torin states you're under his protection."

Even on the best of days, Torin didn't keep his temper under tight control. As it was, he figured he had another, oh, forty-five seconds of patience left. A minute, tops.

"Ms. Araceli?" Xavier prompted.

"Well..."

"A yes or no will suffice, Ms. Araceli."

Chapter Two

Torin silently counted to ten, waiting for her answer.

"I—" She looked at Torin. She swallowed. "We—"

"Choose wisely," Torin warned. He had no claim on her, and they both knew it.

But she was smart enough to realize they'd end up back at the same house tonight. They were stuck together for as long as Hawkeye said or until one of them admitted defeat. Torin figured that would be at least several months, if not years. The next few seconds were critical to her, to them both, to Blake's safety.

Despite his demand that people move away, several couples had gathered closer to better hear what was being said.

Finally, after swallowing, she reached the right choice and said, "Yes, my Liege. We're partners."

"Then the decision to engage in a scene with Master Blake was not yours to make?"

Any other time he might have acknowledged Xavier's skill. As it was, with Blake standing there, onlookers greedily drinking in the scene, and Mira on her knees needing to be punished for her behavior, Torin wanted the drama to be finished and wanted her alone, subjected to his wrath.

"Mira?" Xavier prompted.

"Technically he—"

"*Mira*!" Torin snapped.

She swallowed and then licked her lower lip. She tipped back her head and looked directly at Xavier, avoiding all contact with Torin. "No, my Liege. As you said, the decision to give myself to Master Blake was not mine to make." She bowed her head. "I'm sorry, my Liege." She then looked at Blake. "I apologize, Master Blake."

Apologizing to the whiny bastard who'd been beating her? Torin closed the distance between them and dug his hand in her hair. Pins scattered across the ceramic-tiled floor.

"You broke the rules of the club, Ms. Araceli," Xavier said.

"I will deal with my sub," Torin said.

Always the professional, no matter how much it pissed off Torin, Xavier crouched in front of her. Only the three of them could hear what was being said. "Since it's your first visit to my club, you need to know that Master Torin is well within his rights to punish you for your behavior. It's also at my discretion as to whether or not I will personally punish you."

Torin felt her tremble.

"I'm going to give you a choice. I can turn you over to Master Torin, or I can call you a taxi. If you decide that I should call you a taxi, you will not be welcome at Dark Haven again."

Torin tightened his fist in her hair and saw her wince.

"Thank you, my Liege." She drew in a shaky breath. "I was disobedient to Master Torin."

Master Torin.

Goddamn, his cock throbbed.

She glanced at him. "I'm sorry...Sir."

"I'll leave this between the two of you, then?" Xavier said, standing and looking at Torin.

"I'll be taking my sub to the Medieval Room, if you'll excuse us?" He nodded to Xavier and to Blake. Easy to be magnanimous when you'd won, especially when the loser was cradling his wrist.

Torin kept his fist in her hair, not pulling, just exerting a small amount of pressure.

In all his years practicing BDSM, he'd never touched a sub in anger. He refused to allow her to be the exception. He would punish her because she deserved it, needed it, wanted it, and because it was a house expectation. But he wouldn't do it until his temper was fully contained.

He looked at the blond dungeon monitor and said, "I need a collar and a leash."

Mira gasped. He tightened his grip, silently warning her to keep quiet. She'd pushed him as far as he'd allow.

The man snapped his fingers, and one of the waitresses dashed off. Dark Haven catered to all needs and kept an assortment of toys available for instances much like this one. Tonight he was particularly grateful for Xavier's foresight.

"Turn up the music," Xavier instructed another of the servers.

Loud, thumping music rocked the walls. Tension eased and conversation around them resumed as people went about their business.

"No hard feelings," Torin said to Blake.

"Fuck off, Carter," Blake said. "How the hell was anyone supposed to know she was yours?"

How indeed? He'd never claimed her. Blake rubbed his wrist. "Next time, claim your subs." He looked at the kneeling Mira. "And when you're done with this asshole, look me up."

Torin took a step forward.

Xavier put out a restraining arm. "Enough, Master Torin."

Blake glared at Torin before moving away.

"He's right," Xavier said. "Claim her. If she comes to Dark Haven unaccompanied again, I'll back whoever does master her."

With a tight nod, Torin acknowledged Xavier's order.

Within seconds the blond dungeon monitor returned with a collar and leash. "I'll take it from here," Torin said.

"Yes, sir," the man said, handing over the leather pieces.

"Your sub broke club rules," Xavier told Torin. "And upset one of the founding members."

"She'll be punished," Torin promised. He took his hand out of Mira's hair, confident that she'd stay put.

"As I told Mira, it's my prerogative to mete out the punishment," Xavier reminded him.

"Indeed."

"But I don't want my wrist broken." He smiled.

"Or your movie-star nose," Torin supplied.

Xavier touched his nose instinctively. If he weren't so focused on the sub before him, Torin would have laughed.

"Watch your step, young lady," Xavier said to Mira.

"Yes, my Liege."

Then it was just the two of them. "After tonight we will still be partners, unless you request a transfer."

She nodded.

"But we cannot leave here without your being punished."

"Torin—"

"Master Torin," he corrected. "You forced my hand, Mira."

She sighed. "You didn't have to follow me here," she said. "I was doing fine with Master Blake."

"I'm already pissed, Mira. Don't make it worse," he warned.

"You ruined my evening," she said. If her hands hadn't still been secured behind her back, he imagined she'd have poked a finger in his chest. And here, in the club, he couldn't allow that to happen.

His temper had returned to a simmer when she'd chosen him over Blake, not that he'd given her much choice. The heat was getting turned back up.

"It's the weekend," she reminded him. "And we are not working a case. I invited you to come with me to Dark Haven, and you turned me down. You have no right to go all mondo loco on me just because Master Blake was flogging me, like I wanted, like I asked him to. He tied me to the spanking bench like I wanted him to, and he was hitting my bare ass with just the right amount of pressure. I would have come for him in only a few more minutes."

She'd carefully chosen her words to hit a nerve, and it worked.

"You're not willing to beat me, so it's none of your freaking damn business if I find someone who will. Keep out of my personal life. *Sir*."

The little minx had added the "Sir" more as an insult than a term of respect. The idea of gagging her was becoming more appealing every moment. He leaned in toward her, close enough that he could kiss her. And wasn't that was a tempting idea? A gag, his cock, his tongue—all ways to keep her mouth occupied. "Let's get a few things straight. I'm here now, and I sure as hell intend to beat you."

She shuddered slightly. She wanted to pretend she wasn't affected by him, by his words, his simmering anger, and the tension that had built between them over the last few weeks, but she was.

"Whatever you need, I'll make sure you get it." Torin captured her chin firmly between his thumb and forefinger. He forced her to look at him. "Beating, flogging, spanking, punishment, humiliation, bondage...” He trailed off. “You will not go to Blake or anyone else, and you will not flash your cunt at anyone who wants to see it.” His reaction startled him. He'd never minded playing with other subs in front of an audience. One woman had been a total voyeur; she hadn't cared if he'd posted pictures of her all over the Internet. But this woman... *His*. “Understand?”

“Fuck you,” she said.

He snapped his back teeth together.

“As you said, we're partners. Nothing more.”

“I didn't add the 'nothing more' part, Mira; you did.”

“You can't stake a claim on me without my permission.”

“Which you gave me when you invited me here with you.”

“You refused.”

He sighed, fighting for control over his temper. “You crawled into my bedroom. You publicly chose me over Blake. I'd say you've given permission twice, and now you're just being a brat. Brats get spanked, Mira, and I can make that happen right here, right now.”

“You wouldn't. You can't spank me through this dress, and you've already said you won't have me showing my cunt to others—”

“*Enough*,” he told her, ruthlessly cutting in. “You got what you wanted. Now show a little respect. Fight me all you want, but you can't win.”

They were at an impasse, locked in a battle of wills.

"Ask yourself what you really want," he said. "Do you really want me to turn you over to Blake? Or to Xavier? Or do you want to see if I can give you what you want, what you need? But if you do, it's going to be on my terms."

He waited, knowing how important the next few seconds were. She still didn't wear his collar, could change her mind and have him summon Xavier or even a taxicab.

Her internal struggle was visibly waged on her face. She worried her lower lip. The act was a betrayal of the nerves that she usually managed to disguise. The liquid depths of her brown eyes threatened to drown him. Her desire lay there, exposed. A layer of disbelief was shrouded but not hidden.

"Give me what I crave, Torin."

"Master Torin," he corrected.

"Give me what I crave, Master Torin."

"You're submitting to me?" he asked, pressing for answers so they were both clear. "Willingly?"

Chapter Three

She took a breath and exhaled it in shaky measures. "Yes, Sir."

Satisfied—finally—he secured the collar around her neck. He tightened it to the point he could get just one finger between her throat and the collar.

She looked up momentarily. Her mouth was slightly parted, and her breaths were shortened, whether from fear or anticipation, he didn't know.

"I'm nervous," she confessed.

"I hope so."

"You're not helping to reassure me."

"I'm not trying to reassure you. I'm pissed, Mira. And you will pay for your behavior. Now stand."

"We've never played together before."

"If you think I'm playing now, think again. It may be fun and games to you; it's not to me. Stand up this instant, and don't make me repeat myself again."

Since the gown was a monstrosity of length and fabric, and because her arms were still bound behind her, she struggled to comply. He made no move to help her. The usually graceful Ms. Araceli was out of her element, but to her credit, she didn't protest. When she stood in front of him, head bowed slightly, he said, "Good girl."

She glanced up long enough to glare. He grinned. His partner, his submissive, was a complex woman who intrigued him immensely. She had natural submissive tendencies, and she was clearly a masochist. But she was still a highly trained operative accustomed to being large and in charge. Apparently the three facets sometimes collided. The mix intrigued him.

"I—"

"You look lovely." He didn't think his cock had ever been harder.

He wrapped the leather cord around his wrist several times, then gave it a light tug. She was pulled off balance, and her eyes opened wide.

He liked having her at his mercy, on his leash, the black collar tight and stark against her delicate throat. She'd goaded and pushed until she got what she wanted. But if she wanted to be in control—top from the bottom—she'd chosen the wrong man.

At a fast pace, probably uncomfortable for her in those fantastic-looking, do-me-now shoes, he led her downstairs toward the Medieval Room.

Once inside, he closed the massive door, sealing out everyone but them. There was a window for voyeurs, and he figured Xavier would check on them at least once. As much as he hated the idea of anyone seeing her, watching her receiving his punishment, he also had to respect the club's policies and Xavier's pronouncement. And truthfully, she didn't mind, so why in God's name did he? If she wanted to show her cunt to the world, it was technically none of his business.

So why couldn't he convince himself of that fact?

She'd fired a protective streak in him, one he'd never had for another woman. It was more than just their being partners—something much, much more. The idea of her willingly exposing herself, asking another man to flog her, infuriated him.

“Let's keep the rules straight,” Torin told her. “In here, you're the sub, I'm the dom. There will be no topping from the bottom. Your disobedience, your questioning, your testing were left outside. We're both clear that when we're training or on duty we're partners, and I will respect you as such. For the rest of this evening, you have my permission to respond with a 'yes, Sir' or 'no, Sir.' Or if you prefer, you may say 'yes, Master' or 'no, Master.' You will answer direct questions, and you will not speak without permission. Understand?”

“Yes, Sir. You made your point.”

Good start. He gave the leash a little more slack and said, “Turn around.”

This time she didn't hesitate at all.

“Keep your gaze on the wall.” The walls of the Medieval Room were made from stone. Shackles were bolted into them. He wanted her to focus on the shackles, imagining what he had in store for her.

He removed the bindings from around her wrists, and then he went to work unfastening the dozens of tiny hooks and eyes that held her dress closed. He gave silent thanks that women didn't dress like this anymore. As it was, it took all his restraint not to whip out his pocketknife and go barbarian on her, slicing her out of the yards and yards of material.

"I—"

"You crawled into my bedroom," he said against her ear.

She trembled slightly, responding to him. The knowledge he affected her was heady stuff. "That was different."

"Because you were in control."

She looked over her shoulder at him. He saw a flash of fire in the dark depths of her eyes, and he didn't see a sub. Instead he recognized the woman who showed up for their training exercises, the woman who ran five miles a day, adding punishing sprints to increase her endurance, and who pounded out fifty noncheating push-ups, five more than he did. She could outshoot him, outthink him, and she had never rubbed it in.

She wiggled, trying to turn. "Stay still," he ordered. "I want you looking at those shackles."

He heard her sharp inhalation. Her training as an operative helped her be a better sub, he realized. She had self-discipline that she could call on from the bottom of her soul. Tonight, and others, would be a treat.

He drew the dress off her shoulders and let it fall to her waist. "Good girl," he said when he saw she wasn't wearing a bra. His cock was hard, demanding. He reached around to cup her breasts.

"Torin—"

"Master Torin. Here, I'm your master, and you're my sub. I want you naked, and I'll have you naked. Any questions?" He flicked his thumbs over her nipples. They hardened instantly, and her knees weakened a little. "Stand up straight."

The bass from the music outside the room reverberated through them.

She supported her weight, and he rolled her nipples between his thumbs and forefingers. "You brought me a belt two nights ago," he reminded her. "In your mouth. That was bold."

She didn't say anything.

He squeezed her nipples.

She moaned ever so softly.

He increased the pressure on her nipples until he knew it was painful.

Her knees buckled again, but she caught herself and stood up tall before he had to remind her. "Quick study." Not that he'd expected anything less. "I assume that means you like pain."

She didn't answer.

"Mira?"

"Yes," she whispered.

"I didn't hear you."

"Yes," she said. "Yes, Sir. I like pain."

He tightened his grip on her nipples.

She moaned, but she didn't protest.

"Tell me."

"I like it," she said. "It hurts. S-s-sir!"

He finally relented, releasing her. His cock throbbed behind his jeans. He wanted to be naked, buried inside her.

He unfastened the final hook and eye that secured the dress at the small of her back. The fabric pooled on the Medieval Room's floor. He noticed her ass was slightly red from the force of Blake's blows, and it took all his self-control not to go after the man and finish what he'd started. He reminded himself that Mira had asked for it, but it didn't take the edge off his anger; it only fueled it. “Step out of the dress.”

She did.

Little vixen. While he'd been outside chopping wood for the fireplace, she'd been getting ready. She'd spared no detail.

Even though she couldn't have known it, her choice in lingerie was perfect. Her black lace garter belt and silky, sexy stockings were the stuff of his fantasies. Her high-heeled, fuck-me shoes could not have been fashionable in the Victorian era, but they sure as hell turned him on now.

If he weren't careful, she'd bring him to his knees.

He shrugged out of his jacket and tossed it on top of a bench. He then moved around to the front of her. “Remove my belt.”

Her eyes opened a bit wider, but she reached for the buckle. “Master's cock is hard.”

And getting harder.

She took her time drawing the leather back through its loops. Torture. Pure torture.

She offered the belt to him with one hand, and with the other, she grabbed his cock, squeezing hard.

He curled a hand over hers. “Later.”

“But—”

“No topping from the bottom,” he reminded her.

She obediently dropped her gaze. He could have come instantly.

After taking his belt from her, Torin detached the leash from the collar. “Now that the dress isn't in your way, you can crawl to the wall.”

Her mouth dropped open. “Crawl?”

“Do I need to repeat my order?”

She shook her head. “My stockings—”

“Can be replaced. Crawl. *Now.*”

She sank gracefully to her knees before moving onto hands and knees, doggy-style. He fully intended to take her that way. Soon.

She moved across the uneven stone floor with a flawless class that made his dick physically ache. Her pert rear swayed slightly. He admired the length of her leg muscles, and he wondered how her thighs would feel wrapped around his waist.

When she arrived at the wall, she stopped and waited for further instruction.

“Stand and face the wall. Arms above your head. I want you totally flat against the wall; press your breasts into the stones.”

She hesitated only seconds.

“Legs shoulder width apart.” While she stood there, held only in place by the force of his will and her obedience, he grabbed two sets of restraints from the pegs on the adjoining wall.

He moved in behind her. "You've got a hot body, Mira."

"Thank you…Master."

Master. He liked the sound of that much better than "Sir."

He crouched to wrap the restraints around her ankles and then secure them to the hooks in the floor.

He trailed his fingers up the inside of her right thigh. Her legs trembled. "Are you still wet?" He drew a finger across her pussy lips.

She jerked and gasped, dropping her hands beside her.

"Keep your arms above your head," he instructed her. "You are wet, Mira. Will you still be that damp after I whip you? Or will you be wetter?" He then parted her pussy lips. He pressed the pad of his thumb against her clit. She jerked convulsively.

"I… Please. I need…"

"On second thought, drop your arms. Reach behind you and spread your ass cheeks."

"Master?"

"Do it."

Slowly, she brought down her arms, then reached back to grab her buttocks.

"What's your safe word?"

She spread her buttocks apart. He closed his eyes momentarily to get control of his libido. He wanted to plunge deep inside her, slamming her against the wall,

pounding out his orgasm, and taking her with him. "Mira? Your safe word?"

"Sangria."

"Sangria?"

"Sangria," she said. "It's red."

And it was a drink her country was famous for. Of course. "Anything off-limits?"

"Permanent injury. Strangulation. Knives. Unsafe sex."

"Nothing else?"

"No."

"You're an extreme player, Mira?" *Or she just thought she was.*

"I like to push the edges. I have a safe word."

Fair enough. Unable to wait any longer, needing to possess her, he plunged a finger inside her damp pussy.

She jerked.

He felt a moment of pure male satisfaction. He liked having this woman respond to him so completely.

Torin drew a deep breath. He was in control of the scene, and he intended to control himself as well. "How close are you to orgasm?" he asked softly. He moved his finger, feeling her internal walls constrict around him.

"It's been a long time," she said, her breaths becoming more and more shallow as he explored her insides. "M-Master Blake warmed me up."

Torin growled and impaled her with a second finger. The idea of Blake taking any liberties with this woman, *his* sub, infuriated him. "You're here with me now. You'll not come without permission."

When she didn't respond, he asked, "Am I clear?"

"Yes, Master. But..."

"Problem?"

"I come easily."

"You'll come when I say you'll come. *Keep your ass cheeks parted*!" He knelt to lick her while he finger fucked her.

"Master!"

He stopped short of letting her orgasm.

"Master is a beast."

He grinned but was glad she couldn't see him. She delighted him, made him want to please her. "Did you have permission to speak?"

"No," she said.

"And...?"

"The sub apologizes."

"Apology accepted." He loved the way she referred to herself in the third person; she was suddenly getting into the scene as much as he was. "We'll just add another two lashes for insubordination."

She made a funny sound, somewhere between a mewl and a protest, but didn't say anything else.

He stood then pulled out his fingers from her cunt, trying hard not to think about how badly he wanted to replace them with his cock.

He pressed a damp finger against her anus. Her muscles tightened, but instead of pressing forward and into the wall, trying to escape from him, she took a breath and pressed back in silent invitation.

Lust filled him.

He wanted her. "Bear down," he told her.

"Yes," she whispered.

As she followed his instructions, he pressed his finger deeper, past his first knuckle. She moaned and wiggled. Could she be any more perfect for him?

"More," she begged softly.

He entered deeper, stretching her wider, sinking his finger all the way to the hilt.

"Mas...Master... May I come?"

"No chance." He pulled out.

She groaned in protest.

"Being an impatient sub will prolong the amount of time until you are allowed an orgasm. If you want to come, play it a little more obediently, Mira."

"Yes...Master."

After wiping his hands on a moist towelette, he returned to her. "Arms spread, Mira."

He saw her shoulders rise and fall. Although she hadn't made anything ordinary off-limits, he knew he was pushing a boundary now. They'd never played together before, and all she had to operate on were her instincts. He was pissed, as he'd told her. She was wise to be wary. "I'm waiting," he said softly against her ear.

Slowly, as if it were mind over matter, she moved her wrists toward the shackles attached to the walls.

Beating her was going to be a pleasure.

And the scent of her arousal only made him that much more anxious to get on with it.

Chapter Four

Mira forced a breath deep into her lungs. The breath didn't help calm her nerves. So she did it again.

She'd studied yoga for most of her life. Five years ago, she'd learned to meditate. Every day, even in inclement or blazing weather, she trained physically hard, keeping her body and its responses at their peak. She knew how to manage her stress, her emotions, and her energy. And right now she couldn't remember how to do anything other than gulp oxygen. Her brain felt like scrambled eggs.

She'd wanted this. She'd wanted to play with Torin Carter.

When she'd learned from Hawkeye himself that she and Torin would be partners, she'd almost swooned. She might actually have done just that had she been the type of woman who would ever swoon. As it was, she'd locked her knees momentarily, nodded politely, and pretended to be a professional.

She'd had a crush on the big, bad, mighty Torin Carter for several years, since he'd taught a training course she'd been forced to attend. She'd been young, green, not as physically strong as she'd thought. They'd participated in hand-to-hand combat, and he'd instantly and completely subdued her. Her ego had been as bruised as her body. She had used that experience to fuel her determination to be tougher, to be better. And while she knew he didn't remember her from back then—she'd been just another recruit—she'd never forgotten him.

After the meeting with Hawkeye, she'd been anxious to get back to her Denver apartment. Later that night, alone in her bed, she'd take her bullet vibrator from her nightstand drawer. With the toy set to low, she'd allowed her fantasies about her new partner to run wild. When she'd orgasmed, she'd screamed out his name. Until him, she'd never fantasized about an Irishman. She preferred men who were a contrast to her—blond to her black hair. Fair skin to her darker tone. And she definitely liked men who were more even-tempered than she was. She needed a man who was malleable, someone she could take off a shelf and play with when she wanted.

Torin Carter was the antithesis of what she thought she wanted in a man, what she always went for. Instead of the light green eyes she preferred, this man had searing blue eyes, along with a gaze that seemed to look through her, not at her. He spooked her a bit with the way he seemed to read exactly what she wanted.

Despite her protests, he'd been correct in saying she wanted him. She wanted to be beaten by him, not Master Blake. She wanted to feel the power of Torin's lash. She wanted to know if he was as focused on playing BDSM games with her as he was on his job.

More than anything, she wanted to know if he was man enough to give her everything she wanted and needed when it came to sex.

So far she'd never found anyone who would or could.

Some were good for a spanking, but not for dominating her. One was great at telling her what to do, but when it came to wielding a flogger, he was apologetic and limp wristed. Master Blake hadn't been bad at inflicting the right amount of pain, and he'd been steadily increasing the intensity of his strokes, but she'd heard that outside of the club he was a bit of a wuss. Politeness was one thing; she needed a man who could be in control, always.

"Right wrist first," Torin said, breaking into her thoughts.

His touch was uncompromising but surprisingly gentle as he secured her right wrist in place. Instinctively she pulled back on the tether, testing it. Like Torin, it was unyielding. A ripple of anticipation jolted through her body.

The wall was uncomfortably cold. She was hyperaware of the room's chill, of the door with its window, of Torin's spicy, masculine scent.

He secured her left wrist in place, leaving her splayed and helpless.

Her mother had always warned her to be careful what she wished for. With her temper, Mira always wanted to push the outer limits of everything she tried. In Torin, she might have met her match. His tone when he'd found her had shocked her. She was accustomed to a much more restrained Torin. Even when she'd crawled into his bedroom, he'd calmly wrapped her in one of his robes and escorted her out the door before locking it behind her.

He'd never raised his voice, never betrayed that he cared one way or the other that he'd seen her naked body.

But now she knew. His erection was turgid, and she prayed she'd have it inside her soon. Hopefully he wouldn't be shy about using her anally either. He could be the type of man she'd fantasized about.

Her pussy was still dripping; her clit throbbed.

"How many strokes with my belt?" he asked.

Uh. He wanted her to decide? A chill—part delight, part fear—chased up her spine. Torin wouldn't let her abdicate her role in their play.

"Mira?"

"Eight, Sir?"

"Good place to start. Eight will be sufficient to satisfy the club's demands for punishment, but not mine."

She shuddered.

"How many strokes for allowing Blake to touch you, to see you?"

"When I invited Master Blake to play, I didn't realize I wasn't allowed to do that," she said.

"That wasn't the question."

Her instinct was to protest. How could he arbitrarily enforce rules that she didn't know existed? "Two."

"Three it is."

She opened her mouth but clamped it shut again. He'd simply add more strokes the more she protested. And since she didn't know how hard he would hit her, she figured she'd better err on the side of safety.

"How many total?"

"Eleven."

"How many for coming to the club tonight without my permission?"

She bit into her lower lip. That one she couldn't protest. She had sneaked away from the house. They were partners, and even if an argument had ensued, she should have told him she was leaving. "Three more," she said reluctantly. Fourteen was a lot of strokes from someone you'd never played with.

"Is your pussy still wet?"

"It was. Now I'm suddenly a little nervous," she admitted, "so I'm not as turned on as I was earlier."

He moved in behind her. Using his body, he pushed her hard against the cold, unyielding wall. She felt the scratch of denim and the hardness of his cock against her naked backside. Her breasts were flattened against the stone. Her nipples hardened from the cold and from her overwhelming arousal.

"I'm tempted to just fuck you hard, here, with you so totally helpless."

"*Now* I'm wet," she whispered. He didn't even need to touch her. He could turn her on just with words. He thrust repeatedly against her rear, simulating intercourse. She wanted his penetration, his possession. "Please," she begged. "Please fuck me."

"The beating first," he told her, his breath warm on her ear.

"Master!"

"You'll count them for me, *mo shearc*." He moved away.

"Damn it," she said. "Damn you."

The bastard actually laughed.

He left her weak and needy, on the razor's edge of fulfillment.

He caught her completely off guard, unprepared.

Torin landed the first blow, right under her buttocks, with a vicious upward stroke. She gasped from shock, from sudden pain.

His punishment had been much, much harder than she'd anticipated.

"Count," he reminded her.

"One," she bit out. There'd been nothing erotic about his first smack. Maybe he wasn't as fabulous as she'd thought.

He caught her again, in the exact same spot, with the exact same pressure.

"Mira?"

"Two." She braced herself as much as she could with nothing to hold on to.

The third followed suit, and it was then that she realized his skill. His aim was exact, his timing impeccable. He was a master of beatings.

"This is meant as a punishment," he said, "not as a pleasure beating. Xavier wouldn't approve if I didn't punish you. And neither would you."

"Three," she said rather belatedly.

He added a little more force to the fourth, and she cried out.

"Four!"

"That's my girl."

She bit back her reactive *fuck you*. Letting that out of her mouth, she knew, definitely wouldn't bode well for her.

For the next few seconds nothing happened. He allowed the time and silence to stretch. The only thing she was aware of was her own breath.

"Let me know when you're ready to proceed."

He thought she was struggling to take it? That annoyed the hell out of her. "Bring it on." She waited a couple of seconds before adding, "Master."

"You haven't learned about goading me?"

Instead of hitting her, he tormented her, moving in closer, reaching between her legs, trailing his fingertips up her thigh. He was going to drive her mad. Stark, raving mad.

He pinched her clit. She cried out. It hurt, but deliciously so. She ground her hips forward, all but trying to get off against the wall.

"Stop that. Naughty hussy."

She would have stamped her foot if it hadn't been shackled.

"Where were we?"

"Four," she said.

"Are you ready to resume?"

"Yes, Sir."

"More respectful. Better." This time he caught her across the fleshy part of her butt cheeks.

"Five." *Damn it! It stung so bad. Hurt so good.*

God, she'd wanted this. She'd wanted a man who could give her this, with unyielding force. She liked the pain he inflicted, loved the fact he gave her a few seconds to absorb the sensation before moving on to the next one.

"We have an audience," he told her. "Xavier has been watching for the last few minutes."

That thought turned her on. She did have a little exhibitionist in her, but she respected that he might want to keep her punishment private in future. "I hope he's satisfied. Because you're definitely making me feel punished."

"You don't sound repentant."

She'd have to lie to say she felt repentant.

"Mira?"

Mira had wanted to feel his lash; she knew she would misbehave again to get it.

Before she was fully ready, the beast landed the next one across the uppermost part of her left thigh. The tip of the belt bit into her pussy. She moaned. She groaned. She wiggled, trying to escape. But he'd confined her perfectly, exquisitely.

"So I assume you're not repentant?"

"No," she confessed.

He laughed. "Well then. You've had six strokes," he said. "You've almost satisfied Xavier's club's demands. But you're not even close to satisfying mine."

As he'd talked, the searing pain receded.

He moved to her other side to catch her right thigh; again, the end of the leather monster sliced against her exposed pussy.

"I can smell you," he said.

"Seven…and it freaking hurt," she protested.

"Bad?"

"Bad," she said.

"Poor thing. And that's why your pussy is wet?"

He added the eighth on top of the last two, as if tying them together.

"Those satisfy the club," he said. "And Xavier is gone. The next three are for you allowing Blake to touch you."

The next three were perfectly timed and impeccably landed. Each stripe was on top of the previous one, across her butt cheeks instead of the upper part of her thighs. They hurt like hell, and he wielded the leather aggressively. He gave no quarter, and she asked for none, wanting to feel the full power of his lash.

Each of the three blows dragged a scream from her.

She'd never been beaten so soundly, never felt so overcome with pain, with emotion.

"Now for the ones I owe you."

She squeezed her eyes shut.

She heard the sharp clatter of metal against rock. It sounded as if he'd thrown his belt on the floor.

Before her mind could assimilate, he spanked her, his open palm landing against her already raw skin.

Unbelievably his hand hurt far worse than the bite of leather.

"How many more, Mira?"

"Two."

"Ask me for them."

She wanted to sink into the oblivion of her thoughts, absorb the pain, make sense of it, savor it. But he wouldn't allow her that luxury. "Please, Master Torin. Please give me the spankings I deserve for leaving the house without your permission."

"Where do you want them?"

"On my ass, Sir."

"Not on your cunt?"

Her insides constricted. For a moment she forgot to breathe. The idea of his powerful hand landing on her pussy scared her, thrilled her. And suddenly she had to know, had to know what it felt like, had to have the experience. "Yes," she whispered.

"I didn't hear you."

"Yes," she said louder. "Punish me there."

"Where?"

"My pussy," she said.

"Your cunt," he corrected.

"Spank my cunt, Master."

He played with her first, stroking her labia, teasing her clit, dipping a finger inside her desire-slickened vagina.

She was going to go mad. Mad, mad, *mad.* Her body convulsed. She was so close...

The first stinging blow made her gasp, made her even wetter.

"One more."

She moved slightly, arching her back, giving him better access to her private parts.

"Good girl."

His final slap forced her onto her toes. She cried his name.

Then she felt him behind her, his strong hands forcing her butt cheeks apart even farther, making her entire body strain.

She screamed again when he tongued her. He had to be on his knees, and he was forcing her to fight her orgasm. She jerked convulsively. She groaned when he pressed his thumb against her anal opening. All the sensation was too much, beyond endurance. She knew she should fight off the impending orgasm. She had the skills, but she didn't have the desire. She wanted the relief that coming would bring, wanted to no longer feel the tension that was clawing inside her. "Master! Ohhh, Master! I need to come."

He moved away from her and pinched the inside of her right thigh, but the distraction wasn't enough.

"I'm going to come," she shouted. "Please? Please, may I?"

He said nothing.

Then, without permission, breaking his rules, she shattered, pulling against her restraints, her hips jerking uncontrollably, her entire body convulsing against the rigid wall.

The orgasm was powerful, debilitating, every bit as emotional as it was physical. She was drained, her body limp in her bondage.

His presence overwhelmed her.

Her eyes were squeezed shut, but she saw him as he'd been before he'd secured her to the shackles—tight blue jeans, made even tighter by the size of his erection, scuffed and scarred boots, a black T-shirt with short sleeves, the fabric showing the cut of his biceps and power of his arms.

His scent was consuming, spice mixed with a hint of pure male sweat and the tanginess of a cool Bay Area evening.

But it was the way he'd beaten her that drained her completely.

He'd been relentless, demanding.

He made her hornier than she'd been in years.

"Mira?" he said, his tone was gruff, and it cut into her fantasies. Then, against her ear, he asked, "Did you come?"

She froze. She'd seen this kind of behavior before. Other doms she'd been with had acted the same way, feigning shock and disbelief that she'd come without permission.

She knew intuitively that Torin would have continued to eat her, tongue her, press into her anus until she came. He knew how to touch her, how to encourage the response he desired. Torin Carter had forced her into a no-win situation. Still, Mira was startled into complete silence.

"Mo shearc?"

"Yes," she whispered. "Yes, Master, I came."

"Most unfortunate. Now you truly will be punished."

Chapter Five

He'd been an idiot not to play with her before now.

Mira Araceli was totally responsive, utterly lovely, completely captivating. He wanted her again and again.

Her orgasm had been loud and unrestrained, like the woman herself, filled with passion.

He wanted to fuck her senseless.

And that, he knew, would be even more idiotic.

They were partners. Down the road, they'd be counting on each other. Their lives could depend on the way they interacted. Clouding the issue with sex was beyond stupid.

For once he didn't think logic and reasoning were going to stop him from taking her. This physical demand was undeniable.

After removing her shackles and rubbing her muscles to help restore circulation, he helped her back into her ridiculous gown and the annoying petticoats or whatever the hell they were called.

"Stand still," he said, working on the frustrating number of hooks and eyes. "I prefer you naked," he said. Much easier.

"Yes, Master."

"Goddamn idiot who thought up this outfit."

She laughed.

"I'll ignore that rudeness," he said.

His thumbs and fingers were too big for the tiny metal clasps. In frustration, he skipped a few of them. Good enough.

He picked up his jacket from the bench, and he draped the soft leather bomber over her shoulders. He fed his belt back through his belt loops.

One hand in her hair, her leash wrapped around his wrist, he moved her toward the club's exit, past Destiny.

"Hey, Master Torin?"

He stopped and looked at Destiny, keeping his hand firm against Mira's skull.

"Next time you break our rules and come storming in here in street clothes, Xavier said I get to punish you."

He laughed. The idea of the woman with purple-tinted, spiky, Goth-style blonde hair and a sparkling lip piercing being able to kick his ass was intriguing. "You're a domme?"

"If it means beating your ass, I am."

"I promise I'll follow the rules in future, Destiny."

"Or I get to punish you?"

"Yeah."

Beside him, Mira gave a rude hoot of appreciation. He'd take that out of her hide later too.

Destiny gave a cheery wave. The move jiggled her breasts, which were barely covered by flimsy pink netting. He bundled Mira outside and into his illegally parked car. He'd gotten a ticket for his aggravation, but fortunately, San Francisco's finest hadn't towed his vehicle.

With his cock throbbing, the drive back across the Golden Gate Bridge to the Marin County safe house would seem interminable. But once he had her there... The Hawkeye house was remote and private. He'd be able to fuck her as hard as he wanted; she'd be free to scream as long and as hard as she needed.

He parked the car in the garage, then held open the door into the house. She preceded him, then stopped and turned back toward him when she reached the kitchen. She stood there alluringly, her head tipped back slightly, her lips parted. There were few thoughts in his head, and every one of them had to do with him penetrating her. "Turn around."

He closed the distance and plucked the jacket from her shoulders and tossed it in the general direction of one of the kitchen chairs before unfastening her confounded dress for the final time. When the voluminous amounts of fabric pooled to the tiled floor, he put his hands on her shoulders and gently spun her back to face him. "Kneel."

She didn't hesitate. Part of him wondered how much longer he could stand it before he pounded out his release and ejaculated.

He left her there while he went into the living room to light a fire. As flames licked the logs, taking the chill out of the evening air, he resisted the temptation to stroke himself to satisfaction. When he came, soon, he wanted to be deep in her body.

He returned to the kitchen to find her in the exact position where he'd left her. Her obedience undid him. "On all fours," he told her. "I want to see how red your ass is."

She complied instantly.

"Nice," he said. "The ones on your thighs will make it difficult to sit down tomorrow."

"Yes, Master."

He abraded his thumbnail across the small welts.

She gasped and pulled away. Before he could correct her, she pushed herself back into position.

"The others, on your butt, are almost completely gone." He crossed to a high-backed chair and pulled it back from the table. "Crawl over here, mo shearc." He'd never used the endearment with anyone else. Somehow the "my love" worked with her, for her. "I want you over my lap for a proper spanking."

"Sir?"

"Do I need to repeat my command?"

"No!"

She crawled, her breasts and ass cheeks seducing him. She looked up at him only momentarily before positioning herself artfully across his lap.

"I'm spanking you," he said, "because I want to. No other reason than that."

"Yes, Sir. Thank you, Sir." She braced her hands on the floor. Without instruction, she parted her legs slightly.

He saw the slight glisten of her moisture on her pussy, and he smelled her arousal. He wanted this woman.

Torin parted her lips and played with her clit, watching her squirm, enjoying the sounds she struggled to suppress.

Without giving her any warning, he slapped her cunt hard, his hand open.

She gasped, surged away from his hand, then made another softer sigh and wiggled back into position.

He spanked her hard, on her buttocks, on her pussy, on her thighs. He timed his spanks to arouse, not punish.

A minute and a half later she was begging.

"I need…"

"You need…?"

"Will you fuck me? Fuck me, Master." Her words were breathless. "Fuck me. Please?"

He helped her from his lap. "Lean over the table. Grasp the far end."

She followed his directions, and she even turned her toes slightly inward so that her pussy was presented even more attractively. It would take all his control not to come before he'd even entered her.

He pulled his T-shirt over his head and tossed it near his jacket. He toed off his boots, and he noticed that she moved slightly. "Cold? Impatient?"

"Sorry, Master," she said. "Just…"

"Yes?"

“I'm impatient; the sub is impatient. I want you inside me.”

“I?”

“She,” Mira said with a sigh. “She. The sub. You know, the woman on the table, waiting to be fucked. Dying here.”

He laughed. No matter how hard she tried, no matter how much she was into a scene, she couldn't hide her natural personality. And to tell the truth, he didn't want her to.

He grabbed his wallet from his back pocket. All thumbs, he pulled a condom from one of the compartments. Seemed the beautiful Mira wasn't the only one who was impatient.

He dropped his wallet, pulled off his jeans, and stripped down, throwing everything onto the growing pile of clothes on the floor.

His cock was hard, throbbing when he rolled the condom into place. Fighting to restrain himself, he stroked the outsides of her thighs. She sighed. “Do you have any idea how red your ass is?”

“If it looks like it feels, yes, I have an idea.”

“It's lovely.” He traced a couple of the welts before placing a hand between her legs, feeling her dampness.

“Take me,” she said, moving her hips back.

As if he could wait any longer.

Torin bent his knees slightly and pressed his cockhead against her opening.

“Yes,” she whispered.

She was amazingly damp and ready for him.

He took her in a single stroke. He filled her, felt her internal pussy muscles clench around his cock.

This woman could be the death of him.

He reached across her, grasping her wrists.

"Ride me, hard." Belatedly, she added, "Master."

He held back his orgasm, making sure she came first. It was more difficult than it should have been.

Torin was known as a generous lover, but with Mira—it was about possession. He wanted her; he didn't want anyone else touching her, tasting her. He wasn't sure he liked the feeling. Having a woman, any woman, get under your skin was a bad move. The danger increased when the woman was your partner.

"Master!"

He heard her breaths, little gasps of air. He could feel her fighting her orgasm like a good little sub. "You may come," he told her.

"Torin!"

He drove into her, hard, impaling her with his thrusts. There was nothing gentle or soft about this. It was raw, animalistic, filled with lust. For the moment she was his, and he'd leave her no doubt about it.

She screamed.

Then her body squeezed him tight.

Her climax pushed him over the top. In a hot stream, he ejaculated, the orgasm feeling as if it had been ripped from his testicles.

It was brutal. It was satisfying. It wasn't even close to fulfilling his need to take her.

He withdrew from her. He looked at her for a moment, her midnight dark hair escaping its confines to curl against her neck, her shoulders. She was still pressed against the table. He'd never see oak the same way again.

She remained in place, her hands curled around the edge of the table. The marks of his punishment striped her thighs and buttocks, and her pussy glistened with her moisture.

Oh. Yeah. He wanted her again. And again.

His cock began resurging to life, even though he would have sworn she'd already drained every drop of semen from his body. "Shower?"

"Is water sex involved?"

"Insatiable wench." He helped her to stand, giving her a moment to regain her equilibrium before once again exerting his dominance by saying, "For your impertinence, you can get your lovely tush back on that table."

"Master?"

"This time I want you to lie on your back, Mira. Spread your legs. I want to watch you masturbate."

MIRA'S BREATH WAS shaky.

Her partner, and now lover-slash-dom, demanded more than she'd ever given to another man.

She turned to face him, and it was her first view of him completely naked. Her mouth dried. The sight of him nude didn't disappoint.

She'd known he was lean and muscular—she'd seen him workout in a T-shirt and shorts, but the flatness of his stomach and the definition of his biceps were incredible. She imagined those muscles flexing as he beat her, and she intuitively realized he'd held back a lot when he'd punished her. Torin was a raw, powerful man. He had harnessed that energy when dealing with her. She wanted, recklessly, to know what it was like when he didn't hold back, when he allowed emotion to affect him.

Dark hair arrowed down the center of his chiseled chest, stopping just above the thatch of pubic hair. His cock, even half-flaccid, was impressive. She hungered, suddenly, for him to take her again.

Already the experience with Torin Carter had exceeded any expectation she'd had. She'd used her vibrator several times and fantasized about him, and even those wild imaginations hadn't even come close to the reality of the way he touched her, tasted her, mastered her.

Through the years she'd played with any number of men. Now she realized they'd all had one thing in common. She could manipulate them.

This tall, dark Irishman wouldn't tolerate subterfuge, and that thrilled her as much as it frightened her.

"Now," he said, his voice was roughened, like a diamond sliding across sandpaper.

"Uh..."

"Problem, sub?"

She was always bold, and it sometimes got her into trouble. "I haven't yet seen Master's hot ass."

He laughed. Slowly, he turned around.

Oh, dear. God.

His ass was as tight as the rest of him. His thighs were muscular; his calves were well defined.

He was beyond dangerous to her, mentally as well as physically.

He finished the rotation, then nodded toward the table.

Following orders wasn't easy. She wanted to touch him, kneel before him, take his cock in her mouth, and suck it until he was hard enough to fuck her again.

She climbed onto the table and lay on her back.

Wordlessly, he repositioned her, putting her feet on the table and tapping her knees so she spread her legs wide.

This was a much more revealing position, leaving her exposed.

"Do you fuck your ass when you masturbate?"

She raised her eyebrows "Not usually. No."

"Fuck your ass with your fingers, Mira."

A frisson of excitement danced through her. No man had ever pushed her boundaries the way he did.

"Show me how you like to be pleasured," he said.

Feeling oddly self-conscious, she reached between her legs and stroked her fingertips across her pussy. She was damp. Her heart was racing.

Her eyes closed as she searched for a rhythm to take her to release. Then she remembered he hadn't given her permission to orgasm, he'd just instructed her to masturbate. She opened her eyes to find him intently watching her, his arms folded across his chest. His blue eyes were like chips of a glacier. In that moment he looked truly masterful. She felt weak inside, wanting to be dominated completely by him. “May I come?” she asked quietly.

“I'll let you know when I decide.”

She continued stroking her pussy, feeling it growing damper and damper. She moistened her forefinger and began to push it against her anal whorl.

“It's a total turn-on to watch you, Mira. My cock's getting hard again.”

Using her heels on the table as leverage, she lifted her hips slightly, realizing she was presenting an even more obscene image.

“Nice,” he said.

She inserted a second finger into her rear and began to move them in and out.

She closed her eyes again, and self-consciousness was lost in the sensation of pleasuring herself while he watched her.

An orgasm, and its delicious tension, spread through her.

Her breathing changed, becoming more labored.

She fought to hold off the climax, grinding her bare heels onto the oak table. But then he was there, painfully squeezing her nipples between each thumb and forefinger.

She was so needy, so close...

Still keeping the pressure on her nipples and squeezing her breasts, he leaned over to eat her pussy.

Mira came with a scream.

Chapter Six

Mira woke up the next morning, tired, sore, well used, with a smile, facedown on the mattress and... *Unable to move?*

She pulled on her wrists slightly, realizing she was tied in place.

She pulled against her ankles, realizing they too were secured.

A bit frantic, she opened her eyes.

The room was dark, but at least she recognized where she was: Torin's bedroom in the Hawkeye safe house. She was completely alone.

She heard the sound of running water and inhaled the spice of hot, fresh coffee.

She was safe, but there was no way she was getting out of her bondage.

It was a testament to how hard she'd slept and to his skill that he'd managed to truss her up without her being aware of it.

She barely remembered anything after the scene last night on the kitchen table. He'd carried her to his room over her protests. She preferred to sleep alone, always had. Even when she was in a fairly serious relationship, she rarely had sleepovers, telling the men in her life that she could be called away at any time, day or night, and she hated to disturb them. She'd lied. Truth was, spending the night and having breakfast together were intimacies she didn't want. She enjoyed having a nice, orderly life. Men—relationships—mucked that up completely.

She liked bondage on her terms. She enjoyed being punished when she wanted to be punished, relished being the one to dream up the scenes. For one dom, she'd gone as far as to script what she wanted and send him an e-mail in advance.

Torin Carter, damn him, had his own ideas. Like leaving her spread eagle, facedown on the bed while he had coffee and a shower—after promising her water sex that had never materialized.

So while she'd fantasized about having a man who would push past her boundaries, Torin's actually annihilating them annoyed the hell out of her.

She wanted a cup of that strong, bold coffee with a dollop of heavy cream. Breakfast would be good too. Control over the situation would be the bow on the present.

And since she couldn't control the situation until he got his ass back in the room, Mira schooled her thoughts, trying to rein in her annoyance. She measured her breaths, deeply in, slowly out, focusing on one thing: control of her mind, if not her body.

Unbelievably, she heard him singing in the shower. *Singing* while she was left alone with her thoughts and memories.

Against her intentions, she thought about the way he'd stormed into Dark Haven last night and nearly broken Master Blake's wrist. Torin's temper would be hot, if she went for that kind of thing, which she was suddenly realizing she might. To have a man she desired so intently go after her...

And then the way he'd shackled her to the wall, beaten her, fucked her...

Horny, Mira began to move her crotch against the sheets.

She thought of his hands, the way he'd touched her... His mouth, the way he'd eaten her pussy...

"Naughty sub, humping the mattress just like you tried to get off against the wall in the dungeon."

She froze.

How had she not noticed he'd stopped singing and turned off the water? The room seemed to echo with the silence.

"You didn't come, did you?"

"No," she whispered, turning her head to the side to look at him. *Oh. God.*

He wore a white towel around his hips and nothing more.

Droplets of water clung to his bare chest, and his hair was slicked back, making his cheekbones all the more prominent. His eyes seemed more frosty than they ever had before, and his lips were set in a firm, nonteasing line.

The man who'd been singing a few moments ago had been replaced by a stern dom.

She hadn't thought it was possible to be more turned on than she had been earlier, but clearly she'd been wrong. He didn't have to touch her for her to become aroused; he only had to speak with that toe-curling brogue.

"Don't mind if I check? Subs aren't allowed orgasms without permission from their masters. I assume you were aware of that?"

When she didn't answer, he asked, "Mira?"

"Yes."

"Tell me," he said, keeping her gaze ensnared.

Softly, her voice roughened by sleep, she said, "My orgasms belong to you."

"Good girl." He crossed the room, the towel riding lower on his hips. He sat on the bed and stroked the insides of her thighs.

This was totally different for her.

She'd never had a scene that carried over from the night before. She'd never considered herself a true submissive, just a woman who enjoyed a taste of kink and knew how to play the game. That he'd tied her up while she slept and left her there while he showered bothered her a bit. That he was still exerting dominance this morning left her scrambling. He was taking this thing too far, past where she wanted to go—past the point where she was in control.

When he touched her pussy, she gasped.

"You're wet," he said.

"Yes."

"Lift your hips."

Her restraints made it difficult to comply.

He teased her clit mercilessly, and she pulled against her bonds. When she was on the verge, he grabbed a pillow and pushed it beneath her stomach.

"I was thinking about you while I was in the shower," he said. "How much I want you again and again. And how hard I'm going to fuck your ass."

Her heart missed its next few beats and then slammed them all into a sudden surge of adrenaline.

As best she could, being tied facedown to the bedposts, she watched him. He opened a nightstand drawer and pulled out a bottle of lube and a condom.

He dropped the towel.

His cock was hard, thrusting toward her. For a few seconds she forgot to breathe as she watched him roll the condom down the length of his erection. He squirted a dollop of lube onto his fingers, then knelt beside her on the bed.

He slowly inserted one slick finger into her anus, allowing her time to accommodate his touch. "Relax," he said, sweeping her hair from her neck, tangling his fingers in it.

She dragged her breathing back under control.

"Ready?"

She knew she could refuse. He was totally controlled, despite his obvious arousal; she had a safe word. But she did want this—*him*—despite the small panic caused by his continued dominance. "Yes," she said.

He inserted a second finger, followed by a third. He stretched her, holding his fingers apart. It hurt, not badly, but enough that she wanted him to back off. She was going to ask him to stop, but he leaned over and kissed her exposed nape, distracting her.

"You're doing well, mo shearc."

A hundred pleasurable sensations danced down her spine.

He was attuned to her reactions. The moment she relaxed and surrendered, he began to move in and out, patiently simulating sex.

"Yes," she finally said. "I want your cock."

"Where?"

This man was relentless. He was going to drive her loco. "Up my ass," she said.

He moved slowly. He touched her, soothed her.

She'd never been taken like this, while she was tied down, helpless.

She was aware of him on his knees between her legs. He withdrew his fingers. Then she felt the unyielding firmness of his cockhead against her opening.

"Doing okay?"

"Just take me!"

He laughed and possessed her by slow measures, firm and steady, starting shallow and reaching greater depths with each stroke.

She liked anal sex, but she'd never had it like this before.

It wasn't all about him; he made the act about her pleasure, kissing her, reaching beneath her to caress her clit. "Torin—"

"Master," he corrected.

"Master! I want—need..."

"Come," he told her, pulling all the way out and then surging forward, taking her in a powerful motion.

She screamed as an orgasm crashed over her.

"God, woman, you're sexy as hell." He placed one arm beneath her hips, lifting her off the pillow slightly, holding her prisoner as he continued to ride her.

She felt sore and used, but she wouldn't be satisfied until he came.

She heard his breathing change, felt his cock swell slightly. She bore down hard, and he climaxed with a pure male grunt of satisfaction.

He continued to hold on to her long past the time her breathing returned to normal.

"I didn't sleep last night," he said, "thinking about doing that with you."

"Master fucked his sub hard."

He laughed. "More where that came from, Mira." He pulled out, and he disappeared into the bathroom for a few moments.

She heard the water running, and she closed her eyes, her thoughts in a whirl.

Now what?

Did they train together? Did he expect that these scenes had changed their partnership? *Had they?*

Torin returned to the bedroom with a warm, damp cloth. He pressed it against her anus, soothing her.

That had been missing in all the other scenes she'd participated in—the aftercare from her dom. Generally she hit the bathroom on her way out of a man's house, then called out a cheery good-bye over her shoulder.

Torin, it seemed, was having none of that. She was surprised how much she liked and appreciated the tender gesture.

Once she was cleaned up, he sat on the edge of the bed and released her right wrist from its restraint. “You're a lovely sub,” he said, massaging her skin until circulation returned.

“You don't suck as a dom.”

He swatted her rear, and she yelped. She was definitely sore from last night's beating.

He unfastened the rest of her bonds and then helped her to stand. He pulled her against him, her breasts pressing against his muscled chest.

It felt nice. Right.

He caught a hand in her hair and pulled her head back.

He claimed her mouth, kissing her deeply. He tasted of coffee tempered by a hint of sugar, then drizzled with sin.

She responded and rose onto her tiptoes, leaning wantonly against him. He pressed his free hand against the small of her back, holding her tight. She wiggled about a bit, feeling herself growing more and more aroused beneath his sensual assault. Torin Carter made her want to be a *very* naughty girl.

He slowly ended the kiss. Her mouth felt raw and ravaged. Hungry, she wanted more.

Torin looked at her intently. The color of his eyes never failed to startle her, but what she hadn't noticed before yesterday was that they revealed his thoughts and emotions, whether they were angry ice or aroused smoky blue.

"We need to talk," he said. "I'll brew a fresh pot of coffee while you get cleaned up and put on some clothes."

"Talk?"

"About what's next."

She steeled herself.

If he said that their having had a BDSM scene was a mistake, she'd have to agree with him. Reluctantly. The scenes had been hot. The man knew how to give it to her.

But the emotional cost was high. He'd taken everything she'd offered and then some.

And if he said he thought they should end their partnership, what then? She wanted to work with him. Lord knew there was a lot she could learn from him that would make her better at her job, a more valuable asset to Hawkeye, Inc.

"Mira?"

She nodded. "I'll meet you in the kitchen."

He kissed her forehead before releasing his hold on her hair.

His idea, apparently, of putting on clothes was to pull on a fresh pair of jeans, leaving them unfastened at the waist.

How could she think, let alone talk, with him looking so devilishly sexy?

"Ten minutes, Mira, or I'll come looking for you."

She hurried to the shower in her own bedroom, the promise of fresh coffee more appealing, for the moment, than misbehaving and provoking him into another spanking.

When she exited the shower, she saw he'd left a cup of hot, steaming coffee on the granite vanity. He'd added the exact right amount of creamer, and steam rose from the surface. His powers of observation made him good at his job. No way would it still have been steaming if it hadn't been nuked in the microwave for thirty or forty seconds after adding the cream—the same way she did.

She wondered if he'd stood there for a few seconds and watched her shower through the glazed shower doors. The idea turned her on; it implied an intimacy she liked.

After a long sip of hot coffee that drained a third of the cup, she dressed in faded-to-white denim jeans, a soft sweater, thick socks, and her favorite running shoes. He was braver than she was when it came to facing the Bay Area's morning chill.

She finished the coffee, hoping the caffeine would clear the cobwebs from her head. She needed to be at her peak to face Torin. Cup in hand, she pulled back her shoulders, exhaled from her diaphragm, then joined him in the kitchen. "This seems to be empty," she said, more to break the tension than anything else.

"I can handle that." Along with brewing strong-enough-to-stand-a-spoon-in-upright coffee, he'd cooked a pile of bacon and a panful of eggs, and he'd kept a plate warm for her in the oven.

"You've been busy," she said. "Thanks."

He slid the plate onto the same table where she'd masturbated herself to orgasm last night, and told her, "You need to keep your strength up. Sit."

Still bossy. She picked up a piece of bacon and chewed off a bite as she slid into the chair.

He poured her a fresh cup of coffee. She could get used to being spoiled like this.

After she'd cleaned off half her plate and drained another cup of coffee, he leaned back against the counter and regarded her with his arms folded across his chest.

"While we're partners," he said, "you will not engage in BDSM scenes with anyone else but me."

She put down her fork. "I'm not sure what you mean by that."

"If you need to be beaten, I'll make sure you're satisfied."

"Working together doesn't mean you have any exclusive hold on me sexually."

"Yes," he said. "It does."

He might have been halfway across the room but she knew not to underestimate him or the Irish temper he was restraining. Her own temper started to flare. "You could try asking."

"I could. But I won't. This is nonnegotiable. My rules, or tell Hawkeye you want to be reassigned."

"He'll want to know why."

"So tell him. Tell him you're a pain slut, Mira, who needs to have her ass reddened regularly, and it compromises our mission."

"You never said that. You just went all mondo caveman and started issuing orders." She clenched her jaw and shoved back from the table. He had her backed into a corner, trying to take away her choices, and he was offering no way out. "Is this your idea of us *talking*? You stand there and issue orders, and I'm supposed to smile like an empty-headed idiot and agree with you? You're an ass, Torin Carter."

He grinned.

Damn him. *Fuck him.*

"You have no right to dictate who I play with, who I sleep with."

"Mira, mo shearc, you started it when you crawled into my bedroom with a belt between your teeth. Until that moment, you were free to do whatever you wanted, with whomever you wanted." He pushed his hips away from the counter. "But you offered your sweet ass to me, and I decided to accept. So deal with it." In a few fluid movements—the kind that served him well in crisis situations—he was across the room. He took her by the shoulders and pulled her up from her chair.

She was breathless, angry, and aroused. For the first time in her life she had no idea what to do with the snarly knot of emotion. She wanted to slap him. She wanted to run the hell away from him, forget anything had happened between them, and take back control. Most of all, she wanted him to fuck her.

This kiss was unlike his earlier one.

He dragged her onto her toes, dug a hand into her hair, and pulled her head back, keeping her painfully imprisoned.

"Mine," he said. He took her mouth, staking his claim.

His kiss was hot, searing, punishing. She fought her response for as long as she possibly could, keeping her body rigid and her responses under tight control.

She felt his hard cock against her pelvis, demanding her capitulation. She couldn't. She wouldn't.

Living her life on her terms was more important than his demands.

He was relentless. His tongue sought hers. His hand in her hair kept her from running away.

He dominated her ruthlessly.

After a few seconds he softened the kiss and her resistance.

He probed, sought, asked.

That kind of power—his power—subdued her.

Against her own instinct for preservation, she began to respond to his kiss. She willingly offered her mouth as well as her surrender.

Within moments she found herself falling into the natural order—*his order*—of things.

It infuriated her. She was a woman in control of her own destiny. Or she had been until she met Torin.

By coming on to him, what the hell had she started?

Chapter Seven

Fuck and a half.

Torin didn't let women get to him. He avoided emotional entanglements, and he preferred the anonymity and lack of commitment that went whip in hand with one-night stands.

Now he knew why.

This spitfire had gotten under his skin. He liked, wanted, needed a woman who was as resourceful as she was strong, who was as giving and submissive as she was carnal and honest in her sexuality.

Mira Araceli was all those things in one exotic, sexy package.

He admired that she knew what she wanted, that she went after it.

His balls tightened as the need to possess her intensified. He put a hand on her rear and moved her impossibly closer to him.

He'd clearly pissed her off with his heavy-handed proclamation that he was in charge, that he would be the only one beating her sweetheart of an ass, but damn it to Dublin and back, he was furious too.

He told himself he had no claim on her, save their being work partners. He shouldn't care who the hell beat her, who fucked her. If she wanted half of Hawkeye's team to tie her up, it was none of his business.

But the idea of anyone but him making her scream as she came made his Irish blood seethe.

He'd meant it when he said she was his to use. As long as they were assigned together, he'd be the only one seeing her naked body. He'd made that clear. She might fight it, but she would ultimately capitulate.

As his anger abated, he felt a shift in her response. She no longer struggled against him. Instead she became compliant. She surrendered to his strength and determination.

Unbelievably that just made him crave her more.

He tasted the sweetness of her surrender and its hint of promise...

Slowly he ended the kiss.

He continued to hold her against him, one palm on her rear end, his other hand tangled in the thickness of her hair.

She looked up at him. Her eyes were wide, luminous. Last night the brown depths had been molten, imploring. This morning they were confused, half-angry, half-dazed with the need to submit.

Her mouth was parted and reddened from the brute force of his kiss. No amount of tenderness would erase the swelling.

Her chin was tipped back, her head tilted to the right.

"Have I made myself clear?"

“Your way or your way, Lord and Master?”

His jaw clenched. “Yeah,” he said, his voice deceptively easy. “My way or my way.”

“You've made yourself clear.”

“On your knees,” he said.

She blinked. Her mouth opened as if she was going to protest. As he released her, he put his hands on her small shoulders and pushed her toward the floor.

Yeah, this woman might be fiercely independent, but she was also a natural submissive. She could have told him to go to hell or asked for a new partner. Instead she was on her knees, her appealing mouth only inches away from his crotch. Her hands were behind her neck, which caused her breasts to thrust forward. “Tell me what you want to do right now.”

She looked up at him. “Besides actually talk about how we'll continue to work together?”

“Besides that.”

“I want…” Her voice was slightly husky, the way it had been last night when she'd stopped fighting him and recognized him as her master. The sensuality of it made his erection strain against the denim.

She shook her head, and her magnificent hair fell in mussed disarray around her shoulders and trailed down her back. “I want to unfasten your jeans and take your cock in my mouth.”

“Do it.”

She moved deliberately, not looking away even as she pulled down on his zipper. “And I want to suck you dry.”

He had no intention of letting another man within fifty feet of her.

She lowered his zipper the rest of the way and then pulled his pants down.

“Master is already hard.”

Being hard seemed to be a constant state when she was around.

She took his cock in hand and stroked him until a drop of precum appeared at the slit. She licked the length of his cock, then touched the tip of her tongue to the droplet.

She made a soft purr of satisfaction, and he had to resist the need to slam his dick down her throat.

“Would Master mind opening his legs a little wider?”

This was what made her such a perfect slut. She wasn't afraid to ask for what she wanted. There were some women he'd had scenes with who were like puppets. They wanted to be told what to do, when to do it, how to do it.

Mira posed a whole new set of challenges to him, to his authority. Give him a woman with spirit and fire any day.

He stepped out of his jeans and spread his legs. She moved in a little closer. She cupped his tight balls in one palm and then pressed a finger against his perineum, that sensitive area between his testicles and his anus.

“Love the way Master smells,” she said. “Masculine.” She took his cock deeper into her mouth, sucking, pulling, drawing.

It was all he could do to hold on to control. He wanted to let her set the pace, but it was difficult not to just fuck her until his cum filled her mouth.

Taking a breath, he closed his eyes. Looking at her made him even hornier. In order to let her lead, he needed to just focus on the sensation.

He felt her forefinger against his anus. Involuntarily, his muscles tightened. But she was as relentless as he could be.

She left his cock momentarily, long enough to moisten a fingertip. “Relax.”

The temptress pushed her finger into his ass. No other woman had ever done that. The sensation of her finger against his prostate while she sucked his cock pushed him over the edge.

His penis swelled in her small mouth. He held the back of her head while she licked below his cockhead.

He was done for.

His orgasm spilled hot semen into her mouth. As he pulsed, draining his balls, she swallowed. She gave little groans of pleasure that kept his climax going.

And she literally sucked him dry.

His cock went flaccid in her mouth. She licked every last drop of sticky liquid before gently removing her finger from his ass.

In that moment he questioned who was dom and who was sub. He'd do anything to keep her happy and have her give him a blowjob like that again.

She slowly drew back, and when she looked up at him, she licked her upper lip and smiled. Yeah, she knew exactly the power she had over him. Which only left him one option. “Time to work out.”

"Hope you ate enough to keep your strength up. Master."

He helped her to her feet. "See you in the exercise room in ten minutes."

He pulled on his pants and watched her saunter from the room. There wasn't a better word for it. She moved her hips provocatively, played with her hair, and took her sweet time.

She wanted to be noticed, and it worked.

He went into his room to grab a pair of shorts and put on some running shoes.

He was aware of her in her bedroom, the sound of the closet door closing. As much as he was trying to harness his libido, he was unable to picture anything but her naked ass up in the air, her body completely available for him to take.

By the time he hit the state-of-the-art gym, she was already there. She'd cranked up the stereo system. Lady Gaga blasted from the speakers, the song's beat seductive.

Mira was doing sprints on the exercise bike—one minute of full-on cardio, two minutes at a more casual pace—building endurance. She'd opted for so-skimpy-they-should-be-outlawed shorts and a white sports bra. Up until now she'd worn exercise pants that hit her calf and long-sleeved shirts. The sports bra showed her nipples. And the way she'd pinned up her hair showed the dew of perspiration on her back. He hit the treadmill at a nine-mile-an-hour pace. That ought to distract him.

Usually it would have. He'd find a rhythm and forget about everything, tuning into his breathing, pushing his body past the point he'd been the day before.

This time the self-discipline didn't work.

Mira cooled down, slowing the bike to an easy pace. Then, a few minutes later, she hopped off the seat. Her shorts had ridden up higher, and she didn't straighten them. They were about as good as a thong at this point.

She wiped off with a towel and then dragged over a mat to a place near the mirror, and only a few feet away from him.

She lay on her back and began to lift her legs in time with the song's beat.

He increased the treadmill's incline punishingly. Sweat dripped down his spine, but it had less to do with the heat and exercise than it had to do with Mira, who'd now grabbed a stability ball. She lay on top of the ball, her shoulders and upper back supported by the ball, her legs spread, giving him a good view of her feminine parts.

Enough was enough.

He hit the Stop button. His heart rate was still elevated, his breathing ragged. But he had enough energy left to deal with his misbehaving sub. "Last night I promised you shower sex," he said. He grabbed her around the wrists and pulled her to her feet.

"About time," she said with a grin.

He raised a brow. "Provoking me?"

"Me?" She had the nerve to blink several times in innocence. "Just hot and sweaty…Sir."

"My bedroom," he said. He'd created a monster. "You may crawl, Mira."

"Of course," she said, instantly dropping to her hands and knees.

Once again, she won. She took her time crawling toward the door, exaggerating her movements, stopping once to readjust her shorts. The adjustment didn't make the nylon any less provocative.

He had a feeling if he bent her over that exercise ball and spanked her, she'd just behave even more scandalously.

In his room, she pulled off her clothes while he adjusted the water temperature.

The shower wasn't big enough for the two of them, which made it more than a little entertaining when he squeezed in the stall with her.

"May I wash Master's back?"

He grabbed the bar of spicy soap from the dish and handed it to her. He turned away from her and enjoyed the hell out of the way she ran her slick hands over his shoulders, across his shoulder blades, made circles on his back, then traced his spine up and slowly back down.

She soaped his buttocks, then crouched to wash his legs. Boldly she ran her hands back up again to cleanse his anus and scrotum.

Every touch was delicate, and her nails glanced off his skin. It was enough, just enough, to make him hard again.

He turned back to face her and took away the soap. After putting it in the dish, he adjusted the showerhead so that the water hit his back instead of her face. Capturing her chin between a thumb and forefinger, he wiped water back from her face. Her lips parted in a quiet "thanks."

Torin placed a leg between her thighs. As if it was the most natural thing in the world, she settled her pussy against him. "Hump my leg," he told her.

"Uhmm..."

"You were naughty enough to fuck the mattress this morning," he reminded her. "You've got three minutes to bring yourself off."

"And...?"

"If you don't, it will be a long time before you're allowed the opportunity again. I've been generous in allowing you to come. Don't push me."

She tilted her body forward a bit and wrapped her hands around his neck.

"This feels totally naughty."

"It is."

She approached this task like she did all the other assignments he'd given her—gamely—if a bit nervously.

She moved against him a few times, her breasts swaying. After about thirty seconds, she gnawed on her lower lip. "I need a different angle."

"Make yourself comfortable. Time is ticking. And don't even think of trying to fake it. I'll know."

Mira rose onto her tiptoes. Using her hands, she spread her labia and leaned into him again, pressing her clit against his thigh. She moved slightly and then groaned.

"Better?"

"Oh God."

He took that as a yes.

Her eyes closed, and she tipped her head back, getting into it more. Just watching her was enough to make him hot for her body again. "You've got about a minute and a half left," he told her.

"I..."

He took mercy on her. He reached behind her and pushed a finger deep into her ass.

She screamed, but he knew it wasn't from pain.

She moved faster and faster.

"Grind it out," he told her.

She did, rocking, making smaller and smaller circles on his thigh. He felt the tiny nub of her clit against him. Water sluiced over them both, and steam rose over the shower door.

"You've got twenty seconds to orgasm," he said softly against her ear. When she didn't respond, he asked, "Mira?"

"Yes," she gasped. "Yes..."

He drew her earlobe into his mouth.

She leaned even closer to him, and he supported her entire weight. He moved his finger in and out of her rear entrance, fucking her.

"Torin!"

"Take it, baby," he urged her. "Come."

There was no faking that orgasm. Her cry came from deep inside, and the slick of her cum against his skin was moist and real.

Her response thrilled him, made him feel possessive in a way he'd never experienced before.

She was right; they needed to talk: about the future, about what effect their BDSM relationship would have on their ability to work together.

One thing was certain: now that he'd had a taste of her, he had no intention of letting her go.

Chapter Eight

An hour later she found him outside. He was swinging an ax, splitting a log. He'd cut down a small forest since they had arrived. It had nothing to do with needing to be warm. The house had central heat and a pile of wood stacked inside as well as out.

She admired the raw athleticism it took to split the wood. He wore a black T-shirt, and it emphasized the way his muscles rippled and moved with the exertion.

He looked up, obviously sensing her presence. He drove the ax partway into a log and then took off his safety glasses and pulled off his leather gloves.

The man was pure sex appeal.

He was strong and firm. She'd learned that he was relentless in getting his way, to the point of nearly breaking Master Blake's wrist. But he'd been completely gentle with her when he'd cleaned her up after ravishing her anally earlier this morning.

She didn't want to give him up sexually, nor could she conceive of giving up any part of herself or the job she loved.

"We've got a call," she told him. This, more than anything, was the moment of truth. This was their first mission together. Their safety, even their lives could depend on the way they worked as a team. And if he treated her as a submissive instead of a partner, the results could be devastating.

He nodded. "Fill me in," he said, following her back to the house.

"Black tie required," she said. When he raised a brow, she added, "Seriously. Word came from Ms. Inamorata herself."

"Don't suppose you know her first name?"

No one knew her first name. Hawkeye's right-hand woman was damn good at her job, and that included keeping secrets. The office pool to guess her name had five figures in it. Whoever won would have enough money for a heck of a vacation or a down payment on a house.

"Where are we headed?"

"The Grand Hyatt. Trace and Aimee Romero have a personal security client attending a fund-raiser." Trace and Aimee were two of the best. Aimee was the younger sister of the enigmatic Inamorata. A brainiac if there was one, she was a scientist who had recently taken up running ultramarathons in addition to supporting her new husband, Trace, on occasional Hawkeye, Inc. assignments. The whole ultramarathon thing made Aimee's brainpower suspect, in Mira's opinion. "There's been a death threat against their client."

"Anyone I know?"

"Nathaniel Sinclair."

He whistled and nodded. “No wonder they're calling in backup.”

“Inamorata is e-mailing the hotel layout to us.”

“Be ready in half an hour?”

She checked her watch. “Less if we can manage it.”

He headed for his room, and she went into hers.

“Mira?” he shouted less than a minute later. “Skip the underwear.”

She rolled her eyes.

When she didn't respond, he called out, “Excuse me?”

“I heard you!”

“And what you meant by that was, 'yes, Master.'”

“Yes, Master!” she called dutifully. More importantly, she skipped the underwear. She told herself it wasn't because she was being obedient, but because her black dress would look better without them.

Twenty minutes later she checked the smallest of her three guns for bullets and then tucked the pistol in her handbag alongside a tube of lipstick.

She stopped in the bedroom that now served as a command office, and printed off the hotel layout before joining Torin.

He was waiting for her in the living room, checking his cuffs.

Damn. The man was completely devastating in his tuxedo.

His hair, the color of midnight, flirted with his collar. His eyes seemed all the more electric against the dark clothing. “Show me,” he said.

“Show you?”

“Bend over.”

“Torin...”

“Bend over, Mira, and lift your dress.”

She questioned whether she should actually comply. They were on duty, and they needed to head out.

He waited her out.

Finally, with a sigh, she placed her pocketbook on the coffee table and then turned around, raised her dress, and showed him she'd followed orders.

“Lovely.”

Her insides tightened. Against her will, her pussy moistened.

“Your obedience will make tonight's punishment much less painful. Shall we?”

She stood and smoothed her dress into place.

She shook her head to clear it. He was already at the back door; his hand was on the knob, and he was waiting for her. Obviously he was better at separating business from pleasure than she was.

“Grand Hyatt?” he asked.

“We'll meet Inamorata in the hotel's kitchen.”

He snagged the vehicle keys off a hook and offered them to her.

“You want me to drive?”

“I assume you know how?”

She bit back an instinctive smart-ass reply to his smart-ass question and handed him the printout from Inamorata.

In the SUV, he turned on the GPS and programmed it for the hotel.

She remembered their ride home last night, with him keeping his temper caged while he drove home silently. Neither of them mentioned that, however. Now that they were on the road, they were both all business.

She had the valet park the car and took a deep, steadying breath before heading into the lobby. She saw Trace there. None of them acknowledged each other.

Torin cupped her elbow and led her toward the kitchen.

Ms. Inamorata was there in her pencil skirt, hair pulled back. She had surveillance equipment on one of the stainless-steel work areas, and she efficiently handed them each an earphone.

After a tech made sure all the wiring was secure and in place, Mira and Torin each went through a sound check.

Inamorata asked, "How's the partnership coming? Any trouble working together?"

Mira wondered if the woman could see something. "None," Mira said.

She nodded crisply. "Hawkeye is usually right on in his assignments, but if it doesn't work out, feel free to ask for a new partner."

"Not necessary," Torin said.

"You're a couple tonight. Aimee will be arriving with Mr. Sinclair. She'll be his date for the evening."

Mira had done her research while Torin showered. She'd already known Sinclair was a media magnate. He owned newspapers, magazines, a cable network, and he had a San Francisco hotel named after him. He wasn't popular with everyone, though, because of his politics. He was running for office, and some thought he was trying to buy the election and push his liberal agenda. That hadn't made anyone mad enough to want to kill him, though, especially in California. It was his testimony fifteen years earlier that had sent a mobster to prison that was the issue. Several other people had refused to testify and had gone to jail for contempt of court rather than take their chances. Sinclair was campaigning on his bravery, and it had been effective until said mobster had recently been paroled. It turned out that a decade and a half hadn't tempered his attitude any.

"Questions?"

Mira and Torin exchanged glances. They both shook their heads.

"Your first assignment together," Inamorata said. "With luck, it will be an uneventful evening."

"You have reason to believe it won't be," Torin said.

"Rumors are Alberto Leone is in the city." Inamorata showed them recent pictures of the man. "Bad shots, from a newspaper, I'm afraid." She spread out a few more pictures on the stainless-steel table. "Other family members. Known associates."

Mira and Torin studied the snapshots.

"I'm attending as a guest, like you two," she said. "Cocktails are in fifteen minutes. Here's your official invitation. Our guys are manning the doors."

She handed over the card to Mira, and without another word, Inamorata moved off.

"Suppose she's wearing a butt plug?"

Mira gasped.

"Let's go prepare to meet the man of the hour."

* * * *

For the first time, Torin struggled with an assignment. He wanted to make sure Mira was safe. Yet he knew she was fully capable of taking care of herself. Hawkeye, Inc. had made sure of that. And Torin himself had had a hand in her training. She was strong, smart, resourceful. She didn't need him to look after her.

He was the problem.

He wanted her wrapped in cotton wool somewhere safe. The Leones were a tight-knit family who took care of their own. He didn't want Mira within a hundred miles of them.

She followed him to the lobby. He made eye contact with Trace before placing his fingers intimately in the small of Mira's back and guiding her toward the hotel's elegant ballroom.

A live band played forties music, and champagne flowed freely. Obviously no amount of money had been spared.

They went through the formality of having Hawkeye operatives check their invitation. He noticed that Inamorata was already in place. Outside of Fort Knox, this was one of the tightest places in the United States tonight.

He and Mira mingled. This was the nature of their jobs. Often twenty-three hours and fifty-five minutes of boredom interrupted by five minutes of "oh, shit!" And occasionally nothing happened to interrupt the boredom. Ideally that would be the case.

"We should separate," Mira said.

When hell froze over.

From their vantage near the bar, he kept a watchful eye on the door and on the guests arriving.

The night showed no signs of getting interesting, which was fine by him. He was ready to bury his cock inside Mira's willing body.

There was a buzz of activity near the door, and he kept his gaze there.

"Ladies and gentlemen," the evening's emcee announced, "your next senator, Nathaniel Sinclair!"

Shouts of approval and loud claps filled the ballroom. The media magnate came in with a wave, Aimee at his side.

Sinclair made his way to the stage and said a few words of thanks. He seemed completely at ease, without a care in the world.

In a security nightmare, he left the stage and started glad-handing all the attendees. People queued up to meet him, and they blocked a smooth exit. Torin figured Aimee would unobtrusively move Sinclair toward safety and keep her body between him and the guests as much as possible.

"I'll be back," Mira told him.

"Mira..."

"I want to meet him."

She walked off.

Since he could scan almost the entire crowd and see the door at the same time, he remained in the same general vicinity.

He kept a surreptitious eye on Mira.

She stood in the line with several other women, and she appeared to join in the conversation.

He noticed that she took one of the women by the arm as if they were old friends. Mira started talking loudly. If he hadn't been so in tune with her expressions and reactions, he might have missed the subtle look she shot him.

As it was, he keyed his mic to alert the others and headed her direction.

"I'm sure I've seen your picture before," Mira was saying.

The woman's stiff smile, obviously surgically enhanced, started to fade. "You're mistaken," the blonde said.

"Are you a movie star? Can I have your autograph?"

Torin moved in, cutting off the woman from her other friends. "Everything okay, honey?" he asked Mira.

"I think this woman is a movie star!"

Torin shrugged like a helpless male. "I'm sorry. She's an autograph hound. If you'll humor her..."

The woman had a sheen of sweat on her upper lip.

"Here, I have a pen right here," Mira said. She opened her purse. "Oh. No!" She got louder and more animated. "I don't have a pen. What am I going to do? Do you have one?" she asked the woman. "Can I borrow yours?"

She was drawing the attention of a lot of people, and Aimee whispered something in Sinclair's ear, then kissed him on the cheek, looking like a lover who was anxious to have her man all to herself. He shrugged, as if unable to resist the womanly wiles.

Inamorata moved toward Sinclair.

"Darling, I'm so excited! She's going to sign an autograph!" Mira gushed at Torin.

The blonde snapped. "I don't have a pen."

"Just look," Mira implored. "Please?"

Her expression more a snarl than even a politely civil smile, the woman made a show of opening her pocketbook.

Mira acted. She jostled into the woman, forcing her to loosen her grip on the purse.

Crap!

Mira's instinct had been completely correct. He keyed his mic. "Gun!"

The woman reached into her purse and grabbed the revolver then pointed it straight at Mira.

Pandemonium erupted in screams of hysteria.

Mira, gaze determined, leaned over and surged forward.

The gun discharged. The roar deafened him.

Chapter Nine

Pain shredded Mira's upper arm. It seared and burned. But she was focused.

She rammed her body full force into the blonde's painfully thin frame.

She knocked the woman over, and Torin moved into action, pinning her to the ground.

Trace Romero was there in seconds, securing the assailant's wrists while Torin hustled over to Mira.

"She winged me, Torin," she said. "The bitch winged me."

"Saw that. I made sure she is staying down."

"My hero." Her body refused to support her weight, and she couldn't stand up. "You mad? I wasn't sure I was seeing what I thought I was seeing." She struggled to keep him in focus. Then the world went black.

When she opened her eyes again, she was on a stretcher in the hotel ballroom. An IV drip ran into a vein, and Torin stood next to her, his jaw set in an uncompromising line.

She hurt like hell. And there was no one she wanted to see more than him.

A paramedic strapped her to a stretcher, and she struggled for the control she always had. “My dry-cleaning bill's going to rival the national debt,” she said. “I like this dress.”

He shook his head. “I'll buy you ten more.”

“And go shopping with me for them?”

“You're pushing it, Araceli.”

She tried to grin, to keep it light, but she couldn't. They seriously needed a talk. If it had been him who had been injured, how would she have reacted? How did they keep their jobs separate from their real lives? One thing was sure: she wouldn't give up her job, her freedom, or her independence for him or any man, no matter how good the sex was, no matter how much she wanted to experience his lash. She cared about him—loved him.

That thought made her light-headed again.

She didn't love Torin Carter. The man was strong and dominant, demanding. His world operated by his rules, and he offered no compromise, especially when it came to her and their BDSM games.

“I'm riding in the ambulance,” he told one of the paramedics.

“Sir—”

“I'd save my breath if I were you,” she told the young woman. “In an argument with him, you can't win.”

“At least your brain didn't get damaged,” Torin said with a slight smile.

Inamorata efficiently walked over. “Nice work, Araceli.”

“Except for the part where she got shot,” Torin said.

“Grazed,” Mira corrected. “The slug just took a chunk out of my arm.”

His blue eyes reminded her once again of a glacier. Cold. Determined. The concern she'd seen earlier had vanished. He'd blazed past anger. Now his temper was on a shortened leash. The sweat on her back chilled.

“You,” Inamorata said, pointing at Torin, “can shut up.”

Mira couldn't have said it better herself.

* * * *

Mira exhaled.

The last week had sucked. She hadn't required surgery. The doctors had just stabilized her and used some fancy new glue to put her back together. Treated and released.

Clearly Torin didn't see it that way.

He was still behaving as if she needed to be protected, and she'd already resumed weight training.

He hadn't spanked her, hadn't touched her, hadn't kissed her, hadn't made love to her. He'd slept in his own bedroom to be sure he didn't bump her arm at night. He'd fed her, kept her in coffee and food and ibuprofen, and he made sure she didn't overexert herself. And she was tired of it.

She joined him in the office.

He was obviously pretending to work. But she'd seen the hint of an online poker game before he hit a key to switch back to a spreadsheet.

"We need to talk."

He spun in his chair to face her.

"The way I see it, we have two choices, maybe three."

"Go on."

She licked her lower lip. This would be so much easier if he weren't so remote. He remained in his chair, arms folded across his chest. "You can ask for a new partner. We can stop playing BDSM games."

"And the third?"

"We can end both." She gave a brave, fake smile that faded instantly. Her voice shook as she added, "But we can't go on like this. I'm almost completely recovered. And I have this to say..." She tucked her wayward hair behind her ear and pretended not to notice her hand trembled. She drew a breath. She had to say what was on her mind, had to get it out. She didn't want to live with the regret of having kept her mouth shut. "I want it all. I want to remain partners. I want you to spank me. I want you to fuck me hard."

"Mira—"

She interrupted. "All of life is risk, Torin. All of it."

His posture didn't invite her to continue. His spine was rigid, his mouth unyielding.

"You cannot go off half-cocked. You didn't trust me."

"I didn't trust *me*," she corrected. "There was just something about her... The way she was looking at Sinclair..."

"You didn't trust me," he repeated. "Partners run ideas past each other. Hawkeye might have found you were not at fault, the press may call you a heroine, and the police department may give you an award, but I disagree."

Her blood seemed to slow in her veins.

"You put your own self-interest ahead of the partnership."

His cold words fell harder than any lash he'd ever used. "When I believed I was likely right, you were there instantly. No harm. No foul."

He stood and took a few steps toward her. "And that's the problem. You see it your way and no other."

"And you see it yours," she protested. "Like you said, Hawkeye's investigation found that I'd acted appropriately. We can talk about this. Reach a compromise. Isn't that what partners do too?"

His arms were folded implacably. "Partners trust one another. As for BDSM games—" He flicked his gaze down her body, from the top of her head to the tips of her toes, lingering on her breasts and crotch. "Without trust, I have no interest in those either."

"Torin—"

"I won't beat you senseless at Dark Haven whenever both of us happen to be in San Francisco at the same time, and I won't spend my nights wondering who you're fucking, whether you're taking stupid risks with a new partner."

Her heart stopped momentarily, and her knees felt weak. “So option number three?” Her voice was hardly a whisper.

“You're not going to give up working for Hawkeye,” he said flatly.

“No.”

He nodded.

How could she have been so blind? Of course he'd already chosen option number three. He'd already left their relationship. He was only still here because Hawkeye had placed her on a leave of absence. He wouldn't walk away until she was completely healed and his reassignment came through.

He might have been a wonderful caretaker, but she should have realized the significance of his refusal to touch her. Everything he'd done had been out of a sense of obligation. It was what partners did. Her heart seemed to break into a thousand tiny pieces. “I mean nothing to you?”

“Not true. You mean too much to me. I can't live with your recklessness.”

“So that's that, then?”

Instead of answering, he walked around her. He left the room and closed the door behind him.

Shattered, she collapsed in the chair he'd just vacated and stared numbly out the window, no longer able to think.

* * * *

Torin cursed himself for being ten kinds of fool.

He was five miles into a punishing outdoor run, and he wasn't even close to leaving the demons behind.

She was right that he was rigid in his thinking. No one but him would call her a fool for her actions. No one but him was in love with her. And that was the biggest problem. Somewhere along the line he'd fallen in love with the stubborn Mira Araceli. It'd be easier to cut off a limb than leave her, but he didn't have a choice.

Eventually they'd both get on with their lives.

He just wished the devastation on her face didn't haunt him.

Finally, after another mile, winded, he turned back around. She'd be cleared to return to duty in a few days, a week at the most. He'd get a new partner, a new assignment.

And so would she.

The idea pissed him off.

If he were honest with himself, he would admit there wasn't much about her that wasn't pissing him off at the moment.

She couldn't be cleared soon enough to suit him.

When he returned to the house, he discovered she'd closed herself in her bedroom.

He didn't like the lack of interaction. But he needed to get used to it.

He stayed up later than he usually did, waiting to see if she'd join him in the living room or maybe head to the kitchen for an evening snack. As far as he knew, she hadn't had dinner, not that it should matter to him. She was a big girl, capable of making bad decisions all night long.

Finally he gave up and headed for the shower, remembering the sex they'd had in the small stall, the way she'd ground her hot little cunt against his thigh, the way she'd screamed out her orgasm as he'd inserted a finger deep in her rectum.

His cock was hard, demanding. He'd gritted his teeth and endured it most nights since her injury. Some nights he'd masturbated, but the vixen had supplied the fantasies that made him ejaculate in a hot spurt.

He turned the water to a colder setting and then waited until goose bumps raised on his skin and then turned off the faucet. He towel dried his hair but left his body wet and went into the bedroom.

She was there, waiting for him. She was naked, on all fours, his belt held between her teeth.

His body reacted instantly, his cock straining with an erection.

His mind lagged a few seconds behind.

When rational thought returned, he knew he should send her back to her room. But his body was having none of that. Blood surged, demanding release. “Why are you here?”

She removed the belt from her mouth. She kept hold of it, though. “You said I mattered to you.”

“It's too late.”

“You were right,” she admitted. “I was foolish. Reckless. I wanted to prove something, that I'm strong, capable, independent.”

She kept her legs parted. He forced himself to focus on her words, but he had a hard time not responding as a dominant. Her pussy was spread wide, and he wanted to possess her. He wanted to use that belt on her rounded ass, punish her hard for the stupid risk she'd taken. He wanted to return things to the natural order.

"And the truth is..."

He saw her swallow and look down before continuing.

"The truth is I love you. You—we—matter more than what I want. I realize I am stronger, more capable when you and I collaborate."

"I'm not a bastard, Mira. I was well within my rights to expect that you would share your thoughts and feelings with me about what was happening that night downtown. Despite what you may think, even if you're in a submissive role, I don't think of you as weak or stupid. I'm not the type of man who expects his woman, his sub, to keep her mouth shut. I respect your brain. I'd be insulted if you thought I didn't want you to use it."

"Thank you for that."

"I never expected or wanted you to lose yourself to be with me."

"I'm asking, begging, for a second chance, as your partner, as"—she took a breath—"as your submissive."

"Mira—"

"Beat me," she pleaded. "I heard what you said, and I believe you. You weren't the problem; my own beliefs were. Of my free will, I'm asking you to allow me to submit to you."

He was undone.

She looked up at him.

"You will be punished."

"Yes..."

"For your lack of trust."

"Yes..."

And then the truth. "For scaring the shit out of me."

She leaned back on her haunches and spread her legs even farther apart.

"Because of your wound, I won't restrain you," he said.

"It's healed."

"You will be tied by my will."

She was silent.

"Your choice, Mira." He knew what he was asking from her, and she knew it too. He'd put her in position, and it would be up to her to keep herself there. Being restrained was often easier, because the sub could let go emotionally and physically, surrendering to the pain. He was demanding she be a full participant the entire time.

Without saying another word, she offered him the belt. He took it.

She crawled to the bed and positioned herself, her torso on the mattress, her feet on the floor. She stretched out and crossed her arms at the wrists.

She spread her thighs wide and turned her toes inward, exposing her ass and her pussy to his punishment.

"How many strokes do you deserve?"

"Ten, Master," she said without hesitation.

His cock tightened. He'd expected an answer of six, maybe eight. But ten would have been his choice.

He landed the first stripe from the leather just beneath her buttocks, across the top of both thighs. She gasped but remained in place.

He placed the second one slightly higher than the first. This time she moaned.

Inexorably he worked up a bit higher with each of the next four stripes.

"Are you counting, Mira?"

"Six?"

"Good girl." He crisscrossed the next two on the full globes of her rear. "Your ass is beautifully red," he said.

"Thank you, Master."

Her hips swayed seductively. He was captivated. It took all his restraint to focus on her punishment instead of taking her and riding her hard.

"Please," she said, "finish my beating and fuck me."

How could he resist?

He laid the last two on her already moistened pussy.

She jerked against the pain, but she didn't try to escape his lash. She kept her wrists crossed, her legs parted.

"Turn over," he said to her. "I want you on your back. I want to look at you as I take you."

He helped her reposition so she didn't have to put much weight on her injured arm.

"Take me," she said.

He stroked her pussy, and she was wet. He grabbed a condom from the nightstand and fumbled with opening the package.

Seconds later, he'd sheathed himself in the latex, and his cockhead was poised at her opening.

"Yes," she whispered.

She was perfect. Submissive yet in charge of what she wanted. She was ideal for him. He knew they'd have disagreements going forward, but he believed her when she said she'd communicate with him in the future. What they shared together was more important than what either of them individually wanted.

He sank into her in a single, possessive stroke.

She wrapped her legs around his waist, inviting him deeper.

He took her as his own.

She reached up and dug her fingers in his hair, holding his head close. "Kiss me," she demanded.

He did, but he allowed her to set the tone, and her kiss was fierce, as if making up for lost time and simultaneously staking a claim on the future. Fine by him. He met her tongue and returned the kiss with his own intensity.

Sparks ignited when they were together; he liked it that way.

Finally she ended the kiss and closed her eyes

He rode her, filling her, impaling her, imprisoning her. He felt raw and savage in a way he'd never felt before. Her breaths came in frantic pants, and she whispered his name.

"Take it, baby. Come for me."

She did, shuddering and crying his name, her internal muscles drawing out his climax. His balls tightened, driven by her responsiveness.

His body stiffened as he ejaculated deep inside her.

Her lips were swollen; her eyes glassy. "You're mine," he said.

"Yeah?" she asked, full of sass.

"Yeah."

"Prove it."

He would. Again and again and again. "You sure you know what you're asking for?"

She shuddered, and it was obviously in delight and anticipation. "I"—her smile seemed to tremble—"I think so. I hope so."

He pulled out of her, grabbed a damp washcloth from the bathroom, and cleaned her up.

He knelt on the floor near the bed and hooked her knees with his arms, positioning her so her legs rested on his shoulders. "Are you sure you know what you're asking for?" he repeated.

"Oh God," she said with a tiny whimper.

Using moisture from her still-damp pussy, he lubricated two fingers and slowly worked them up into her ass.

She gasped.

"You sure you know what you're asking for?" he asked yet again.

"I..."

He inserted fingers from his other hand into her cunt.

"Torin!"

"Master Torin," he corrected.

"Master Torin," she said.

He who'd never wanted a sub, he who'd preferred a different woman every night was now besotted. Completely. Totally. In addition to keeping her, he was planning to collar her publicly at Dark Haven. There'd never again be a question of whom she belonged to. "Still want me to prove it?"

"Yes!"

He fucked her hard in both places, and when she was on the edge, he closed his mouth over her pussy and sucked hard on her clit.

Her heels dug into his shoulders, she thrashed and screamed on the bed.

He didn't settle for wringing one orgasm from her body; he demanded a second and a third. "Still want me to prove it, mo shearc?" he asked when she lay there panting, her head thrashing from side to side.

"You win," she said, her voice ragged. "I think I've met my match."

He was going to have a wonderful time showing her they were a *perfect* match.

~ * ~

Sierra Cartwright

Born in Northern England and raised in the Wild West, Sierra Cartwright pens book that are as wild and untamed as the Rockies she calls home.

She's an award-winning, multi-published writer who wrote her first book at age nine and hasn't stopped since. Sierra invites you to share the complex journey of love and desire, of surrender, submission, and commitment.

Her own journey has taught her that trusting takes guts and courage, and her work is a celebration for everyone who is willing to take that risk.

If you'd like to encourage Sierra Cartwright to tell us more, she would love to hear from you. Feel free to email her at sierracartwright@hotmail.com, or check out her website at http://www.sierracartwright.com.

Loose Id® Titles by Sierra Cartwright

Available in digital format at www.loose-id.com and other retailers

The HAWKEYE Series
Danger Zone
Bend Me Over
Make Me

* * * * *

"Met Her Match (A Hawkeye Story)"
Part of the anthology *Doms of Dark Haven*
With Belinda McBride and Cherise Sinclair

* * * * *

"A Good Sub Would…"
Part of the anthology *Doms of Dark Haven 2: Western Night*
With Belinda McBride and Cherise Sinclair

Available in print at your favorite bookseller

Danger Zone
Bend Me Over (with Make Me)
Doms of Dark Haven
Doms of Dark Haven 2: Western Night

EDUCATING EVANGELINE

Belinda McBride

Chapter One

DARK HAVEN.

The sign was small and subtle just over the door of an inconspicuous building. After blocks of running, Eva had merged into a large group of men and women who wore Victorian attire like hers. It didn't look like a private party, so she followed them inside the club, praying she'd find her haven from the hunters who were just blocks away.

The group moved quickly inside, clearly accustomed to the place.

"Do you have a membership?"

She blinked, looking down at the cute...and scantily dressed receptionist. Eva cleared her throat. "Uh...no..." The girl's breasts were clearly visible through the Goth-inspired Victorian outfit that she was barely wearing. The girl smiled, and a diamond winked like a brilliant beauty mark over the side of her upper lip.

Gotta love San Francisco.

"That's okay. Is this your first time at Dark Haven?"

Eva nodded, brushing a loose strand of hair from her face with a gloved hand.

"No problem, then. Membership is five dollars, plus tonight's entry fee. Just fill out the paperwork. By the way, my name's Destiny."

Somehow she doubted that was really the receptionist's name, but heck, her name wasn't her own either. She paid and then scribbled a false name and address on the form, grateful that they weren't checking IDs.

Eva looked around the dark little reception area. The place was clearly a club, most likely a dance club. Music reverberated through the walls. She heard muffled laughter, and the occasional woman's squeal punctuated the air. A bulletin board on the wall held flyers for alternate-lifestyle events in the area. Eva's stomach sank. Was she in a sex club? She looked back at Destiny.

"Restrooms and lockers are to the right. If you have any questions, look for a staff member; the DMs have bandannas on their left arms."

Eva decided to skip the ladies' room. There was no doubt that the people following her would venture into the club soon enough. She didn't need to get cornered in a toilet. Hesitantly she stepped through the curtains and into the main room of the club.

Immediately she was assailed by the pungent mix of sweat, alcohol, perfume, and sex. Lots of sex. Adrenaline and the bite of fear saturated the air.

Her skin prickled; phantom hackles rose in panic. She blinked, trying to focus on the room and the myriad of possible dangers within. A woman's scream carried faintly from downstairs, and Eva's wolf growled. Blindly she turned to run, to escape. She found herself surrounded by people moving into the club and nearly staggered to the floor. A hand steadied her elbow; another patted her rump. She jumped away, barely hearing their laughter.

Run! The wolf whirled and spun in panic.

Just yards away, a woman was lying prone over a man's lap. Her skirts and petticoats were pulled up, leaving her bottom bare. With a *crack*, he slapped her ass bare handed. A strangled cry left Eva's throat. Against another wall, a naked man was suspended from chains that dangled from the ceiling. A collar circled his throat, and a complicated ring held his penis upright.

She whimpered.

Bodies in ruffles and frills and frock coats milled around tables. Some danced, and some leaned together in intimate conversation. The civilized behavior was a paper-thin veneer over the raw lust that drenched the atmosphere.

Too much. The sensory overload was too much. She tried to make a run for the door and slammed into a broad expanse of velvet and silk and man and the most wonderful fragrance in the world. He was sandalwood and vanilla and something she couldn't define.

Eva screamed, and her scream was echoed by that of the woman who was being spanked.

She screamed again.

Hands gripped her upper arms, and she began to struggle; her feet were caught up in the long, trailing skirts of her dress. A booted toe connected with a shin.

“Damn! Take it easy, sweetheart!”

“Sorry! Stop! I need to go!” She twisted in his grip.

Strong hands lifted her clear off the floor. “Sweetie, look up at me. Now!”

His voice was deep and compelling, and it cut through her panic. She shook her head, doing her best to bring herself back under control. For a moment—just a moment—she rested her forehead on his chest, inhaling deeply. The yummy scent of the man helped distract her from the surrounding chaos. Eva's entire body reacted to that fragrance. To her great humiliation, she was growing aroused and wet. She blinked hard and looked up into his face. His beautiful face.

“Now that I have your attention, can I help you?” His nostrils flared. He leaned a bit closer, his face coming dangerously close to her throat. She whined in panic. And then she bared her throat in surrender.

What the fuck did she do that for?

“You're scared witless. Follow me.” He lowered her to the ground and turned away, clearly expecting to be obeyed.

On trembling legs, Eva followed the stranger until they reached a little room that opened into one of the walls. As soon as the door closed, the music muted, and the scents faded to a tolerable level. She panted, fighting down the panic that still played at the edges of her consciousness. Gazing around, she gulped. The room was the exact duplicate of a police interrogation room.

She knew; she'd seen the inside of those a time or two.

“This is a bondage club.” He looked serious, but she could see he was stifling a smile. It was there in a dimple that flashed in his cheek.

“Thank you. I think I just figured that out,” she said wryly. Good God. Of all the doors she could have ducked into, she'd chosen a bondage club's.

The man gave her space, taking a seat on a battered table that dominated the center of the room. She couldn't miss the chains and shackles that were conveniently anchored to the floor.

“It's all for play here. Adult play, but still, everyone's here because they want to be.”

Eva bit her lip and glanced away from him. He was tall. Of course, everyone was tall compared to Eva, but this man would be tall next to most people. His wide shoulders were clad in a precisely tailored Victorian suit in dark coffee brown. His lush, wavy hair was the same color. A waistcoat of gold and green brocade winked out at her. The colors of the waistcoat matched his hazel eyes. He was handsome enough to immediately put her defenses up. His cheekbones were sculpted; his nose, straight and slender. His lips were just short of being full and were beautifully shaped.

In Eva's experience, the pretty men were usually pretty damn worthless.

But the way he smelled...

“I know what the club is all about. I don't have a problem with what goes on here.” Eva had plenty of knowledge about the scene; it was the surroundings that gave her problems. The place crushed the breath from her body. She shivered in delayed reaction. She wasn't shivering because of the presence of this much-too-handsome man. Hell, maybe she was.

"Why don't you tell me what you're doing here at Dark Haven? You're dressed for tonight's theme. Did someone pull a prank on you?"

She faltered, glancing away. How to explain her situation? She opted for the truth. He probably wouldn't believe it anyway.

"I was being followed. They were waiting for me outside where I work. I saw some people coming in here, so I followed them."

His casual posture suddenly looked alert. "Followed? Who was following you?"

He didn't ask why. There were many reasons a woman would be followed in the city, and none of them were good.

"I don't know. Some men. Maybe three. I managed to shake them for a few minutes."

She gathered her courage, deciding to trust him.

"One was following me by scent."

"Shit." He'd gone white. "Abraxas is in San Francisco."

"I didn't know that's what they're called. But I thought I'd lost them a few years ago. I thought I was safe here." Tears prickled her eyes, but she would not have welcomed his comfort. He was too strange, too male. She breathed deeply, calling up her female pride.

"Now I've led them to you."

"You've led them to my pack. Several of us are here tonight. Patrice wanted to come for the Dickens thing." He looked at her speculatively. "They won't be looking for us, so their tracker won't fixate on anything but you."

Eva took a breath. "I should go, then. I know this city. I can lose them down in Chinatown."

"No, we can hide you here. Right under their noses." His eyes took on an eerie glow. Immediately Eva stifled an impulse to retreat. As a general rule, she never let others decide her actions or dictate to her. But this man was an alpha; her wolf could sense it. He'd switched from Good Samaritan to predator right before her eyes. She'd rarely encountered other shifters in her life, and she'd never met an alpha before. He was a complication she didn't need right now.

"How?" She swallowed. Her voice was just a whisper. He was examining her, his bright gaze lingering on her stocking-clad legs and then moving up her body. She should take offense at his rude behavior. Instead she felt wobbly—weak.

"Remove the cloak."

She raised her chin at the command. He held her gaze, backing her down, and she looked away.

Eva reached up and untied the bow at her throat. The heavy velvet cloak slipped to the floor and puddled around her feet in a crimson pool. She stood impatiently as he evaluated her.

"There. If they get a look at you now, they won't recognize you at all." His gaze now wandered her figure. "Corsets are generally worn under the dress." He was hiding his smile again, and that seductive fragrance filled the air. Eva shifted, mortified at the arousal that pulled low at her belly. She'd never reacted to a man before—not like this.

"I worked at a corset booth at the Dickens Faire today. This is how we display the merchandise. The corsets..." Eva trailed off; her voice was thick and husky. When she peeked up at the alpha, he was staring at her with frightening intensity. She didn't glance down, aware of how the snug lingerie pushed up her ample breasts so that they strained against the pink silk of her blouse. Her deep purple skirts flared out from beneath the lacy pink edge of the corset. Her stockings were held up by frilly lace garter belts that attached to the corset. Her clothing had seemed fun and silly when she'd put it on. Now she wanted to strip, to bare her skin for the alpha.

He straightened, approached her, and then walked slowly around her in a circle. He reached out and stroked a strand of hair that curled next to her cheek.

She growled at his presumption. He ignored her anger.

"It's your scent that's going to be the problem. And there's one obvious solution to that tonight." He came to a halt in front of her, just inches away. Eva had to look up to see his face.

"And what's that?"

He looked at her intently, as though evaluating her worth. "Do you want me to help you?"

His voice had dropped to a whisper, and behind his eyes, the wolf was rising fast and hard. Her wolf reacted, causing the hair on her arms to stand up. She clenched her hands, fighting off the urge to flee—or to roll on the floor at his feet. She glanced at the door, wondering if she could make it before he caught her. She looked up at him again.

"What does your help consist of?"

He stared at her steadily. "Do you want my help? They could be here in the next minute. Think fast."

"Yes! I want help... But what do you want in return?"

For a painfully long moment he didn't answer.

"If I help you, I will keep you hidden from these people. Plus, I will teach you things that your alpha would have taught you if you had one." He reached out and clasped her chin between a thumb and finger. "I'll bet you can't even identify them by scent, can you?"

She glared but had to be honest. "No."

"How did you know they were stalking you?" His index finger was stroking her skin slowly.

"I don't know. I just did. Sixth sense, maybe."

"No such thing among our kind."

He let go of her chin and ran a finger over her cheek. She did her best not to flinch away.

"I will help you. I will teach you, but you must obey me without question. Do you understand?"

"In here? In the club?"

There was a light knock on the door. Neither looked in its direction. His thumb dragged over her lower lip, coming away with the sparkle of her lip gloss. He carried his thumb to his mouth and tasted the sweet gloss. She shivered and felt a tug of arousal at her belly. Her nipples went hard, and he was gazing at them, which made her skin go hot. She knew exactly what he wanted from her. Her body was intrigued, but was she willing? Would her wolf submit?

Her gaze boldly dropped to his groin, but his formal coat was buttoned closed. It didn't matter; she'd suddenly identified that delicious fragrance. It was his arousal. She didn't fool herself. It wasn't her; it was the situation that had him excited. He probably went hot with arousal the moment he walked in the door of a place like Dark Haven. Now he was getting off on her fear and the possibility of her surrender to him. He was a dom, and she was fresh meat.

“I'm not into this stuff. I don't like pain. Being helpless... Let's just say it taps into my fight-or-flight response. That could make me shift.”

“Don't worry. I won't let that happen. And we won't do anything that you don't want to do. Those are the rules.”

It seemed to Eva that he was making up his own rules as he went along.

The door opened and then settled closed again.

“That was a dungeon monitor. They make sure that nothing gets out of control. They're very responsible here.”

“How will my posing as your sub tonight protect me?”

“You won't be posing. And it will help you because your scent will be lost in here. They might know that you're in the building, but they won't be able to pick you out. Plus, as I mentioned, I'll teach you.”

“What? What will you teach me?”

He stepped back, drawing out of her space. Immediately she felt cold.

"I'll teach you survival skills. I'll teach you not only to hide, but to use all your senses. If you're very good, I'll teach you to hunt.

"Tonight? All that in one night?" She forced a skeptical smile.

"If you behave. If you do everything I tell you to do." He was back at the table, leaning casually against it. All the sexual pressure had receded like an invisible wave. He wasn't going to coax her anymore. She had to push back a smile. He'd come on like a tidal wave and was now pulling back, denying her of his presence. He was flirting.

"If you want, you can meet a couple of members of my pack later. I can put you in touch with others like us. You won't have to be alone anymore."

"How do you know I'm alone?"

He grinned, causing her heart to stutter. "I know a lone wolf when I see one." He paused, letting her think about that. "I like lone wolves. They're always tougher at the core than those of us who've been raised in a pack. Always willing to take a risk. And when they find their place in a pack, they place a higher value on it."

She wasn't ready, not yet. Not for a pack, but especially not for him. Her heart pounded. If she said yes, her entire life would be altered this night. If she said yes... Her gaze dropped to the shackles. How could she submit? It went against every fiber of her being! Desperately, she changed the subject.

"Who are they?"

"Abraxas?"

She nodded. The name was familiar. It was probably the name she'd heard her mother speak of all those years ago.

"On the surface, they're a legitimate international company that deals primarily in medical research. Unfortunately they actually exist to do research on us and on others who are different. From what I've heard from the new Truckee alpha, they're trying to bioengineer soldiers with various paranormal skills. They've got hidden labs all over the world."

Eva looked away from the alpha, not willing for him to see the impact that information had on her. Those people had taken her mother. God only knew what they'd done to her and what they planned to do to Eva once they caught her. *If* they caught her. She clenched her hands, anger trumping any grief that she felt. All those years ago, she'd been a helpless kid. She'd sworn vengeance for her mother but known that it was a vengeance she'd probably never see. Now she had a name... Abraxas.

"How long have you been able to shift?" His voice was soft but firm.

Eva blinked quickly, gaining control of her emotions. "A couple of years. I lived up in the park, and one night I woke up trapped in my sleeping bag. I remember being surprised that I could see so well in the darkness."

"That means you're sexually mature. They want females of childbearing age."

That meant they would never stop hunting her. As long as she was alone, she was a target. She needed every tool, every weapon that this alpha could give her. It would be worth any price that she had to pay.

Eva looked at the stranger, and oddly, he didn't seem unfamiliar anymore. His scent was embedded in her brain. She knew every plane of his face. If she let her imagination run free, she could picture the hard brown body under the suit. His wolf was dark brown; its eyes, molten gold. Her fingers tickled with the feel of his fur under her hand. He would be swift...

"What's your name?" If she was going to submit to a stranger, she should at least know that much about him.

"Harte Sommers." He reached out and offered his hand. She had to move to him to shake it. He was certainly a manipulative bastard! Yet his hand was warm and strong, and he didn't let go.

"Evangeline Jones. Call me Eva."

"Jones?" He quirked a brow, smiling slightly.

No, that wasn't her real last name. She'd left it behind when her mother had been taken. There were plenty of Joneses listed in the phone book. Details like that slowed down the hunters.

She looked down at where their hands joined; his skin was the warm brown of someone with genetics other than Anglo. Her skin was the lily-white of Ireland and Scotland. Someday she hoped she could find her missing family and learn exactly who she really was. For now, she was Eva Jones.

She looked at Harte, awaiting his instructions. Her jaw was so tight it ached. Submission went against her nature; Eva had no illusions about that. But for tonight, she would bend.

She saw a flare of triumph in his eyes, and the stirrings of hunger laced his scent. Again her body responded to his. He already knew her answer. He pulled her to stand in front of him. They were so close she could feel heat rising from his body.

"Yes or no, Eva?"

Back to that. Could she really submit to this man? Granted, he was an alpha, but hell, Eva had always had issues with authority. While she'd never returned to school once her mother had disappeared, she'd attained an education of sorts, haunting libraries and slipping into the shadows in university lecture halls. For years she'd studied kendo under a noted fight-master. Unlike the other students, she'd never called the man "sensei," in spite of her great respect for him.

If this man wanted her to call him "Master," could she do it?

"Yes."

That was all she needed to say. The rest would follow. If he truly could teach her to survive on her own, then it would be worth the humiliation.

"Tonight you will begin to learn two sets of rules. The first are the rules of this world, the behavior of a submissive toward her dominant."

Eva nodded. She hadn't lived in San Francisco without learning about the alternate lifestyles that flourished here.

"The second set of rules is more important to you—to us. It is the protocol of the wolf pack. Much of that is already imprinted on your genes." She glanced at him and then glanced away.

"See? You avoid holding my gaze because I'm dominant to you, as you will be dominant to some. Your head is turned away slightly. Doing so opens your throat to me. Do you understand what that means?"

She fought the impulse to back away. "It means I'm offering my throat—my jugular."

"Would you do that if your wolf didn't trust me?"

The floor nearly opened under her feet at that revelation. Her heart raced, and the hairs on her neck rose. "If the wolf didn't trust you, I'd not give you my throat. I'd never look away."

He nodded in approval. "Back to the rules out there. While you are my submissive, you will keep your eyes cast down. Don't speak unless you are spoken to. If you wish to speak to me, call me 'Master.'"

Her jaw tightened.

"That one doesn't work for you?"

Wordlessly, she shook her head.

"Sir, then."

Sir. That, she could do. She did it in the store all the time. Eva nodded, keeping her gaze averted. It seemed he was willing to be flexible.

"When I introduce you to other dominants, you will formally address them as 'Master' or 'Mistress.' Save for my pack and a few select others, I won't introduce you to submissives."

He folded his arms. The dark frock coat pulled tightly across his arms and shoulders. Once again she was unable to hold his gaze.

"You aren't a complete stranger to this world, are you? You've been curious enough to do a little research."

Her cheeks flushed in embarrassment. "I make corsets for a living. I have to know a little about fetish."

"Good. That will make things easier." He reached out and ran his thumb over her bottom lip again and then slipped it inside her mouth. Eva froze, feeling the tip of his digit hook over her bottom teeth. Confused as to how to react, she remained perfectly still. Using his thumb as a hook, he pulled her closer.

"Now, Eva, we begin your education. The first thing you will do is remove your clothing." He smiled, seeing rebellion cross her expression. He slipped his thumb from her mouth and stood back, a wicked smile on his face.

"All of it. But leave the corset and thong. Stockings and boots too. I like those."

She took a deep breath and reluctantly began to disrobe. She growled softly the entire time.

Chapter Two

Harte had no idea how he managed to survive that short time in the interrogation room. When the little wolf began to unbutton her blouse, he leaned back against the table, gripping the edges hard. If he didn't, he'd either grab her and take her down to the floor right then, or grab himself and get much too far ahead of the game.

Initially she was embarrassed as she undressed, but as she struggled and pulled her blouse free from under her corset, her fair skin flushed, and she bit her plump bottom lip. She stepped out of the long purple skirt, then glanced at him and blushed. She wasn't bashful—she was pissed as hell. That turned him on even more.

The pink-and-white-striped corset cinched her waist and cupped her breasts lovingly. The pink matched the cotton-candy streaks in her black hair. She wore a matching thong over the top of the garters.

She might not have dressed with sex in mind, but she knew what needed to come off first. Her fragrance surrounded him, and he nearly went dizzy with arousal. She was cotton candy and musk, and her arousal was laced with fury. That was good; as long as she was angry, she wasn't afraid.

Finally she stood before him, defiant in her feigned submission. Later it wouldn't be an act, but for now, her willingness to put herself into his hands was enough. It wasn't enough to keep the wolf from howling in his brain and scrabbling to break free.

Want!

Harte had scented her the moment she'd stepped into the building. He'd been negotiating a scene with a young human when he'd caught her fragrance. He'd probably been rude to the sub, but he'd apologize later. At that moment it had become imperative to track his prey.

Her scent had been laced with adrenaline when she'd entered the building and then panic as she'd stepped into the club. He'd managed to catch her just before she bolted.

Mate!

No, not mate. But a damned alluring female just the same. Mating was for life, and Harte was far from ready for a lifetime commitment. He had enough to deal with in managing his unruly little pack of wolves.

But she'd stumbled into his life with Abraxas on her trail. It was his obligation to do what he could for her. For the moment, that settled the wolf. Right then Harte knew that if he let her go after tonight, he'd regret if for the rest of his life.

Abraxas. He needed to call Chase Montenegro of the Truckee pack. His people frequently came to the Bay Area; they needed to be warned. They'd help if Harte needed it.

The Truckee pack was a collection of misfits and basket cases, but Harte couldn't deny that Chase and his betas were the most powerful, intimidating group of wolves that he'd ever encountered. When Chase had initially taken over the alpha position in the weak and disorganized Truckee pack, everyone had laughed at the foolish arrogance of the young nobody. But within weeks, Chase had shown up on Harte's doorstep, offering friendship and the invitation to join his pack, if Harte were so inclined. Harte hadn't been inclined, but with Abraxas on his doorstep, the alliance might go a long way toward keeping his own pack safe.

Eva shifted uneasily, and Harte realized that he'd been staring, his gaze lingering on the swell of her breasts, the flare of her hips. She was tiny but luscious.

"Take your hair down."

She looked slightly annoyed at his command but obeyed. It tumbled around her shoulders, a cloud of ebony black waves spiked with pink that was nearly the same color as her lip gloss. Briefly he indulged in the fantasy of her shining, pouty lips wrapped around his cock, then set it aside. In spite of the promise that he'd extracted from her, if she showed the least reluctance to engage with him sexually, he'd respect her wishes.

Right. Who was he kidding? The wolf was howling to the sky, beating its rear foot in ecstasy at his brief fantasy. He'd push her as far as she'd go, and then maybe a bit further. If he didn't get his cookie, then Harte would reacquaint himself with his hand. Yet if he could only break past that brittle human shell, her wolf was ready and waiting.

He stood looking down at her, appreciating the way her gaze automatically slid to the side. Some dominants got off on the obedience of their subs, and with humans, he did as well. But with one of his own, it was the language of the pack. She was a strong female bowing to him, giving him her throat. That was what wound his clock. Later, though, she'd hand him his ass on a platter if he didn't get her under control now. But then, he wasn't planning on a later, was he? The wolf certainly was. That realization nearly sent him out the door.

But little Eva was woefully lacking in survival skills, and Harte had only one evening to teach her what young wolves picked up automatically among their packs. She was smart, though. Hot tempered as well.

"Pick up your clothing and bring it to me."

She gracefully bent to scoop up the skirt and blouse, then carefully deposited her purse on top of them. She crossed to the table and held the garments out for him to gather.

"Get into position."

Anger flared in those blue eyes, but she didn't object to his command. Harte pushed her a little, letting the innate power of his alpha flow outward to add just a touch of compulsion. Her eyes widened; she'd never been exposed to a dominant wolf before.

Eva cautiously lowered herself to her knees and looked up for further instruction. Her eyes showed her inner conflict, but to his gratification, she didn't argue. "Spread your knees just a bit more, and place the backs of your hands on your thighs as though in supplication." It wasn't the norm in the club, but it was the stance his wolves took during the occasional discipline he administered. She automatically bowed her head.

“Very good. Now rise and follow me. Bring your clothing.” Harte led her back into the club, idly noticing that Master Simon was busy on the stage with a flogging demonstration. A very proper-looking woman in blue brocade stood in the doorway, fixated by what she was seeing.

Fresh meat. Someone would have fun with her tonight. He'd have homed in on her if not for his little wolf.

He scented Eva's rising anxiety; obviously the club was overwhelming her. He led her to the locker rooms. “Go do what you need to do for the evening. I'll take care of your clothing and purse.”

She started to object and then most likely remembered that she didn't have a lock. Besides, it was unlikely that the Abraxas hunters would search the men's room.

* * * *

She was waiting outside for him, standing self-consciously in her little corset and granny boots. Her cheeks were flushed, and her fingers laced together in front of her. To top it all off, she held her chin high, defying anyone to approach her. They returned to the entrance, and her anxiety quickly spiked.

“What bothers you most about the club?” He moved her to the side, and they watched the crowd. Master Simon had left the stage and was speaking with the woman who'd been watching his demonstration.

"The music. I don't go to clubs. It's too loud. The crowds make me uncomfortable."

"What else?" He had a feeling he already knew, but she had to pinpoint the problem herself. Mistress Alexandra sauntered by. She was dressed in formal men's clothing. Her sub followed, wearing nothing but a collar and leash.

Eva's fear surged and then receded as the women passed. Harte reached out and ran a soothing hand down her spine.

"Is it the collar and leash?"

She looked at him. Her eyes were huge. There were collared subs all over the room, many on leashes.

"To many, the collar is almost like a wedding ring or some other symbol of commitment. It's a great honor for a sub to accept a dom's collar."

She swallowed hard.

"However, to us, it's innately abhorrent. I also have to suppress my discomfort with the practice."

"Why? Because it's demeaning?"

He reached out and wrapped his hand around the back of Eva's slender neck. With a growl, she twisted away.

"It's a dominance zone. If you watch natural wolves—even some dogs—you will see that they lay their heads over the necks and shoulders of others to show dominance. It's very threatening. Even the most submissive among us cannot cope with a collar."

"Oh." She frowned as she examined the room, relaxing perceptibly. "How do you adapt to that? When you're here, that is?"

Harte waved at a group across the room. "I'll show you what we do."

EVA WAS STUNNED at how quickly he'd pinpointed her anxiety and how much sense his explanation made. She looked around, noting the collars and wrist cuffs on some of the subs. Dominants wore more clothing and sometimes had floggers hanging from their wrists or belts. One domme in a red velvet hunting jacket sauntered by with a riding quirt in hand.

She sensed movement in the crowd and realized that whoever Harte had signaled was now approaching. It was a man and woman, both attractive and fully dressed in elaborate costumes. A leash dangled from the woman's hand. At the end of it was a beautiful young man wearing breeches and knee-high riding boots. The leash was attached to his wrist rather than to his neck. Her skin prickled when she realized that these must be members of Harte's pack. Eva fought the impulse to growl threateningly.

The woman claimed her attention first. She was of moderate height; her dark hair was fashionably highlighted and twisted in a chignon. Her Hispanic origins showed in her caramel-colored skin and exotic, dark eyes. She was regally dressed in deep maroon velvet, with rich, creamy lace ruffles at the throat and sleeves. The man she was holding hands with was blond and tanned. He looked like a surfer, with sparkling blue eyes and a well-toned body. From the cautious expressions they wore, they were already aware of her wolf.

Their sub was just as beautiful up close as he had been from a distance. Golden brown hair spilled over his shoulders like waves of honey. His arms were muscular; his chest and belly were well developed. Automatically she knew that this prime bit of male was their omega, the bottom-ranked member of the pack. His gaze slid away from hers, and his smile was sweetly genuine. Immediately she liked him.

"I won't make you kneel before them, but remember to show respect." Harte didn't look at her as he spoke. Eva gritted her teeth and looked down at her hands. The woman spoke first.

"You picked up a stray." She didn't sound unfriendly, but there was an edge to her voice. Eva glanced up, and their eyes locked. The other woman looked away first. Eva stifled a surge of satisfaction.

"Eva, this is Patrice. She and Brian here are mates. Kevin is our omega. He's agreed to sub for them tonight." She glanced at the young man, and he flushed; his gaze met hers tentatively. That seemed odd for an omega wolf. She gave him a smile, and he ducked his head away. His smile was genuine, but his submission was as feigned as hers. He was humoring his temporary doms. He might be a sub, but his submission had to be earned.

When she looked up at the other man, he held her gaze. Eva looked away first. He wasn't quite up to Harte's level of dominance, but he was trying.

"I was just explaining to Eva why the collars make her uncomfortable. I wanted her to see how we treat our submissives here at the club."

Kevin held out his arm so that she could see the broad leather wristband that was attached to the leash. Eva leaned closer to examine it and pulled up short when she felt rather than heard a low growl. She glanced up at Harte to see what she'd done wrong.

"Ask first, Eva."

She flushed and nodded. "Sir, may I examine his leash?" Instinctively she knew to ask Harte rather than Patrice.

He gave a curt nod. Eva bit the inside of her cheek to keep from saying something smart-ass.

I can do this.

Once again she looked at the wrist cuff, lifting his arm this time. It wasn't nearly as offensive as the collar.

Okay. If he wants me to, I can deal. Tonight anyway.

"I can also wear a chain around my waist. That doesn't bother me too much. I won't wear a harness, though." Kevin gave a mock shudder and crossed his hands in front of his body. A slight tug on his leash put him back into position behind Patrice.

"Brian is my second in command."

She nodded in the blond man's direction. Something about the beta and his mate rubbed her the wrong way. They were saying and doing the right things, but something was slightly off with them.

The music in the club changed as a domme took the stage. She was dressed as a schoolmarm. A young man wearing only breeches waited in a posture of patient submission—he was on his knees, his head bowed. Evidently he was her student and was about to be caned. Eva grinned. That made her remember school, which led to thoughts of her mother and the day two men in black suits had forced her into a van. Everyone on the street had seen it happen, but no one had stepped up to help. Her smile faded.

A crowd of newcomers surged into the room, and Harte jerked his head, leading the small group back to the interrogation room. Once he had closed the door, Eva welcomed the comparative silence. He leaned against the table, and Brian pulled a chair over for Patrice, then took one for himself. No one offered Eva a chair, though her feet were beginning to grow sore.

Kevin sat on the floor at the far end of his leash and leaned against the wall. For the moment the rules of the club were being set aside. Eva sighed and slid to the floor next to Kevin. The industrial carpeting was rough on her bottom.

"Eva here didn't come to Dark Haven tonight to play. She was being followed. I'm pretty sure by Abraxas."

As one, they all looked at her.

"Dark suits? Bad haircuts?"

She nodded at Brian, noting his expertly cut hair. He probably spent more on his hair and tan than she did on her clothing in a year.

"Damn it, Harte. We've stayed under their radar till now." Patrice shot a glare in her direction. Eva bit her lip and kept her mouth shut. "Now we'll have to contact the rest of the pack and make sure everyone goes on alert." She had a phone out and was rapidly texting on the tiny keyboard.

"She couldn't have known that we were here, Patrice," Kevin said mildly. That didn't seem to soothe her or her mate. Both glowered at Eva.

"I'm going to take her in hand tonight, teach her a little about our world."

Yeah, Professor Harte Sommers probably had some lovely things on his syllabus for her tonight. Eva glared at the opposite wall. She felt a subtle wave of power and glanced up at Harte, who was gazing at her. His expression gave nothing away, but she knew he was reacting to her disrespect.

"I don't want you guys leaving. I think they've got a tracker after her. If that's the case, it'll be fixated on her. Don't do anything to draw their attention when they show up. Just get their scents, memorize what they look like, and take note of when they leave. When they go, we go too."

"Hunting?" Patrice sat a little straighter. Brian had a chilling smile on his face. Kevin studied his linked fingers.

"I'm calling Chase Montenegro. It's about a two, maybe a three-hour drive from Truckee. With his people, we'll have the manpower to deal with the hunters."

"Why call in those freaks?" Brian looked angry. "We can handle it! Our people can be in from Calistoga before Chase can come down from Truckee!"

Harte narrowed his eyes and glared at the other man. Brian wilted visibly.

"Do you question my judgment, Brian?" His voice was soft and threatening. Once again Eva felt that wave of power wash over her skin. This time it was stifling and ominous. She swallowed hard. She'd tasted his amusement and maybe his lust; she didn't ever want that anger directed at her.

Eva thought they might fight, but after a long, tense moment, the blond man backed down. He did so a bit grudgingly. Eva was not impressed. Surely Harte had better candidates for his beta?

"Why should we help her?"

Harte folded his arms and looked at Patrice. He didn't bother to answer. Like her mate had, she backed down, gaze gliding away. Eva could smell the woman's anger. She shifted to her knees, ready to leave and face the hunters on her own. If this was pack life, she didn't need it.

"It helps us to help her, Patrice." Kevin looked up at the alpha, seeking permission to continue. Harte nodded at the omega. "She might be their primary target, but they'll eventually find us, unless we deal with them quickly."

"Shut up, Kevin. You agree with every fucking thing he says!" Patrice yanked sharply at the leash that she still held. Kevin looped his hand and clasped the leather leash, tugging back so that he had slack.

"Yes. He's my alpha."

This was the first time Eva had ever seen pack dynamics at work. It wasn't that different from other situations she'd been in. Patrice, Brian, and Kevin were like angry siblings, challenging their parent and each other.

Eva cleared her throat. "What's a tracker?"

Patrice snorted contemptuously. "They're the scum of the earth. That's what."

Eva ignored the other woman and looked at Harte.

“Trackers are a product of the labs, Eva. They're usually human mixed with a shifter of some sort, often coyote or wolf. Sometimes they even splice canine genes into the mix, mostly for the sake of developing a tracker that fixates on a scent.”

“Are they shifters like us?”

“Nothing like us.” Brian's voice was low and feral, filled with hate. She looked from the beta to Kevin. His skin was flushed. Something about this conversation was bothering the young omega. Suddenly her skin prickled, and she shivered. She looked up at Harte and spoke.

“They're here. Inside the club.”

Chapter Three

"Damn. I meant to have you downstairs before this." Harte rose and helped Eva to her feet. His hand lingered on hers, and the expression on his face was intense. "I don't want her alone. You three stay close to Eva while I call Chase. Take her downstairs. Try to get her into one of the theme rooms till I come down. Kevin, since you two are both bare skinned, before you leave this room, make sure you cover her scent."

Brian stifled a smirk, and Patrice growled in anger. Kevin scooted closer to Eva and threw his arm over her bare shoulders. She went rigid—partly in embarrassment, partly in fear. He patted her arm, and she relaxed as the warm musk of his fragrance mingled with her own. Maybe it wouldn't be so bad. Hopefully he wouldn't pee on her.

"How did you know they were here, Eva? Did you scent them?" Harte studied her carefully. His nostrils flared, and he glared at Kevin. The omega was following his orders, but the alpha wasn't reacting well to Eva's proximity to him.

Eva grinned and snuggled closer to Kevin.

She shrugged. “Don't know. I felt them outside when I was leaving work. This was the same.”

Harte crossed to the door and opened it slightly so he could peer out. “It's damn crowded.” He waited for a moment.

“Bingo. Two black suits are headed to the bar. Since they saw you in that cloak, they aren't going to be looking for you nearly naked.” He smiled smugly. Eva growled, and Kevin laughed.

“Okay, get her down the stairs. I'll be there in a minute.”

Within a second, Eva was surrounded by three warm bodies; Kevin kept an arm around her waist, Brian led, and Patrice followed. She was painfully aware that they looked like a pair of dominants with their subs in hand. They moved to the right and started toward the stairs.

“You've never been to a dungeon before?” Kevin felt good next to her. Warm and comforting. When she shook her head, he continued, “Okay, don't be freaked. It'll be quieter down there, but the scents will be stronger. Your wolf will react. Just stay calm.”

She swallowed hard, nodding. As they approached the bottom of the stairs, she heard the steady, rhythmic sounds of leather on flesh. The occasional moan or squeal jolted her. She took a deep breath and then wished she hadn't. The air was redolent with sex and adrenaline. Next to her, Kevin also took a deep breath. He shivered, and she was fairly certain that it was delight that moved him. The front of his breeches tented outward.

The dungeon had a hushed atmosphere, and nearly everywhere she looked, Eva saw bodies. Bodies on wooden frames, bodies on swinging contraptions. To her left, a naked man was strapped to an X-shaped cross. Another man had a flogger in either hand and moved so quickly that the floggers seemed blurred. The sub's back was red and welted, but he seemed oblivious. In fact, he seemed to be in a state of bliss.

"Sub space," Kevin whispered. "He's moved past the pain into an altered state." She nodded and wondered if it was like a runner's high.

"Wait here. I'll see if there's an empty station." Brian didn't speak above a whisper. Judging by the intensity on the faces of those playing nearby, it would be bad to break their focus.

Kevin moved her against a wall, and automatically she turned around, then realized that they stood with their backs to a window. To her mortification, a couple writhed on a bed just on the other side of the glass. She turned back quickly, her cheeks hot with embarrassment.

"What's wrong?" Kevin turned and saw the couple who was having sex mere inches from where they stood. He chuckled and turned Eva to watch. "That's why they chose that bed."

Eva wanted to turn away but found herself unable to stop watching. She'd seen and heard people having sex before; privacy was hard to come by on the street. But these two were oblivious to their audience. No...they weren't oblivious; they were *enjoying* their audience.

The man pumped into his sub faster, her back arched, and they cried out in climax. Even with the window between them, Eva scented their arousal and the mingled scents of their release, and she responded. Her nipples drew tight under the silk cups of her corset. She shivered and turned back to the room.

"The evening's still young, Eva. You'll be seeing lots more. Soon." Kevin winked and took her hand, pulling her toward the other end of the room

She paused at a table where an older man was using a pump to apply suction cups to a woman's back. The woman was in a blissful state—her eyes were heavy, and she was smiling dreamily. She was secured in a web of rope that was exquisitely beautiful. Eva wanted to stay and watch more, but Kevin tugged at her hand.

When she saw their destination, her eyes grew large. A huge bed was suspended from the ceiling. It was curtained with hanging chains. Damn thing was big enough for a dozen! A woman lay in the center of the bed, lazily stroking the erect cocks of two very happy men.

"Climb up." Brian bodily lifted her onto the bed, ignoring her struggles. Without another word, he stalked away. Kevin followed her onto the bed and sat cross-legged, then pulled her into his arms. "We're mixing your scent with a lot of other people's. Just settle in and enjoy the show."

Eva couldn't help but notice that Kevin was certainly enjoying the show. After a few minutes, he grinned, leaned back, and located the woman's breasts. He licked at her nipples and then, coming back, took a quick swipe at one of the men's cocks. He gave her a naughty grin.

"I'd like to do that to you too, but Harte would kick my ass all the way back to Calistoga."

Eva flushed, imagining Harte in a possessive rage. For just a second, she was unable to breathe.

"That's where you're from? Calistoga?" Anxiety settled in her belly. That was too close for comfort. Yet Eva couldn't avoid the flutter of pleasure at knowing that Harte's territory was nearby.

"Yup. We can escape up into the hills for runs now and then, and most of us work there. Harte owns several businesses. Spas mostly."

"Spas? Like the Calistoga mud-bath kind of spa?"

"Exactly. You can come and soak in mineral water, sit in a pool of mud, or get a facial or massage."

"And what do you do?"

He grinned. "I give the massages."

"I'll bet you do."

He chuckled and directed her attention to a station just outside their hideout. "That couple met here at Dark Haven. He bid on her at an auction, and they've been together ever since. They even got married here."

"No way!" She watched as the young husband finished the last touches on an elaborate webbing of rope that held his wife immobile. The woman was passive, allowing him to position her as he pleased. Once he was satisfied with his work, he opened his bag and removed a scrap of fur. He then set several canes and whips out in neat order. After stepping up behind her, he ran a long cane up the inside of her thigh.

"He'll warm her up slowly with lots of touch. Some can take pain right off the bat; others have to move up slowly."

"I don't understand any of this. I don't understand the need to submit."

"You probably aren't a sub like me. Truthfully, subs can be hard to come by. You faced down Patrice pretty easily and stood up to Brian, but you bow to Harte."

"I don't know why," she grumbled.

"He's alpha. And there's something between you two. How'd he get you undressed, anyway?"

She clenched her jaw and didn't answer. She was still stinging from the bargain she'd made with him. She too was wondering how he'd gotten her out of her clothing so easily.

"Are you going to sub for him tonight, Eva?"

"Yeah. I guess."

His arms were wrapped around her waist, and she leaned back against him. He was sexy, but more than that, the omega was comforting in the most sensual fashion.

"Lucky," he whispered in her ear. "Very, very lucky girl."

Chapter Four

Harte approached, looking every bit the wolf that he was.

He was no longer wearing his jacket, and his white shirt was loose and unbuttoned. He had a large sports bag slung over his shoulder. His powerful body gleamed under the dim lights. He was heading straight for her. Kevin chuckled but still dropped his arms from her body at Harte's warning look. Seems the big guy didn't share well.

Behind them, one of the men grunted. She heard the slapping of flesh, knew there was a lot of sex going on, but still, she couldn't take her gaze off Harte. Someone climaxed, flooding the small space with the scent of semen. Kevin slid off the bed and held out a hand to assist her down. She landed on shaky legs and then watched as the men talked quietly. Kevin flashed a wink and left, winding his way through the stations. A moment later, he vanished up the stairs.

"He's keeping watch at the head of the stairs." Harte's voice was low and intense. "Patrice and Brian are in the crowd, keeping an eye on the men. If they come down here, don't panic. Don't even look at them. Your entire focus is on me."

"Can't we just leave?" Anxiety settled hard in her gut.

"There are three inside. One or more, plus the tracker, outside. Besides, this is an excellent training opportunity."

"Training?"

He stared hard at her. She swallowed, feeling a flutter of fear laced with perverse arousal in her gut. Where was the anger? The indignation that had kept her together until now?

"I allowed you to speak out of turn, but from this moment, you are on notice. You will ask permission to speak. You will address me as 'Sir.'" He took her by the elbow and guided her to an empty station. "Step up to the St. Andrew's cross, Eva. Face the wall."

Her anger returned in a rush. Eva jerked her arm from his hand. She stepped away, ready to leave him there, high and dry.

"Eva. Now." A wave of energy came off him, dangerous and threatening.

"No." Her throat was tight and dry. So what if she'd made a deal with him? It had been under duress. She glanced around the room, looking for an exit other than the stairway. There was a fire escape at the far end of the room.

"Planning to run outside wearing nothing but a corset?" He lifted a brow, and the wild energy receded. "I'm sure the hunters will enjoy that."

She froze.

"Come here, Eva."

Her feet were heavy, almost as though they were anchored to the floor. Step-by-step, she moved closer to Harte and to the wooden frame. Faster than the human eye could follow, he moved in and nipped her on the jaw. He shook her slightly and then released her.

Humiliated, Eva rubbed her stinging skin and dropped her gaze to the floor. It was the same punishment a wolf gave to a puppy. To add insult to injury, his big hands encircled her neck. With a hand braced under her jaw, Harte lifted her from the floor. She didn't choke, but the feeling of absolute helplessness overwhelmed her. She remained perfectly still until he lowered her to the floor.

Without further urging, Eva stepped up to the cross and put her hands into place. To her embarrassment, she wanted to grovel at his feet, wind herself around his legs. She wanted to bury herself in his scent.

Shit.

"What are your limits?"

She shook her head and then watched as he secured her wrists snugly to the frame.

"Don't play dumb, Eva. If you don't tell me, I'll have to find out myself." She set her jaw, refusing to answer. Truthfully, she'd never pondered limits. She'd never visualized herself on the wrong side of the flogger.

"Earlier you promised that you would turn yourself over to me completely. Do you trust my judgment?"

She pondered the question. Of the three pack members she'd met, she liked only Kevin on an instinctual level. He trusted Harte. Maybe she should too.

“Yes, Sir.”

“Then we'll explore. Since you're wolf, your triggers and limits will be different from humans'. For example, humiliation and objectification won't sit well with you, will they?”

“God no! Sir.” He was down at her feet, placing straps around the leather of her booted ankles.

“But you might have a higher tolerance for pain—real pain. Is that correct?”

“Yes, Sir.” There was no getting around the fact that she'd lived a rough-and-tumble life. She was a tough little bitch, if she said so herself. She swallowed hard, steeling herself to ask a question.

“Sir?”

He was kneeling next to the bag he'd been carrying and was rummaging through the contents.

“Do you have a question, Eva?”

“Yes, Sir.”

“Go ahead.”

“Do you plan to have sex with me?”

He stood up, circled the cross, and ended up next to her. He leaned down to whisper in her ear. “Is there a reason I shouldn't? Have you had a past trauma? Are you a virgin?” He was close, so close that she could nearly turn her head to brush his lips with her own.

She shook her head.

“If we get to that point, I will certainly ask. Does that make you feel better?”

She looked up at him, fascinated by the molten gold of his eyes. The wolf was close, but he had exquisite control. "Some. Sir." She remembered something else. "What's my safe word?"

"'Red' to stop. 'Yellow' if you just need some breathing space."

She nodded.

"Eva. I expect you to use your safe word if you need to. Everything will come to a complete halt. That's not a threat. It gives us a chance to reevaluate what we're doing. If you use your safe word, you won't be punished; it isn't a bad thing."

She took a deep breath and let it out. "Thank you." She was glad for that last bit of information. She could approach the scene with a little more objectivity. Stopping if she needed to wasn't a failure.

"Ready?"

Like she had a choice? Eva nodded. Ready or not, this was it. Harte leaned against her; she felt the warmth and weight of his body. Darkness settled as he placed a mask over her eyes. Eva fought down the panic that rose with the blindness. Her world narrowed to the scent of Harte and the hard, smooth surface of the wood against her cheek.

HE'D POSITIONED HER so that her feet were wide apart and just a few inches farther back than her shoulders. That gave just enough slope to her shoulders and back and brought her little bum out appealingly. From the corner of his eye, he caught a glimpse of Kevin on the bottom stair. The omega flicked his gaze up to the other room.

So they were coming? That was fine with Harte. It was just what he needed at the moment. He was dangerously close to losing his self-control with Eva. As a dom and an alpha, he was all about control. As a wolf, he was all about losing control, and Eva tapped into his wolf like none ever had before.

He lifted a leather flogger and then set it down; he chose one with wider strips instead. He didn't want to start her with a flogger that would sting. In spite of her tolerance, tonight wasn't about pain; tonight was about teaching her to merge with her wolf. It was also about stripping away those layers of grief and pain that shone from her blue eyes. She couldn't join with her wolf until her emotions were laid bare.

Frankly, Harte didn't know why he was so desperate to have her complete obedience. It wasn't like she was pack. Though if she wanted to join his pack, they'd be facing negotiations of a completely different sort.

Wouldn't that be interesting? As fast as she'd stared Patrice down, he'd have a new alpha female within the week. Yes, she was that strong in character. She just didn't know it yet.

He swung the flogger, getting the feel of it, letting Eva hear it whisper through the air. She went taut in anticipation of the blow, so he let it settle gently on her shoulder. She flinched, expecting pain, but received only weight. He slid the strands of the flogger down her back and over the rigid corset, watching and scenting as she reacted. He repeated the movement on the other side and then back to the start. On the fourth swing, he struck hard across her buttocks, and she gasped.

Damn corset was in the way, but for now he left it, enjoying the way it manipulated the shape of her body. The heels of her boots served the same purpose, giving extra length to her legs and a sway when she walked. He began to bring the flogger up to speed, brushing the leather tips over her shoulders and arms and down to her hips and bottom. Abruptly he stopped, pleased with the light pink tone her skin was taking. There wouldn't be much pain, but the increased blood flow to her skin would heighten its sensitivity.

He made a production of searching in his bag, rattling and shifting items around, while in reality he already had what he needed. He stepped up close enough that he knew she felt him in her space. Instead of a blow, she received a kiss on the neck.

She shuddered, and Harte scented liquid arousal. Reaching around, he then traced his hands over her belly, imagining the corset coming off inch by inch, revealing her ivory skin and rounded breasts. He fought the urge to grind his cock into her ass, to cover her and take her right there. His shaft was hard and heavy; the wolf paced and whined in desperation. Succumbing just a little, he trailed the tip of his tongue up her neck and ended at the shell of her ear. He leaned in, pressing his erection against her bottom. He held a long feather between his fingers and trailed it along her skin.

“Can you smell them? Hear them?”

She shook her head.

“Use your senses, Eva. You can smell me, can't you?”

He saw legs encased in black suit pants making their way down the stairs. His hackles rose as the scent of the first man flooded his senses. "He smells like gun oil and hair product. Old Spice and sautéed onions. His right shoe squeaks just a little."

He moved to her right and ran a hand down her cheek, smiling as she instinctively followed his touch. He'd been right about pain; the light flogging hadn't fazed her at all. She continued to instinctively challenge her bindings. She didn't like being helpless. On impulse, he swatted her ass with a bare hand.

Her wild-anger scent told him that she didn't like that at all. He'd found the chink in her armor. He grinned and laid his head next to hers. He felt the blood pulsing through her veins and pressed a kiss on her throat. He caressed her lips with the feather.

"Can you locate him?"

She frowned, cocking her head and focusing on her senses. "I hear him to my left. He's not on the stairs anymore. Sir." Her whisper was as soft as his had been.

"Very good." He turned her face and kissed her lightly. He then slapped her face sharply. She pulled her head back at the abrupt transition.

"That hurt!"

So he did it again. She jerked hard against her bindings.

"Be still!" he growled.

She took a series of deep breaths and stopped struggling. He didn't praise her obedience. Moving away, he then reached into his bag and brought out a cane. With the tip, he stroked up the length of her stockings, watching as she reacted to the feel of it on her inner thigh. She squirmed and then went very still when it passed lightly over her labia. Grinning, he pressed it up a bit tighter, watching her jump as it settled directly over her clit.

Without any preliminaries, he removed it and flicked it smartly over her ass.

"Shit!" She wiggled, trying to avoid the sting, but Harte was persistent, varying the blows, never falling into a predictable rhythm. He loved watching her shimmy and flinch, a private dance just for him and the slender, flexible wand.

A scream rang out, nearly shattering his concentration. At the station next to him, Master Patterson was laying into his sub hard—no warm-up, no warning. The man's face was stoic, and his sub for the night faced him as he flogged her breasts. She stared intently into his face. Some were like that, and that was Patterson's style; he liked to administer a hard beating. He'd seen subs line up for the older man's services, and Patterson would tirelessly oblige.

"She's just venting. Remember, she's here because she wants to be. If she needs to stop, she'll tell him." He'd noticed that Eva's attention had also been diverted.

"I know. She smells...excited."

He stepped close again and ran his hands up her bare shoulders. His breath ruffled her hair. "What else do you smell?"

"You."

That was a bit obvious. "And?"

"Someone furious. Angry." Harte glanced around and spotted Master Torin marching a new sub to the Medieval Room. He wasn't dressed for the theme, and

Harte stifled a grin at the thunderous expression on the human's face. His little sub had pissed him off royally.

Torin was bagged and tagged.

"There's only one hunter down here. He's...down by the bed where Kevin took me." She paused and swallowed. Harte returned to his bag and pulled out a bottle of water. He opened it and gave her a sip, visually checking the bindings around her wrists while she drank. He'd take her down soon, after the hunter left.

"How do you see the world around you, Eva? What senses do you use?"

She paused to swallow her water. "Sight, hearing, smell."

"No, that's the human way. They see, hear, smell, touch, and taste. We work in a different order." She was attentive now, her focus completely on him. "Like wolves, we rely on our sense of smell, followed by hearing, sight, taste, and touch. It sometimes varies, but that's the general order."

He took the bottle he held up to her and set it on the floor. While he was down there, he wrapped his hands around her ankles, just above the bindings. Slowly he ran his hands up her calves and circled around to the outsides of her thighs. She was very still, and her fragrance was sweet and alluring. Slowly he circled to the insides, finally cupping her mons through the silky fabric of her thong. She was wet.

"You're drenched. You're dripping into my hand."

"Adrenaline does that. So does fear."

"But you aren't afraid, are you, Eva?" He rested a cheek against her bare buttock, then rolled in to give her a light nip. She jumped. He kissed the spot he'd nipped, and moved his fingers, sliding the scrap of silk aside. She went very still. He slid one finger through the slick folds of her labia, hissing when she flexed automatically. She made a small, animal-like sound. He doubted that she was even aware she'd made it.

His fingers brushed lightly over her clit and then circled back to her entrance. He pushed the tip of one finger inside, caught the juices, and pulled them backward to her ass. He pressed lightly just to check her response. She tightened and jerked away from his hand. Harte chuckled at her reaction. This was going to be fun.

Harte stood and began to loosen her restraints. "I'm taking you down now. Don't take off the blindfold. Just get your balance."

When she looked steady on her feet, he led her across the room to a padded table. It was low enough for her to drape over comfortably. "Panties off." She looked reluctant but didn't hesitate to obey, and reached out to orient herself to the table as she slid the thong off her hips. He carefully guided her into place and then used the shackles that were bolted to the floor to hold her immobile. They had a spreader bar and held her feet far apart.

Carefully, slowly, he unlaced the back of her corset, admiring the exquisite work of the piece. She sighed as it came off, and he sighed at the sight of her tiny waist and slender back. He still hadn't seen her breasts. He'd save that treat for last.

There was a drop cloth under their feet, and Harte decided to make use of it, pulling a half-burned red candle and a lighter from his bag. When he lit it, her head came up anxiously. He watched the wax pool under the wick and then stroked her back, relaxing her just a bit. He reached out, centered the candle over the curve of her spine, and tipped it, watching the red wax drip onto her ivory skin.

She screamed. Finally.

"YOU FUCKER!" SHE didn't scream the words, not exactly, and she kept her face buried in the vinyl of the table.

"What was that, sub?"

Eva shook her head wildly, trying to process the sensations that were sparking along her skin.

"You fucker, Sir!"

In reply, another trickle of fire hit her shoulders and dribbled down her back. She stomped her feet as much as the shackles allowed. Her fisted hands pounded on the table.

"Are you saying your safe word?" His voice was low and silky in her ear.

"No!"

"Good." Another spatter of wax hit her back and trickled toward the crack in her ass. Now that she'd adjusted to the shock, it wasn't so bad. Eva went still in surprise. In fact...

"Sir?"

"Yes, Eva?" He sounded a bit disappointed, like perhaps he had expected her to call a stop to their play.

"It only hurt because I expected it to burn, right?"

"Very good. And I appreciate your stifling that scream. A second black suit just came down the stairs. However, there is that little matter of language..."

She went still, trying to catch a scent that was slightly familiar. All of a sudden, it hit her. "Black licorice. Cigarettes. A gun." She ignored the comment about her language. It would come back to haunt her soon enough.

"That's right." His hand slid down between her legs again, and his fingers glided into her slick pussy. Her eyes nearly crossed at the sensation. Her ass tilted, and inwardly she cursed at her body's eagerness to take him. Her wolf was awakened; she'd called on it to scent, and now it was up and aware of the alpha who was wreaking such havoc on her body and mind. Never in her life had she felt so connected to the animal.

She shivered, feeling the sudden need to shift, to escape out into the foggy streets of the city. Surely she could shake the tracker if she could only run...

The tickle of fur started on her skin, beginning on her neck and chest. Eva whimpered in fear. What if she shifted here in front of witnesses?

"Sh... You're all right, Eva."

A wave of warm, reassuring comfort flowed over her, helping Eva to push the wolf back. He covered her from behind, his huge body wrapping her in an embrace that nearly brought her to her knees. Harte stroked her throat and whispered softly in her ear until the urge to shift passed. She panted with the effort it took.

"Excellent, Eva. You controlled that well."

She'd done it with his help. Usually Eva avoided any situation that might trigger her wolf. She'd never been able to pull it back once the shift started. She sighed in relief.

"A reward for doing so well..." His tongue stroked slowly down along her throat, further adding to the confusion of sensations that Eva was experiencing.

Harte moved away, and she immediately missed his presence. Just a second later, she felt him kneeling between her legs with his back to the table, his face turned up into her crotch. She tried to pull away—she'd never allowed that before. "No..."

He ignored her, and his tongue slowly passed over her vagina, up to her clit. He flicked his tongue quickly, taking her up the slope of arousal so fast that she gasped. A heartbeat before she could no longer hold back, he stopped and dipped a finger into her juices, then trailed up to her ass. Why the hell was he so fixated there? She squeezed hard.

"Relax, Eva. Let me in."

She shook her head mutely.

Once again he was tonguing her, taking her back up to the peak. She plunged and bucked and moaned in frustration when he stopped. His wet finger returned to her ass. It pressed and slipped in a tiny bit.

"Push against it, Eva."

"Fuck. Fuck!" She twisted, still fighting the finger when his mouth began its cruel torture yet again. She whimpered, lost in the sensations that flooded her body. Her back was heated from the wax. Her belly was heavy and tight from the blood flowing to her pelvis. Her legs were locked into place; she couldn't even protect herself. Her pussy clasped on emptiness, and his damned finger was now up to the knuckle in her butt! He pumped in and out as his tongue flitted over her clit. When he pulled the finger out, a second joined it on the way back in.

She was coming and coming fast with him there between her legs.

"Come, Eva."

She fought it with everything she had.

His free hand swatted her ass, and the climax began deep, wrenching hard through her belly. She didn't pant or whimper; Eva let out a deep, hearty groan as the orgasm drew out endlessly. She couldn't bring herself to be mortified when the burn turned to pleasure, and she rose to meet his pumping fingers. Her hands clutched at the far edge of the table; her fingernails dug into the vinyl. When it finally peaked, she froze, completely unable to breathe or move or to even think. Finally she gasped and ground her clit against his face, desperately chasing the last, fleeting sensations of the shocking release.

Eva dropped her head to the table, panting and spent. After a moment, she felt movement as Harte unbuckled her feet. He rose and stood at her side, gently stroking her back. He picked the hardened wax off her skin and slipped off the blindfold.

"That was..." She trailed off, too confused and drained to summon words.

"I know. There's nothing quite like it, is there?" He leaned down and kissed her—their first kiss, and she tasted herself on his mouth.

"Thank you, Sir."

"Oh, Eva. Don't thank me now. There's still the matter of your language."

Chapter Five

"Do you need a drink? Bathroom?" He helped her up onto the table, smiling when she curled up on her side. Her dark hair cushioned her cheek, and he found it difficult to look away. She looked young enough to be in her teens, but she was sexually mature, putting her in her mid- to late twenties.

She shook her head, but Harte wasn't fooled. She needed a break—just a short one to cool down from that climax. He glanced around. The two Abraxas hunters were talking quietly, doing their best to look at every woman and still not draw attention to themselves.

They were failing. A DM was cautiously watching them from across the room.

He caught sight of Kevin hovering anxiously at the bottom of the stairway. Once the omega had his attention, he swiftly moved to join Harte and Eva.

"The one upstairs went outside. Brian and Patrice followed like they were going out for a smoke. He met someone else in a black car. He argued with them and then came back inside."

"Were they able to hear anything specific?"

Kevin shook his head. "They just seem to know she's still in here. They aren't to leave until they've got her."

Harte frowned. The men had already walked past Eva several times. The only thing that had him worried was the pink streaks in her hair. Even in the updo, they'd been glaringly obvious. Down here, the dim light muted the color. But eventually they'd spot her.

Kevin looked down at Eva's still form. She appeared to be dozing.

"Are you two almost finished? The other two are getting antsy."

Harte felt his jaw go tight. Soon—very soon—he and Brian would be coming to blows.

"They can just continue to stay on alert. I'm not finished." He relented a bit, not wanting Kevin to feel the brunt of his anger. "She's identified two of the hunters by scent so far. Her hearing is perking up, along with her sense of smell. I can't just turn her back out on the street defenseless. Besides, we should stay put till Chase and his men get here."

Kevin's green eyes flicked in her direction. "She's not a sub. You could teach her without going through all this."

Harte smiled. "She's not a sub, but she's submitting to me. And...there's something there. I can feel it—almost taste it. I think she's alpha herself." He shrugged his shoulders. For the first time, he found it odd that he confided in his omega rather than his beta. The beta who was currently upstairs sulking.

On impulse, he reached out and clasped Kevin by the hair, pulling hard. The young man's eyes glazed with pleasure. He didn't know who'd trained Kevin, but he or she had been a class act. The only time Kevin displayed any major anxiety was when his hazy origins were brought up. He'd been through rough times, and they'd left their mark. Yet the young man was surprisingly secure and balanced. His former master had built the young man up rather than torn him down.

From the corner of his eye, he saw one of the hunters returning up the stairs. The other was headed in their general direction. Harte pulled Kevin close, so close their lips brushed. He watched the hunter from behind the screen of the omega's honey-colored hair.

"She's your mate, Harte. That's why you need to dominate her." Kevin's voice was soft to his ear. "Your wolf already knows. You've already claimed her. I can see it in your face."

Gently he brushed his lips over Kevin's. By pack tradition, the young man was his if he wanted him. Theirs, if he someday chose to share him with his mate. Just the thought of Eva with Kevin made him want to tear the omega's throat out. Eva was his.

Carefully, Harte pulled himself back under control.

"It doesn't matter what my animal thinks, Kevin. Eva's never learned to listen to her wolf, and as soon as I let her loose, she'll run. All I can do is give her the tools she needs and hope she runs with me instead of away."

He relaxed his hold on Kevin and let the young wolf loose. "Thank you, Kevin. You're doing good tonight." The omega glowed with the praise. He returned to the stairs, a smile lingering on his face.

Harte sighed and turned to where he'd left Eva resting on the table. Her eyes were open. She'd been watching with interest.

She sat upright. Her corset lay abandoned and forgotten, and Harte froze at the sight of her almost fully nude. Her legs were neatly folded back, still encased in her boots and stockings. Her breasts were pale and round, tipped by dark rose nipples. Her belly was soft, belying the raw strength that she possessed. Her mons was shadowed with dark curls. He knew many men preferred their women to shave, but she was perfect the way she was.

He was fixed to the spot where he stood, staring at her. She blinked slowly. Her ridiculously long lashes shadowed her eyes.

"She's beautiful. Are you keeping her?"

He turned to see Master Xavier at his shoulder. Damn! He'd been so distracted that the club's owner had walked right up on him! He swallowed, watching Eva react as both men gazed at her, talking about her within her hearing.

"If she'll let me, yes. I'd like to keep her."

She seemed to remember the minimal training he'd given her, and her gaze dropped to the tabletop. He could scent the warmth of her embarrassment.

They took a step closer. "Eva, this is Master Xavier. He owns Dark Haven. Since you owe him for tonight's sanctuary, you will call him 'my Liege.'"

Her eyes grew wide, and he prayed she'd keep a lid on her mouth. He could see the curiosity playing behind her eyes.

"Welcome to Dark Haven, Eva. If you need anything, please feel free to ask any of the staff."

She nodded, gave a slight smile, and her gaze slid off to the side. That was involuntary, and Harte had no doubt that she was stunned by her own behavior. Submitting to a human? That was probably a first for Eva.

Xavier's hand on his arm urged him out of earshot of his little wolf. She was probably getting fed up with being left there. As he watched, she lowered herself to the table again and lay on her side, her chin propped on her forearm as she continued to watch him. She was wild and feral looking. He had a difficult time pulling his attention away from her.

"Harte, we've noted some strangers in our midst tonight. Is she the reason?" Xavier questioned him bluntly. It never failed to amaze him how much the human observed.

Lying would be very bad form, especially to a man he considered a friend. Harte glanced at Eva again and back to Xavier. "She's in trouble, Xavier. I can't just let her run off into the night."

The other man nodded and looked at Eva again. "You just met?"

"Those men were following her. She ducked in here to hide and literally ran into me. The minute we step outside, they'll be on her. I've got help coming."

The black-haired man stared at him enigmatically.

"Just be certain that when anything goes down, it goes down outside, not in here. I won't have my guests endangered."

"Whatever happens, we'll be in control of it. And it won't be inside of the club." Harte gave a wicked smile, fully aware that his eyes had shifted. Xavier might not know exactly what he was, but he'd never judged Harte and his people. "We think too highly of you to do that."

Xavier bowed slightly, and his long braid slipped to the side of his shoulder. "I'm glad that I was able to give her sanctuary, then. You should go back to her now. She's drawing attention."

Harte turned sharply and growled under his breath as an unattached dom approached Eva. He turned to thank Xavier, but the man was already gone. With his hackles rising and the wolf in his gaze, Harte returned to Eva.

EVA WATCHED THE man at Harte's side with some degree of awe. Yes, some humans were innately dominant, but he held a force similar to Harte's alpha presence. He was dressed in black, unrelieved except for the silver and blue vest under his frock coat. His hair was combed back from his face; the braid dropped near to his ass. Under the lights, she could see the high cheekbones of Native American lineage. She let out a deep breath.

Eva looked around, seeing so much more now than she'd been able to take in earlier. In one corner sat a cage; a young woman was crouched inside. She looked uncomfortable in her waist cincher and heels. In another corner, a heavy woman was lying on a table similar to the one Eva was perched on. She was bound to it with clear cellophane wrap. Her dom was between her spread legs, and his entire focus was on fucking her with his fingers.

She looked away only to see a tall man with his pants open, having sex with a woman on a hanging sling of some sort. They were oblivious to watchers. When his pants began to slip down his ass, she sniggered. It was interrupting his focus. He was having a hard time fucking and holding up his pants at the same time.

"Are you alone?" She looked up into the face of a stranger. Frankly she didn't know how he could possibly have missed Harte, but maybe he'd just come in.

"No, I'm with someone."

"Well, your dom shouldn't have left you here like an offering, should he have?" She firmed her jaw and stared directly into his light blue eyes. He was young, perhaps in his midtwenties, and had blond stubble on his chin. His leathers looked stiff and new. He wasn't dressed for tonight's theme.

"I said I'm with someone. Now go away."

His fair skin flushed with anger. His jaw went tight, and Eva recognized him for what he was—a poser. A bully. If they weren't in a controlled situation, he'd strike out at her.

"Go. Away."

The young man leaned over the table, facing Eva. He started to speak and then stopped when a low growl floated through the air.

"She said leave."

Harte's face was dark with fury; his eyes were molten gold. He was barely a step away from wolf, and that exquisite control of his was slipping. Eva swallowed. Part of her was thrilled at the possessiveness in his voice; another part wanted to run. If she ran, would he follow? Inside, her wolf rose to meet him.

The blond straightened slowly and turned to face Harte. He might have considered challenging the angry dom but wisely changed his mind.

"Sorry, man. Misunderstanding. My mistake." He was between Harte and the table Eva sat on. It was only then that she remembered she was practically naked. Slippery juices from her orgasm still slicked her thighs. She'd been so high from the climax that she'd forgotten where she was and why she was here in the first place. She found her corset and realized that she'd be unable to put it on without assistance. Great! She was sitting nearly stark naked on a table in the middle of a dungeon while two men were preparing to fight over her. She scooted toward the head of the table, trying to distance herself from trouble.

Just when she thought they were going to burst into a fight, a DM stepped in.

"Hey there, Master Harte. MacKenzie. Is there trouble?"

"No trouble. Mac here was just leaving. Heading home. Weren't you, Mac?" The blond looked ready to argue and then thought better of it. He gave a stiff nod.

"Well, if you're leaving, I'll see you to the door." The DM winked at Eva as he left. She saw the glint of a collar peeking out from the open neck of his shirt.

"He's a sub? And he's bouncing that guy? Sir?"

Harte was still caught up in fury. His breathing began to slow; his eyes slowly regained their hazel color. By the time he spoke, he'd regained his temper.

"Being a sub doesn't mean you're passive or weak. He's just wired to be the bottom in his relationship. Kevin's another good example. He's tough and a good fighter; he simply has no drive to challenge the other wolves. In personal relationships, he enjoys the power that he gains from being the sub."

She'd heard about that before, the power of the submissive. Harte might be calling the shots, but if she said stop, he'd obey her without question. It was a comforting idea and empowering as well.

He scooped her up in his powerful arms and lifted her off the table. He was treating her as though she were precious and fragile. He settled her on the floor, watching critically to be certain that she was steady on her feet.

She glanced at the front of his trousers; she could easily see his erection straining against the fabric. Eva didn't even try to hold back her smile.

He reached down and picked up his bag. He tossed the abandoned corset to her. "Rest time is over. Back to work."

Chapter Six

They walked toward a series of rooms situated to the side of the dungeon. The doors didn't lock, so Harte slid open a small peephole to make sure the room was empty.

"You'll like this."

Eva entered a small space that was fashioned to look like an exotic tent. Silken hangings of vivid, luxurious colors lined the walls, and the floor was covered with heavy oriental rugs. A hookah was displayed on a table in the corner. Pillows and throws made of silk and velvet were strewn over the floor. A rich, thronelike chair sat at one end of the room. She could easily imagine a sheikh lounging there, choosing from his harem.

"Take a seat." He gestured to the floor, so Eva settled on one of the huge pillows. Harte sat with his back against fabric-covered wall.

"So talk to me."

She looked at him in puzzlement. "About what?"

He rested his head against the wall. "I just tied you up and whipped you. Then I dribbled hot wax on your skin and gave you a very public anal orgasm. You crossed some major boundaries, and I need to know what's going on in your head."

"Sir?"

"Yes, Eva?"

"May I take off my boots?" He nodded his permission, and Eva untied the laces, then removed the boots with a sigh. "I've been on my feet well over twelve hours."

Without comment, Hart moved over and began to massage her aching feet. She tried to jerk away, but he growled softly, telling her that perhaps his control wasn't as complete as she'd believed. When he pulled massage oil from his bag, she sighed with bliss. He carefully unfastened the garters and rolled down her stockings. He warmed the oil with his hands before smoothing it onto her skin.

"If anyone else in the world tried any of this with me, I'd have had their head."

"I knew you were a dangerous woman."

He grinned, and her heart melted just a bit. She reclined and stared at the ceiling. In the relative quiet of the little room, she could make out noises from upstairs: footsteps and muffled voices as well as music and the sound of the pipes in the walls.

"I can hear Brian's voice. I can't hear what he's saying, but I can hear him," she said.

He rotated her foot, stretching her hamstring.

"He's up to no good, you know. He and Patrice. I hope they don't have many followers in the pack."

"Some. We're a bit scattered. I keep the ones like Kevin close to me. Make sure they have jobs and a chance at school. The ones like Brian and Patrice don't depend on me so much, so that makes it easier for them to rebel."

"They all need you. A wolf pack is a social structure. They all need the approval and support of their alpha. You need them to need you."

He smiled but didn't look up at her face. "You know an awful lot for a lone wolf."

"You're the one who told me it was in my genetic wiring. I just think maybe you're being a little too human. Too civil." She looked at him soberly. "You're alone at the top. That can't feel good."

She reclined on the pillow and let the wonderful sensation of Harte's hands flow over her. She closed her eyes, picturing the club in her mind. Mentally she tracked the movements of Harte's wolves and the Abraxas hunters.

"I never realized that I could isolate so much information. The jumble of sounds and smells always overwhelmed me. Now when I remember leaving the faire tonight, I clearly recall the scents of the two men who were down here." She wiggled her toes as he pulled at them. "I remember hearing their whispers. They were upwind of me."

He worked quietly for a while. Finally he put the oil away and wiped down her feet with a towel from his bag.

"Not the third?"

She shook her head. She'd never gotten a bead on that one.

"I was...surprised by what you did to me tonight."

"What part?" He was back against the wall, giving her space. She looked over at his body; it gleamed in the dim light. Suddenly she wanted to touch him, to run her hands over the sleek muscles of his chest. Once again her gaze settled on the ridge of his erection. She'd climaxed, but he hadn't. She scented his arousal. It had to be uncomfortable, but Harte seemed at peace with it.

"When I was blindfolded, I anticipated a blow, but you stroked me. The whips hurt a bit, but they were arousing." She rolled onto her side and looked at him. "The wax was hot but not painful, yet my brain told me it burned." She knew the term for what he'd been doing to her. They called it "mindfuck." She'd expected pain and instead received pleasure. He'd been messing with her head. "It was scary and exciting and..."

"And..." he prompted.

"Intimate. I've never allowed anyone control me that way."

She didn't want to talk about the climax. She didn't want to tell him that she'd never allowed a man to go down on her before. All those years living hard, sometimes days—even weeks—passed without her being able to take a shower. She'd always associated her genitals with being unclean. Tonight he'd performed oral sex and capped it all with a finger up her ass. He was right—she'd crossed some major boundaries in the past couple of hours.

Eva sighed. How could she communicate all this to him when she barely understood her own reactions?

"Have you ever been hungry, Harte? I mean honest-to-God it's-been-days-since-you-ate hungry?"

He swallowed and shook his head. His eyes glowed, catching the dim light.

"Sometimes I ate scraps out of Dumpsters. Sometimes I begged. A lot of the time I was dirty, and the people around me were dirty. I could smell them... Intimacy was a huge issue. Yet I hungered for touch. I still do, but old habits..." She closed her eyes.

"Eva, you coped well with everything except one punishment. I don't know that you were even aware you reacted as strongly as you did."

She looked up at him in surprise. "The wax?"

He smiled grimly. "No, not the wax. I doubt you even remember what it was." He looked her over steadily. "In fact, I would say that you stayed in remarkable control this evening. And staying in control was not what I wished for you." His eyes looked dangerous and feral. Goose bumps ran down her arms. Nervously she showed him her throat.

"I'm sorry."

"I'm not. It just means that we aren't finished." He smiled slowly.

Great. Just great. She was hot and horny. All she wanted right now was to lie on her back and feel his weight between her legs. She wanted his naked skin against hers. She wanted to fuck.

But he wasn't finished playing his games.

"Yes, Sir." She rolled to her knees and assumed the position of submission, waiting for his next instruction. He left her there long enough that her knees began to ache. He rose gracefully from the floor and crossed to the chair, then sat like a king on his throne.

"Come to me." She started to rise. "On your knees, sub."

Her heart picked up its pace. Eva settled back onto her knees and made her way to where Harte sat waiting expectantly. He watched her curiously, as though expecting her to react with something other than obedience. She bit her tongue, marveling at her own compliance. Was this the training, or was she truly submitting to Harte?

Soon enough she was on a cushion, kneeling between his spread legs. When she dared to look up, he'd unzipped his pants. His rigid, erect phallus jutted from the fly. His waistband was still fastened.

"Lick me."

Her gaze shot from his face back to his cock, and instinctively she licked her lips. Eva didn't like being on her knees before anyone. She didn't like being forced to subjugate her will like this. Nevertheless she shifted a bit closer and reached up to grasp him in her hand.

"No hands. Clasp them behind your back."

She looked at him, barely disguising her frustration. She straightened her posture and linked her hands behind her back. She leaned in and tentatively ran the tip of her tongue from the base to the head of his cock.

He was uncut and long, but wide enough to fill a woman. When she ducked her head for another pass, he hooked one leg up over the arm of the chair. This close, she scented his sweat and his musk and the mouthwatering scent of his arousal.

Again she licked, swirling her tongue over the shiny head of his cock when she reached the top. She flicked her tongue into the slit, taking the salty taste of his precum. With her lips, she worked the foreskin back, nibbling the tiniest bit.

Her creativity was a mystery, as she'd only gone down on a man a couple of times in her life. Perhaps it was the command that he'd given to not use her hands. Or maybe it was just Harte. She licked long and slow and then quick and fluttery.

He didn't make a sound. He simply looked down, watching her through hooded eyes.

Eva worked at his pants with her teeth, carefully making space for his balls to be revealed to her ministrations. Harte's first sign of frustration was when he pushed her head away, adjusted himself, and offered them up like ripe fruit. She licked and nuzzled before blowing lightly over the velvety sac. She gently worked one and then the other into her mouth, sucking lightly. He gasped.

"Enough."

She leaned back, feeling a bit of triumph to see that sweat glistened on his torso. Eva knelt humbly between his legs, looking down at the floor, a satisfied smile on her face.

HARTE GLARED DOWN at her bowed head. He used his displeasure to hide his complete loss of balance. He'd been so close to the edge that he'd literally felt the climax cresting; it was ready to swamp him still. He took a moment to gather his control.

"I told you to lick my cock."

"I did! Sir."

She looked more than a little peeved at his displeasure. It was only a mask on his part. She'd well and truly upset his applecart. But there was punishment to be applied. She'd obeyed him to the letter, but not to the spirit of his command.

Little vixen.

"I said lick. You did a bit more than that."

"But..." she protested in righteous indignation. He lifted a single brow. "Yes, Sir." Her head dropped again, and her shoulders sagged just a tiny bit. "I was just trying to please you."

"That was pleasant. Incredibly pleasant. But I didn't tell you to suck me. I told you to lick me."

He was quite certain she got his point. She didn't like it, but she understood. She also understood the opportunity that her disobedience had offered him. She caught her bottom lip between her teeth.

"Get up on your feet."

She rose, looking humbled and a bit confused.

"Now lie over my lap."

"What?"

He smiled at her outrage. He'd flogged her, caned her, pushed her into a public orgasm, and *now* she bristled with outrage!

"You know what I just said. Over my lap."

She took a step back; for a moment, he thought she'd refuse. "Are you using your safe word, Eva?"

He watched as she considered it. He waited, watching the emotions flow over her open face. He'd been right earlier—spanking was her hot button.

"No, Sir." She still didn't move, so he waited. He counted her breaths. She was gathering her courage, one deep breath at a time, stifling her outrage and humiliation. She took a step to his side and carefully lowered herself over his knees. When she was settled, Eva's cute little bum was offered up to him like twin peaches on a plate, and he couldn't resist stroking her smooth, fine skin. The pink had faded. Even if he'd marked her with the cane, she'd have healed by now.

Alluring as she was, Harte recognized this as a critical point in their evening. He rubbed her ass, feeling her stiffen.

Crack!

"That's one." The skin on her arms pebbled. If she'd been in her wolf form, she'd have her hackles up.

Crack!

"Count for me."

"T-two." Her voice was raspy. She exuded fear, panic, and fury. He gently rubbed the pain away. Normally he'd move this up an erotic notch, but not this time. Eva's emotional state was too precarious.

"I'm going to ten. Keep counting."

By the time he reached seven, her voice was tremulous. At ten, the tears began. She lay over his lap like a limp rag, the skin of her bottom pink and rosy.

"How many times did you swear at me?"

"I don't know." Her voice wavered. "Four… I think four."

"Count them." He spanked quickly, pausing just to let her get the words out. He leaned down and kissed the rosy skin on her bottom. He hadn't spanked her that hard, just enough to sting and bring up color.

Harte gathered her in his arms and cradled her like a child.

Gently he kissed her forehead, and the real storm began. Sobs racked her body; tears ran freely down her face. The spanking had brought her to a state where she could free herself in a cathartic storm. This had been his goal the entire evening. As a dom, Harte's goal was always to push his sub into an emotional as well as a physical experience. Until Eva unburdened herself, she'd be unable to see him with the eyes of her wolf.

He wondered when she'd last cried.

He rocked her a bit, stroking her hair, not minding in the least that her crying was noisy, that her tears were wetting his chest. The panel on the door slid open as a DM checked on Harte and Eva. Her arms were wrapped around his neck, her face buried in the crook of his neck.

"It's okay, Eva. Let it out. You're safe now." Carefully he rose and settled her among the pillows and silks that mounded the floor, smiling when she clung to his neck. "Sh... I'm not going anywhere. I just want to get you a tissue. Or maybe two."

She covered her face and laughed a tiny bit. He returned with the box and handed it to her, then settled onto his side as she wiped her face and blew her nose. Finally she lay to face him.

"Why'd you do that?" She was inches from him. Her blue eyes were reddened with tears, but she was beautiful. So beautiful. He reached up and stroked her full lips, then leaned in for a kiss.

"Your emotions were all bottled up. You were frightened, and that fear goes back years, doesn't it?"

Her lips trembled, but she didn't look away. "I can't remember not being afraid. Ever."

"Grief. Anger. Something terrible happened. Did you cry then?"

She shook her head. "No. Never. I could never show any weakness. If you're weak, you're a victim."

"Will you tell me what happened?" He waited, wondering if he'd truly managed to break down any walls tonight.

"They took my mother—Abraxas. I was just a kid..." She didn't cry as she spoke, but grief throbbed in her voice.

Another kiss. A tiny smile. She could tell him more later.

"How do you feel?"

She continued to study his face, and he wondered what she saw there. Did she see the worry lines from the fine line that he walked with his pack? The never-ending fears about the danger of exposure? Her eyes grew dark with knowledge. She saw the loneliness that ground right to his bones. He was humbled before her.

"Euphoric. I feel...weightless."

"That's exactly how you should feel." He ran his hands over her body, marveling at how she fit him.

Love.

That was the wolf. Things moved fast for their kind. His human side wasn't so quick to concede, but the wolf was already gone on Eva. If he took her body and she left him, there would never be another. There would be lovers and bodies, but never another who completed him.

"I whipped you pretty hard out there. I put you up for public display. I made you come to me on your knees and service me. Why did the spanking set you off? It surely didn't hurt as much as the cane."

She moved closer then and curled into his body.

"I didn't remember this till just at the end. When I was little, I ran off. We were living in a crappy old studio in some city—probably back east. I was just a little kid and didn't know any better, but Mom caught me talking to strangers. They were men in black suits. She was so scared… I smelled it all over her. The men were just young Mormon missionaries, and they were asking if I was lost. She didn't know that. To her, they were dangerous." Eva paused and bit her lip. "She took me back to the apartment and made me lie over her knees. She told me what I did was wrong, and then she spanked me. The entire time I didn't cry. When she was done, she got up and turned on the TV for me, and then she went into her bedroom. She cried and she cried." Eva's eyes watered up again. "I never ran off again."

He wrapped her in his arms and held her until the emotional storm passed. He kissed her forehead and then her nose, her eyes. He kissed her lips. She kissed him back.

"I was so good after that. I always did what she told me to do, but she left me anyway." She curled up tighter, tucking her body closer to his.

"It wasn't your fault, Eva."

She shook her head. The words registered, but it would take time for her to release the guilt that had taken root in her soul so long ago.

"Who am I, Evangeline?" he whispered in her ear, praying that she understood what he was asking. She did.

"You're my mate."

Harte closed his eyes hard, feeling the magic of the moment sweep over him. A true mating. He'd never thought to experience it.

"When this night is over and done with, where will you be?"

"With you. I'll be with you."

He sighed, and the terrible knot that had been in his chest for so very long suddenly loosened. Harte felt his heart beat freely for the first time in years.

"Do you promise?" He'd asked for her trust; now he needed to trust her.

In answer, Eva leaned in and kissed him—fully and deeply.

Chapter Seven

Eva rose to her knees, straddled his hips, and leaned forward, then ran her hands over his chest, playing with the flat disks of his nipples. She didn't ask permission. He didn't bother to stop her. She'd earned her time on top. She leaned down, her dark hair trailing over his skin as she licked him. Her tongue etched a trail from his belly to his chest. He lay back with his eyes closed, content to let her play.

He was achingly, painfully hard, but that was a small matter compared to the sudden understanding that had blossomed between them. She explored his arms, running her fingers along the distended veins under his skin. She tasted the insides of his elbows, then finally moved to the side so she could unfasten his pants. He toed off his boots, then settled back to let her finish undressing him. Once he was nude, Eva bent toward his groin, but he clasped her hips and rolled her to her back. Her eyes were wide as she watched him go down on her.

She was uncomfortable with the act, and he exerted all his skill to send any remaining inhibitions out of her head. She was propped on her elbows, her legs draped over his shoulders, and when he looked up at her, she was watching uneasily.

Clearly he wasn't doing his job right. Harte slid a finger inside her channel and pressed up into her G-spot. When she slithered bonelessly from her elbows to her back, he grinned against her swollen flesh. He brought up her arousal, reveling in her transparency, cherishing her honest response. He moved away and stared down at her newfound abandon. This time, he stopped before she climaxed. He wanted to feel the grip of her flesh around his cock when she came.

Eva moaned when he drew away, then opened her eyes as Harte moved up and knelt with his cock arrowed at her entrance.

"Yes?"

"God yes. Please." She smiled a bit coyly. "Sir."

He couldn't hold back the grin. Harte reached to a low table that held a bowl of condoms, then quickly opened and slipped one on.

"You don't need—"

"Rules are rules. That's why they're here." They were immune to human venereal diseases and carried none of their own. Eva wouldn't get pregnant this time, but just the same, they were in Xavier's house, and his word was law. Harte gently pressed against her swollen flesh before sliding his cock through her folds, making it slick with her cream. Once again, he pressed with agonizing deliberation.

She was groaning, fighting to impale herself on his shaft, but he backed off, only to return slowly. He wanted to savor every second of this first time with Eva.

She lay back in a mound of velvet and silk, her pale skin gleaming in the dim light of the room. Her hair tumbled around her flushed cheeks, and when she opened her eyes, they were dreamy with desire.

"Please, Harte... Inside me..." She wrapped her legs around his hips, pulling him to her body. She reached her hands out to him, but he was too far away. He grinned wickedly and pulled his hips back.

She groaned in frustration, and when she was unprepared, he thrust, sinking deep into her body, lifting her hips to meet his. She gasped, and Harte let his eyes slip closed, cherishing the moment with every fiber of his being. After a long moment, he opened his eyes and moved forward into her waiting arms.

HE REMAINED BRACED above her body, so Eva was able to look up into his face and watch the fascinating play of his eyes in the dim light. Like a wolf, his eyes caught the light, reflecting it back with a green glow. It was eerie and wild and so beautifully Harte.

Wanting to feel more of his weight, she tugged at him, but he remained above her, his hips rocking against her with a slow, sure tempo. His cock cleaved her in steady, deep strokes. Damn, the man had stamina! She ran the soles of her feet up the backs of his legs, then dug her heels into his hard, muscular ass. That brought him a bit closer, but he stayed rhythmic as a machine, giving her only part of what she wanted—needed. When she felt ready to throw her head back and scream, he varied his movement, rotating his hips in a circle.

That froze her in place and choked the sound in her throat. A flutter of quick, short thrusts threw her over the edge, and her head arched back, her body locked in rigid ecstasy. The climax was unexpected and deep, rippling down her back and rocking right into her womb. He held very still as she used his body to reach her fulfillment.

Afterward she collapsed under him, her body a loose puddle. He didn't stop. Harte began to move once again, leaning away just a bit to avoid contact with her sensitive clit. He returned to his knees, his face a smooth, focused mask of pleasure. Soon Eva was recovered enough to participate once again. She began to rock her hips, meeting his thrusts.

He smiled, and the expression on his face took her breath away.

It was true. He was her mate. A freakish circumstance had brought her into this place and set her right into Harte's path. He was the one man in the world who instinctively knew how to rule her, how to read her, and more importantly, how to find and heal that wound made so long ago to her heart.

She hadn't lied when she told him she felt weightless. Eva knew enough about submission to understand the high that came from giving control over to the dom. But the catharsis that came from letting go of her emotions had been painful and shattering. She'd been devastated—destroyed—and a new woman had risen from the destruction. That woman looked at Harte and saw more than a handsome, desirable man. She looked at him with the eyes of the wolf as well as those of the woman, and she saw forever. She saw her mate.

The power of that emotion overwhelmed her, once again bringing tears to her eyes. Harte saw and leaned over her. He kissed her lips with delicacy and sweetness. She caught his head and brought him closer, willing him to dominate her with every inch of himself.

He finally succumbed. His long, powerful body covered her completely, trapping her with his weight. He buried his face in her throat, nipping, sucking, making her his. His pace increased; she heard the slapping of his skin against hers and felt the sudden dampness of sweat beneath her palms.

"Come!" Her voice was fierce. "Come for me!"

He groaned, rising from her body. His cock powered into her fast and hard, and she met him stroke for stroke. An unexpected climax coiled through her, and Eva fought it back, willing him to surrender before she set it free. She reached down and clasped his ass in her hands, her nails sinking deep, drawing a fine line of blood.

The pain was the last straw for Harte. He cried out, plunging into her wildly, his tempo ragged and unsteady. She felt him go tense even as she teetered at that brink herself. They came together, struggling and cursing, their bodies locked in a virtual battle and then in perfect synchronicity. They clung to one another and shivered out the last gripping spasms before Harte's full weight settled over Eva's body.

When she felt tears trickling down her cheek, she blinked with surprise. The tears were not her own.

* * * *

They lay together like two shipwreck survivors. As she slowly roused, Eva became aware of an ache on her neck. She reached up to find a bite.

"You marked me." Her voice held a trace of wonder. Harte struggled upright and blinked.

"I did." He looked at her a bit warily. "Do you mind?"

She rubbed at it idly. "Does it mean what I think it means?"

He couldn't hold back a grin. "Probably. It means I won't have to worry about Kevin flirting with you quite so much."

Eva frowned. "Oh. But I like his flirting."

Harte just grinned some more and stood, searching for his discarded clothes and boots. He paused as a shiver of power moved through the air. Eva's eyes grew huge, her face drained of color.

"What the hell was that?" Her voice was a whisper.

"That means Chase Montenegro is in the house. He's brought his betas with him. They amplify his power."

"Betas? He's got more than one?" She looked up toward the ceiling. "Brian doesn't amplify your power, does he?"

He shook his head.

Harte pulled on his trousers and moved Eva onto her knees. He searched until he located her corset and carefully began to lace up the back. He didn't cinch her in too tightly; she might need to move soon. He found her discarded panties in his pocket and helped her into those. He shoved her shoes and stockings down into his bag. When he was finished, he turned her to face him.

"Eva, Chase and his men are different. They were created to be specialized soldiers—killing machines. They spent their lives in captivity, only leaving their labs to do what Abraxas made them do. Then one day, they broke free. From what I've heard, they killed nearly all their captors. They brought all the shifters and gifted humans who would come with them and eventually settled around here. When I realized what we were facing here tonight, I called him in. Some of my own pack has arrived as well, but Chase and his men are the big guns. No one knows Abraxas like they do."

She stared at him steadily. "Are they dangerous to us?"

"No. These guys have an almost exaggerated code of ethics, probably because they were raised by people without ethics. Chase can be brutal and uncompromising, but I trust him completely." He pulled on a boot and looked around for the other. "In all honesty, he could crush me as an alpha. Sometimes..." He looked away, nearly ashamed to continue. "My pack—there are some bad characters. Selfish. Greedy. Ambitious. I get tired of it sometimes. I don't have an alpha female strong enough to stand with me. I don't have a beta that I trust at my back. Back when he asked me to merge with his pack, I was tempted."

"Am I strong enough to help you?" She didn't ask defensively. It was an honest question.

"Yeah. You certainly are."

Eva's smile was self-satisfied. She watched as he slipped into his crisp white shirt.

"The plan. We're going upstairs to meet Chase. We'll leave and draw out the Abraxas hunters. My pack will follow them, and then Chase and his men will fill in where they're needed. We'll lead them to an unlit alley. We'll choose where we stand and fight. I want you to be ready. We're going to run. Are you up to it?" She stopped in the process of putting on her boots.

She smiled wryly. "How soon can I shift?"

"You're bait, so you'll stay human. But you'll need every skill you possess tonight."

He looked into her face, seeking fear but finding a budding confidence. "You aren't alone anymore."

Eva leaned in and kissed him gently. "You aren't either. Are you going to teach me how to hide in the shadows?"

"That's next on the agenda." He stood and took her hand. Harte looked her over. Her hair was tousled; her makeup was completely washed away. She was rumpled, flushed, and completely adorable.

And she was dangerous. He knew that at gut level. His little mate had the backbone it took to fight back.

"Let's go." He opened the door and let her precede him into the dungeon.

"Yes, Sir."

He reached down and clasped her hand. When they climbed the stairs, a man in a black suit followed. They pretended not to notice.

Chapter Eight

"Chase. Good to see you."

Eva hung back, not out of observation of the rules that Harte had drilled into her, but rather out of gut-wrenching fear of the man they were facing. Chase Montenegro sat in relaxed comfort at one of the tables, an open bottle of sparkling water in front of him. He was tall, dark, and dressed in an impeccably tailored designer suit. His blue-black hair was swept back from his face; it was on the long side but cut with precise expertise. His dark, intense eyes took in everything around him, including Eva.

Another man prowled the perimeter of the room. She couldn't see him but felt him clearly. Smelled him. He was wild and dangerous. The alphas were powerful and intimidating, but the unseen man was walking the edge of sanity. She moved closer to Harte.

"Eva, this is Chase Montenegro, alpha of the Truckee pack. This is Evangeline Jones." She nodded, and Chase rose to shake her hand.

"Eva is my mate."

Chase looked him over with humor. “You work fast, Sommers.”

“I didn't know what hit me!” To Eva's relief, Harte laughed and turned to brush a kiss on her hand. He then sat down in the empty chair. “The wolf knew immediately. It only took me an hour or so longer to agree. And a couple of hours longer to convince Eva.”

Chase laughed, and Harte glanced briefly toward the stairs. “One followed us up the stairs. Is the other there yet?” Eva slid onto Harte's lap when he tugged on her hand. She was painfully aware of her near-naked state, but the other alpha appeared not to notice.

When she looked at a nearby table, a pair of subs cuddled together. They were completely naked. She didn't look so bad compared to them.

“There are two upstairs now. A couple more, plus their scent hound, are waiting outside. The tracker is our priority. We want that one pulled out alive.”

“Why?” Brian and Patrice had converged on the table. Little as she knew about the etiquette of the packs, Eva knew they'd just been grievously rude to both alphas. At their backs were two more men and a woman in street clothes. They looked stressed and confused. She didn't have to look at Harte to know that he was beyond displeased.

“The tracker is a mutt. It's filth and should be put down like a beast.” Brian's face was suddenly not so handsome anymore. Eva could only look at him in shock. Didn't he sense the raw force of these men? Maybe he was just stupid.

Chase looked up at the beta; a tiny smile played on his lips. When the full attention of the dark alpha settled on him, Brian began to look distinctly uncomfortable.

"The tracker is a victim. It didn't choose its role in life. At best, we can rehabilitate it. At worst, we can keep it away from Abraxas so they can no longer avail themselves of its abilities." His deep voice rumbled just at the edge of hostility, but Chase didn't reprimand the beta; that was Harte's job.

Eva's opinion of the Truckee alpha rose several notches. He wasn't interested in flexing his muscle in front of Harte's pack. He was all business, and there was room for compassion in his world.

Over the music, she listened as Harte spoke quietly with Chase. He signaled a waiter over, and soon they all had drinks. Eva downed her water gratefully. She tracked her stalkers from the corner of her eye, praying that they looked like nothing more than a group of people having a good time. In reality, it was a war council. Harte nodded to Brian to take a seat. His little posse hung back, watching carefully. Patrice was in a rare fury at being excluded. She stood behind her mate's chair.

"What's this show of power about, Brian?" Harte asked.

The beta didn't like being singled out. His skin flushed, and his eyes flashed with anger.

"It's between us, Sommers. Later."

"Are you challenging me for the pack? Do I need to watch my back when I step outside?" He had no intention of dropping the subject. "You haven't issued a formal challenge. We have an outside alpha here to witness the battle. Is that what you wish?"

Brian nearly squirmed. “We're leaving. Tonight. We're setting up new territory here in San Francisco.”

Harte's lips twitched in humor. “A new pack. Here in the heart of the city. I suppose you can run in the park. How brave of you, especially considering that Abraxas is here.”

“Looking for her.” Brian nodded toward Eva. “Once they have her or know they've lost her, they'll be gone. That tracker is tuned to her. Not us.”

“What's the matter, Brian? Don't have the balls to challenge your alpha in a fair fight?”

A tall man with wild auburn hair dragged a chair to the table and shouldered his way in between Chase and Brian. His eyes were fierce and wild and exactly the same wine red color as his hair. He was handsome, but his looks were nearly overshadowed by his feral expression. He was inserting himself between his alpha and a possible threat. This was the one she'd sensed earlier.

“We've decided to split off peacefully. We don't like the leadership anymore, so we're leaving.”

The redhead sniggered and clapped the man over the shoulders. “Peaceful wolves. You just keep telling yourself that, Brian.” He snagged the beta's drink and helped himself to it. Chase looked unmoved as his beta taunted Brian.

“We'll help with the hunters, but then we're on our way.”

Eva saw that the three new members of Harte's pack were hanging back, looking distinctly unhappy. Her gaze darted to Brian and Patrice. Were these wolves being compelled to rebel? Or were they simply distressed about being caught in the act? Perhaps it had been their intention to defect quietly. Eva glanced around the room, searching for Kevin. She spotted him leaning against a wall, ostensibly watching a naked couple dancing seductively on the stage. In reality, he was carefully watching Harte's back.

Next to her, Harte shifted. His body heat had risen a notch. "No, Brian. You've effectively tried to make me lose face in front of another pack leader. You might not want to challenge me, but I think that I'd like to challenge you. We will fight immediately after we take care of business with the hunters."

"Not necessary, Harte. I don't want your pack or territory. We just want to live our lives our way. You can come into our territory just as long as you give us a heads-up first."

"He knows he can't take Harte in a fair fight. He'll try and take you out tonight while you're distracted." Kevin knelt next to Harte's chair, his arm looped over the back. His fingers brushed Eva's shoulder.

"Shut up, sub!"

Kevin smiled at Brian. "Game's over, Brian. Truth is, you probably can't even take *me*. Funny to hear you claiming territory that you have no right to."

Eva looked at the group at the table. The level of tension had risen dangerously. Across the room, she saw a DM standing next to Master Xavier. They watched carefully.

"I think we're drawing more attention than we should." Eva spoke softly. "As far as I'm concerned, you're in my territory, Brian. I've been the only wolf in the city for over a decade. I've fought off every imaginable threat, including vampires and creatures you've never dreamed about. I don't welcome you here. And by joining with me, Harte has a claim on this territory as well. Maybe you should look farther south. I hear Bakersfield is nice." She held his gaze this time, not even feeling the temptation to look away. It was Brian who broke eye contact.

"Little girl's got balls. I like that." The redhead grinned. He clearly enjoyed stirring up trouble.

"Eva, let me introduce you to Sage. This troublemaker is my first beta." Chase's lieutenant reached across the table and extended a hand. She shook it, and her skin tingled with his wild energy. She couldn't help smiling back at him.

"Kevin, take Eva to the locker rooms and guard her while she gets dressed. We need to get out of here." He turned to Eva as she rose. "Leave off the corset and boots. We'll need to move quickly."

The omega nodded and held Eva's elbow lightly. With a nod at his alpha, Sage rose to follow.

* * * *

When she stepped out of the bathroom, Sage and Kevin waited by the door. Harte joined them as they returned to the entrance of the club.

"Are we ready?" Harte rested a hand on her shoulder and tipped up her chin to look into her eyes. "Kevin, take our stuff to the car, then come join us. You and Sage are to find their car. Sage will take care of the driver; you guard the tracker. Be ready in case anything...unexpected happens. Understood?"

“Understood.” Kevin's voice was soft, but there wasn't the slightest trace of fear in it. He vanished into the fog, and Sage stepped back into the shadows, melting from sight.

“Damn.” She stared after him in amazement.

Chapter Nine

Harte clasped Eva's hand. He kissed her lightly, pausing to nuzzle her hair.

"You are a miracle, Eva. I won't let anything happen to you." With the fog swirling around them, she felt as if they were in their own private world. She was frightened yet oddly calm. For the first time in years, Eva knew what it felt like to be part of a greater whole.

"What's going to happen?"

"We're going to let them herd us into an alley, where my people are waiting. Chase and his men are standing by for emergency, and they'll do the cleanup."

"That's not what I meant."

"I know." He held her at an arm's length. "You know we belong together."

She nodded.

"After tonight, we'll get the details worked out. You're part of my pack now. You're free to continue your life, but I want you to come home with me. We've got plenty of time to work things out. Though I might want to, I'm not going to take over your life." He grinned and began walking down the sidewalk, her hand tucked into his elbow.

"You really fought vamps?" He glanced at her and then away into the darkness.

"Sure did. When I was on the street, they'd come creeping in while we slept. Vamps have a really twisted moral code. They go after drunks and junkies, but they prefer criminals. They don't believe in rehab or the justice system. I never hunted them, but they learned not to prey on me and my neighbors in the camps."

They walked silently for a while.

"Now, Eva, are we alone?"

"No, there's someone at the end of the block behind us. He's starting to move quickly. There's another ahead. He's waiting."

"Very good."

"What about Brian and Patrice?" she asked.

"Brian intended to make his move tonight but didn't expect you to come along. He meant to ambush me. Now that I know of his plans, I can exile him rather than hurt or kill him."

"Kill." She automatically tightened her hand on his arm. Over the years, Eva had seen a side of life that most people knew nothing of. It had been hard and cruel and didn't fall in line with human law.

"That does happen sometimes. We aren't human, though we try our best to live within their social structure."

"I know. I'm just...I'm just glad that things worked out this way. He might have taken you by surprise."

"No. I've been expecting it. I just wasn't expecting Abraxas."

There was a deep sadness in his voice. Eva let her hand slip down his arm and clasped his hand. "They change things, don't they?" A wave of guilt washed over her.

"It isn't your fault, Eva. And Abraxas isn't anything new. What is new is Chase's aggressive approach to them. While I didn't join his pack, we struck up a friendship. It was the best possible alliance I could have made."

They came to a corner and waited for the light to change. When it was green, they continued moving. "Kevin has passed us on the next street over. He'll be waiting." Harte didn't look like he was focused on anything but her.

The smell of the hunters was acrid in her nostrils. They reeked of aggression and excitement. She caught the distinct scent of lust as well. She swallowed hard. One of those men enjoyed his job a little too much.

Eva saw the dark entrance of an alley and knew it was their destination. In the heavy fog, they made little noise.

"Now you learn to hunt." Harte guided her into the alley. She pulled the dark velvet cloak tightly around her body, hiding the pink blouse that she wore. She sensed movement and saw Kevin approach.

Instead of speaking, Harte taught by example. He stepped into the shadows, his body blending into the darkness. Eva tucked herself against a wall, feeling the embrace of the night as she went uncannily still.

Were they alone? Her nose told her that Chase and his men were close, but Brian and Patrice were nowhere near. A quiet growl told her that Harte was aware of their absence too. The sound made the hairs on her neck stand up. A surge of power told her that he'd shifted form, and not far away, a pair of reflective green eyes stared at her from where Kevin had hidden. She swallowed and fought back the primal need to shift.

The air went electric. A muted footstep announced the arrival of her stalkers. Heavy breathing told her they were nervous, aware that something wasn't as it should be. At the far end of the alley, a dark sedan pulled up, blocking her exit.

She needed them to move closer, to step into the snare they'd set. Eva swiftly moved farther into the alley, allowing her pale blouse to flash against the darkness.

The hunters moved in quickly.

She melted into the shadows and watched as three dark forms slipped into the alley. They moved swiftly, but to her ears they were loud and clumsy. The dull gleam of metal told her they carried guns. Her nostrils caught the harsh scent of sedative, and the sickly sweet fragrance of gun oil tainted the air.

She squeezed her eyes shut. No matter how tough Harte was, how fast and capable, a gun could still kill a werewolf. It wouldn't even take a silver bullet, just a well-placed shot. When she opened her eyes, all color had leached from her vision; she saw only in shades of gray and black. The alley stood out in stark relief before her. This was the vision she had in wolf form, and she was surprised that she'd been able to call it up voluntarily.

She caught the merest hint of movement in the shadows. That was Kevin, adjusting his position behind a bank of trash cans. She couldn't see Harte at all, but her nose told her that he was moving slowly, steadily in her direction.

The hunters had spread out, guns at the ready. She scanned, seeing two; she'd lost track of the third. Eva gathered her courage and moved from the safety of the shadows. She barely had time to brace herself before the third hunter had her down flat on her back, his hand clamped over her mouth.

"Hello, darling."

Eva's heart stood still and then began to race wildly.

He had no scent of his own. She smelled only the fog and the cold night air on his skin. In the monochromatic landscape of the night, he had no color. She saw a brutally handsome face hovering above her; silvery hair wafted in the moonlight. She struggled, but his strength was inhuman. Like the others, he was dressed in a dark suit, though his dress shirt was black instead of white.

"If you make any noise, the hunters will know where we are. Understand?" His whisper was so faint that she wasn't sure she'd heard him speak at all. He glanced around, and to her horror, Eva realized that the hunter knew exactly where the other wolves were hiding.

"I know all of you can hear me. If you make a move, I'll be forced to play the game and take her head off." He paused and smiled coldly, looking right into Eva's eyes. A sense of otherness flooded her. He was no more human than she. "Frankly, I'm getting a little tired of the game."

The breeze carried the rank scents of the two hunters to Eva.

"I don't have much time. I just want you to take care of the boy." He glanced around once again. "Chase, I know you're here. The boy's a good kid. Take care of him. Please." The request was clearly difficult for the phantomlike hunter to make.

Eva struggled to listen, to scent the air. The other two hunters were nearly on them.

"Little wolf, in just a second, you're going to throw me right across the alley. That'll cover you to run. Get down there to the car. Some of your people are going after him."

Tentatively she nodded. The hunter grinned and winked, and suddenly his weight was gone. He flew backward as though he'd been thrown and crashed into a trash can. All hell broke loose. Eva scrambled to her feet, then ducked and ran to the car parked at the end of the alley.

She heard angry voices, smelled the sudden arrival of many bodies—some that she knew, some that she didn't know. Shit! Harte's pack was attacking the car with the tracker inside! How had the hunter known it would happen? The car's engine gunned. It skidded away, and she bolted from the alley at full speed, heedless of the angry shouts of the hunters. A bullet sang through the air, missing her by inches.

Eva heard the growls of large animals and the panicked shouts of the hunters. The scent of blood assailed her, but she kept running until she reached the street, where she watched as the taillights of the car faded into the fog. Brian and Patrice were attacking the car. They planned to kill the tracker.

A powerful form sailed past her, and she followed the huge wolf, running as fast as her human form allowed. She didn't have time to shed her clothing and shift; she could only follow and pray that the car wouldn't make it far.

In the distance, she heard the sound of skidding. Glass shattered and metal was torn. The growls and snarls of the pack were hushed and muted in their fury. A fight broke out, and a gun discharged. Fortunately the sound was muffled by a silencer.

She caught the panicked scent of the tracker. To her sensitive nose, he smelled like prey. He was injured and frightened.

The black sedan had been forced to a stop at the entrance of another dark alley. Shadowy figures flowed around the car in a nightmarish dance. The body of the driver was freshly dead. The back passenger door stood open, but the wolves were being held at bay by the huge wolf that'd passed her in the alley. It was Sage, following his alpha's orders to protect the helpless tracker. A careless pack member darted in, only to be snatched up and flung to the sidewalk. All the time she'd been in the alley, Sage and Chase had been there as well. She hadn't sensed their presence at all. Yet the strange hunter had known Chase was there.

She caught the stench of fear and heard the keening wail of terror. Whatever else it might be, the tracker was to be protected, and this small clutch of wolves were disobeying the orders of their alpha. Dodging past the shifters, Eva scrambled up behind Sage. Without turning her back on the wolves, she glanced into the car to see a naked white form huddled on the floor of the car.

"Mama!" His voice was shrill with panic. "Mom!"

He was bound hand and foot and shook his head, looking into the night with blind eyes. His scent was an enticing blend of familiar warmth blended with something sharp and unfamiliar—something other. Another wolf drew too close to Sage's powerful jaws; it shrieked as he flung it against a wall. In a heartbeat, the beta shifted and stood naked and wild in the darkness.

As though they'd been compelled, Brian, Patrice, and the others twisted into their human forms. They staggered, and Eva felt a backwash of Sage's power. He'd indeed pulled them into a shift. Fear washed over her as she felt the beta's control stretch dangerously thin. If this was his level of power, what did it take to subdue Sage? As though in answer, Chase strode from the mist. He stepped up to the giant shifter and laid a calming hand on the man's bare arm. Sage dropped his forehead to Chase's shoulder; his shoulders heaved as he panted for breath.

Harte appeared, followed by Kevin. They were naked and bloody, but the blood was not their own. He moved steadily toward his wolves. One by one, they dropped to their knees in front of their alpha. The posture they took was the same she'd performed for him earlier. Only Brian and Patrice remained on their feet.

"You disobeyed my orders," he snarled.

Several of Harte's wolves cringed. Brian defiantly stood his ground. His mate hovered behind him slightly. Interestingly enough, the other three wolves averted their heads from the rebels.

Eva snorted in disgust.

"Brian. Patrice. Start walking. Do not look back."

"You can't!" Patrice started forward, a look of panic on her face. "Our clothing...our possessions..."

"You lose, Patrice. Everything. If you two had challenged me honorably, I'd have let you and your pack leave. Now you're lucky I simply don't kill you where you stand. You have a car. Take it. Leave. Never come back to us again."

Brian growled and faced Harte.

"Now he decides to fight." Sage grinned in wry amusement. He seemed to have recovered now that Chase was at his side

Brian lunged forward, attacking low. Harte met his attack calmly, taking him down almost casually in a smooth throw. Brian came up with a snarl, his fists clenched, and he dived at Harte like a mindless animal.

They grappled, a streak of blood appeared on Harte's rib cage. He cuffed the former beta with a partially shifted hand. The huge paw was graced with claws that no natural wolf would have. Three lines of blood welled up on Brian's torso.

Sage whistled. "Takes a lot of mojo to pull that off."

They went to the ground, rolling and scrambling, slick with sweat and blood. From the corner of her eye,

Eva saw Patrice stiffen, preparing to jump into the fray. She reached out, clasped the other woman's arm, and growled, halting her in her tracks. Patrice bared her teeth but backed off, reluctantly submitting to the new alpha female.

Harte pinned the blond's face to the ground. All around, the night went quiet. Green light from the traffic signal tinted the fog eerily. Eva heard cars in the distance. A siren wailed, and she looked around uneasily.

The street was abandoned; she didn't even sense the presence of street people. The light changed to yellow and then red. The men lay on the ground, motionless except for their breathing.

"Submit?"

Brian must have said something, because Harte hauled him to his feet, his hand wrapped in his hair. Even the tracker in the car had stopped moaning, though Eva decided it was only because the boy had gone senseless with fear. She kept her back to the open door, her gaze on the unfolding drama just feet away.

Harte flung Brian away, forcing the blond down to the ground once again.

"Now go. Never come here again. Ever."

Brian staggered as he regained his footing. His face was twisted with anger, humiliation, and fear. Patrice looked around for support, finding none among her former pack mates.

"You'll be sorry!" Her voice was a soft hiss in the darkness, and Eva suddenly understood where the true power of this couple came from. She knew that Patrice was the one to fear. Her hackles went up in aggression. It was all Eva could do to not attack the other woman.

"Go, Patrice. You made your choice."

Where Brian had slunk away in shame, Patrice kept her head high in impotent fury. She turned and moved with grace and pride. Before long, she faded from sight. The tension in the air slowly dropped.

Eva turned to the car and knelt on the frame of the door. She reached in and rested a hand on the boy's naked leg.

"Are you all right?"

"Mom?"

"I'm Eva. Are you all right?"

"The kid can't hear you, Eva. Can't see you either." Kevin moved into the car from the other door and urged the boy to sit upright. He quickly loosened the ropes from the boy's ankles and wrists. Somehow, being surrounded by naked werewolves seemed normal. However, this boy's nudity was shameful. He shivered, and Eva pulled off her cape and wrapped it around his body like a blanket. He rubbed his face against the velvet, inhaling deeply.

"Mom."

Eva sighed, finally taking him in her arms. He was small and young, though not as young as she'd initially thought. His hair was dark; his skin was fair. They could very well have shared the same mother.

"Eva, we need to get him out of here." She looked up. Harte stood next to her. One of Chase's men was settling into the driver's seat of the car, while the other carried the broken body of the driver back to the trunk.

"We'll get him home and take care of him." His gaze darted around, looking for possible witnesses.

A light growl carried on the night air, and she looked over to where the small, ragged remnants of Harte's pack hovered on the sidewalk.

"Tonight is not a good night to challenge my decisions, Martin." Harte's voice had dropped to a rumble. "I'm not particularly in the mood to listen to anything you have to say."

The man ducked his gaze, as did the others.

"We didn't know what Brian was going to do, Harte. Patrice called us to help with the hunters. We didn't want to be dragged into Brian's challenge." The woman spoke without raising her gaze from the sidewalk.

Eva watched them carefully. In their human lives, they were probably accountants and business owners, but here in the night, they were werewolves. Whatever they sensed about the boy caused a primal reaction that hit them to the core. It was that sharp scent that came from the tracker. It was off somehow.

"What's wrong with him?" She held the boy closer.

"Nothing's wrong, Eva. He's part coyote. They're our natural enemies." Kevin's voice was heavy and sad. He reached out and stroked the black fall of hair away from the boy's face. Kevin sighed deeply.

Chase was still fully dressed; he hadn't shifted. He stood tall and dark, his black eyes glittering in the night. Not a drop of blood stained his body, but death wafted from his very being. "We'll give him sanctuary, Eva. He needs medical care as well as emotional support. We have a doctor. We have other pack members who know what he's suffered."

Automatically Eva glanced at Sage. He looked at the boy with raw grief in his eyes. Chase's pack was different than Harte's. There was probably no other pack like it. Gently, Sage leaned down and lifted the boy from her arms.

Down the street, a long black SUV cruised toward them. Another of Chase's betas was at the wheel. The sedan pulled away, heading toward the alley where the bodies of the Abraxas men lay.

"What did they do to him?" she asked Harte, but it was Sage who answered.

"Maybe they spliced his genes, or maybe his father was just some poor coyote shifter they caught. Their scientists are pretty damn creative."

Chase took the tracker from Sage and settled him in the back of the big vehicle.

KEVIN. HIS SCENT was full of stress and doubt.

"That boy, Harte."

"I know." He threw an arm around the younger man's shoulders and pulled him close. "That was you not so long ago."

"It was bad enough for me. I can't imagine how hard it will be for him."

Kevin was full wolf, but a coyote pack had found him as a young man about the same age as the tracker. He'd been wandering the desert naked and dazed, traumatized from his treatment at the hands of Abraxas. The coyote shifters had taken care of him, raising him until he was a young adult. Their pack alpha had then brought Kevin to Harte, trusting him to take the young wolf into his pack.

It had been hard. He'd had to contend with the ingrained prejudice of the pack as well as its fear that he was a spy. Kevin hadn't been born an omega; he'd been forced into that role to survive. His submissive nature had allowed that adaptation.

"That boy is going to need me, Harte."

"Go. You're right. You keep an eye on that kid. He's going to need your understanding."

Chase came around the rear of the SUV. He was a dark presence in the night. "Are we ready to go?"

"Can you find space for one more? I think Kevin might be helpful with the boy."

"Understood." Chase gave a grim smile as he glanced at the small cluster of wolves behind Harte. "You can't assume that Abraxas doesn't know you're here. Your people aren't safe."

Harte scented the night. Chase's men had already taken the corpses of the Abraxas hunters. In a day or two, those three bodies would appear in another city or even another state. They might never appear at all. But Abraxas would get the message. They'd never found the hunter who had caught Eva. He'd vanished like the wind.

"There's strength in numbers, Harte. We've got space. If you want to stay alpha of your pack, we can get you set up close by. You can even cross the border into Nevada."

He nodded. Chase's suggestion bore consideration.

"If anything happens..."

"If anything happens, it will be too late for the wolf that it happens to." Chase extended a hand, and Harte took it, not shaking, but simply holding it.

"I'll take care of them, Harte."

He nodded and then looked up at the Truckee alpha. "That hunter—do you know him?" He felt Eva move to his side and automatically his arm went around her shoulder, pulling her close.

Chase looked away from Harte, his gaze following the path that Brian and Patrice had taken.

"That's Wraith. I don't think anyone knows him. I suppose that in a way, he's as captive to Abraxas as we were." His gaze returned to Harte. "You won't hear from those two again. He won't go back to Abraxas empty-handed."

"Shit."

"Exactly. He gave us Eva and the tracker in exchange for your troublemakers. As far as he's concerned, you're square."

"Will he lead other Abraxas hunters to this area?"

Chase shrugged and turned to the SUV. "Who knows? They might hold him, but they don't own him. Even back in the labs, Wraith operated under his own agenda."

They watched Chase climb into the truck. Sage had donned a pair of sweats and tossed a pair to Kevin. Eva felt Harte's three wolves at their backs as the SUV vanished into the fog. As though a spell lifted, a cluster of cars approached the traffic lights. Eva realized that she was the only one of the group with clothing. She also realized that Harte was looking at her with heat in his eyes, and his arousal was evident.

"You three go home."

"But Harte..." They moved closer.

"Now! Present yourselves at one o'clock tomorrow. Notify the rest of the pack that we'll have a general meeting at two o'clock." His gaze didn't leave Eva's face. Neither of them watched as the three shifters stepped away, fading into the mist like ghosts.

Chapter Ten

It occurred to Eva that she was profoundly grateful that the night was foggy. She took a step backward and then took another as Harte matched her progress. He was in his human skin, but the wolf was right there on the surface for her to see and scent and touch. He reached out, and she smiled coyly, taking another step back.

“You can't outrun me.”

“I'll bet I can.” She loosened the skirt and let it drop to the ground. The blouse followed. Eva picked up the rumpled garments and carried them deeper into the alley, careful not to turn her back on the man-wolf that was stalking her. She drank in his form; his shining hair dropped nearly to his shoulders, and his skin gleamed under a dim light. He was sweaty and bloody, but that would vanish as soon as he shifted.

Lower, his cock was rigid and erect, swollen with the arousal that followed combat. Seeing her appraisal of his form, he dropped his hand to his shaft, and he stroked it gently, never taking his gaze from her.

There in the darkness, they stood like statues, each willing the other to make the first move.

It was Eva who broke and ran, dropping into her shift with a bit of awkwardness compared to Harte. He came up behind her and nipped her ass, forcing her to tuck her tail and run. Her claws scrabbled at the wet asphalt, and Eva launched herself to full speed, leaping over a shabby car, grinning a doggy grin when she heard Harte's claws scrape over the rusted metal of the hood.

She flew from the mouth of the alley, slowed abruptly on the sidewalk, then skillfully wove between parked cars, careful not to be spotted by late-night travelers. She'd become a wolf on these streets and had learned a few things the hard way. She wished with all her heart that they were across town, near Golden Gate Park or even the Presidio. They'd have had room to run there. But here, the hunt was made more challenging by the need to remain hidden.

She streaked along the sidewalk, wishing she could laugh as she dodged between a pair of late-night partyers who were exiting a leather bar. Exclamations turned to curses as Harte followed, his larger body knocking the men off their feet.

Eva took a hard right, all too aware that Harte was close on her heels... His teeth snapped as he nipped at her flanks. With one hard leap, he had her by the scruff of the neck and forcibly brought her to a halt. Eva panted and whined, twisting in his grip until she rolled to the ground, offering her belly. Harte released her and gently set one foot on her furry chest.

With a sigh, she shifted and looked up at the magnificent animal that held her in place. It was too dark to make out his color, but like her, his coat probably matched his coffee brown hair. Even without light, she could see the molten gold of his eyes. He leaned down and nuzzled her skin, working his way from her chest to her throat, paying special attention to the marks he'd left earlier. His tail came up, waving in satisfaction.

His form shimmered, and Harte shifted with an ease that Eva had never imagined possible. He knelt there on the ground next to her. The expression on his face took her breath away. He rose and reached down to help her to her feet.

They were back in the original alley, and without warning, Eva found herself facing the parked car. Harte's body was hot and eager behind hers. He dispensed with foreplay, manhandling her into position and reaching down to slide his fingers through her labia, grunting in satisfaction as he found her wet and ready. He thrust, the head of his cock wedged into her body, and he pumped again, steady and forceful, parting the tight folds and muscles of her body until he was balls-deep and flush against her ass.

"Oh damn..." Eva buried her face against her arms, all too aware of the cold metal of the car against her breasts and the heat of the man behind her. He pulled out and returned, pressing steadily into her body. By the third thrust, he was moving easily, the head of his cock skating over hot spots that she hadn't even been aware existed.

He held her in place, one hand on her shoulder, one on her hip. He grunted and growled, still too close to the wolf to vocalize his wishes. When Eva tried to move back against him, he forced her face down, keeping her immobile.

He wanted her compliance. He wanted her to submit to him, body and soul. While Harte didn't have ropes or chains to hold her in place, he had the force of his will and brute strength. This wasn't making love; this was fucking. It was conquest. In one evening, Harte had vanquished a dangerous foe, exiled a challenger, and found his mate. The wolf could no longer hold back; it had to celebrate life and victory.

His thrusts were deep and hard. If she'd been human, they would have been painful. But Eva was not a human, and she relished his power over her. Even as he took his pleasure, Harte saw to hers, adjusting her position until she was breathless and groaning with frustrated bliss.

Their skin slapped softly, and their breathing mingled in the night. Eva whimpered, desperate for the culmination that was just out of reach. Without warning, Harte pulled out and dragged her away from the car. He spun her to face him, and she looked up, awed by the raw need, the wild abandon in his eyes. He lifted her, propped her bottom against the car, and angled her so that he was able to penetrate her once again. She hooked her legs around his hips and her arms around his neck.

"You like this better?" He'd slowed a bit, coming back to his senses. Eva dropped her head back and looked up to the sky, where the fog was breaking up just a bit. Their time was running out; soon dawn would come, and the city would slowly awaken. She closed her eyes, reveling in the sensation of Harte's skin against hers, his breath ruffling her hair. She pulled him closer, trying to take every single inch that he could give her.

"I like to hold you."

He slowed his pace, allowing her to feel his shaft as it delved into her flesh. It was heaven. It was care and nurturing, and if the words that he whispered in her ear were truth, then it was love.

Harte pulled away and, looking at her face, examined her as if he'd find the secrets of the universe in the curve of her cheek or the depths of her eyes.

"Is it too soon to speak of such a thing?" He slowed nearly to a halt, buried deep, as though forcing two beings to become one. "Is it too soon to tell you I love you?"

"No, it's not too soon." Eva shifted her legs, allowing herself the space to pull from his shaft and then drop hard. She grinned when he gasped in pleasure. "But if you don't let me come, you're sleeping on the couch tonight!"

Harte looked at her in shock. Slowly his expression shifted to wicked, dark intent, and she knew that he was picturing the possibilities that a good sofa offered. He bent down for a kiss, and his tongue parted her lips, his teeth then nipping and teasing. Once again Harte took control, bracing her against the car as he began a steady, deep tempo. Just when Eva thought she could take no more, that her body was stretched as thin and taut as it had ever been, he changed his angle, and she let out a choked cry.

"Come, Eva. Now."

It washed over her like light and color piercing the blackness of night. Her hearing faded in the rush of her heartbeat, and every muscle in her body went tight, holding her in a vise of erotic anticipation. He thrust hard then and deep, and her back arched and jerked, forcing her pelvis to his.

Somewhere amid the rush he joined her, and for the briefest moment, Eva saw Harte's wolf. They ran together in the foggy night, tongues lolling, feet silent as the hard concrete gave way to the soft loam of the forest floor. They rolled, laughing, and suddenly it was his human face above her again and his slippery, sweaty skin under her hands. One final, exhausted thrust, and they went still, listening to the wind in the trees and the rush of water in a river.

Her head rested in the hollow of his neck, and Eva opened her eyes, expecting to see forest and wilderness. Instead she saw the foggy alley, and she felt the hard metal of the car at her back. When he slipped from her body, the slick heat of his seed quickly chilled on her skin.

Without letting her feet touch the ground, Harte Sommers hunted down her clothing. He carried her away, intent on taking her to his home and bed before the sun finally rose to the east. Long before they reached his car, she was asleep, safe for the first time in many, many years.

Epilogue

Eva rested her cheek on the chain that supported the swing and looked out at the expanse of Harte's property. She'd known he was a businessman in the Napa area but hadn't really understood what that had meant. His house was settled amid acres and acres of grapevines. A forest rose up behind his property and melded into hundreds of miles of Forest Service land. Scraggly black oaks blended into the majestic live oaks, which fell away to make room for pine and fir trees. He sold his harvest to local wineries and owned multiple businesses in Napa, Calistoga, and Sonoma. Some of the businesses belonged to the pack; the rest were Harte's.

She heard his voice, though the breeze was coming from the wrong direction. She was shaded by the branches of a giant live oak, and the fragrance of roses tickled her nose. Eva stretched and yawned. She hadn't been getting a lot of sleep lately.

“Hey, sweetie. You still out here?”

She sent him a droll look. Eva had awakened that morning to a “present” under the trees. Frankly, she figured the gift was really for Harte, who'd strapped her securely into the sex swing and then abandoned her to take a call from Chase.

"Good thing it's comfortable. Otherwise you'd be locked out of the bedroom again."

And of course, every time she locked him out of the room, he figured out some devious way back in. Once he'd climbed up to the deck of their second-floor bedroom on a rickety ladder from the orchard. Another time he'd removed the bedroom door from its hinges.

"Well, you look pretty as a picture there, all spread out and tied up with a bow."

He'd festooned the swing with bright red ribbons. Those ribbons were now looped around her wrists and ankles. Harte busied himself with the swing, adjusting her to the exact angle that he wanted. It was one of the more deluxe models. Fortunately it wasn't remote controlled. He'd have a little too much fun with a remote control!

Harte picked up the manual and then chuckled wickedly.

"What?" She looked at him suspiciously.

"Nothing. Just getting some ideas."

"Great. Just great. I see a lot of this contraption in my future."

Her legs were splayed open, and Harte levered her up so that her pussy and ass were prominently displayed. He dropped to his knees and grunted with satisfaction. She was exactly at face level.

"Mmmmm..." He began a leisurely exploration of her inner thighs, swinging her back and forth, trailing his tongue into her labia. In spite of her indignation, Eva couldn't struggle away from his mouth. He cupped his hands under her ass, then tickled and teased it with his very gifted tongue. Eva sighed and then gasped. She got the feeling that they'd be here awhile.

"What did Chase have to say?"

That earned her a hard flick on the clit. She gasped again. "What did Master Chase have to say, *Master*?"

His finger slipped into her pussy, putting delicious pressure up against her G-spot. She choked, unable to form any more words.

"Chase said that the boy is doing well. He's recovered his hearing but not his sight. Their doctor hopes that when he is mature enough to shift, the damage might be repaired." He pumped slowly and then returned to applying pressure to that spot. "God, you're getting wet. I wonder why?" He leaned forward and dragged his tongue over her clit again. Eva squealed.

"I hope you aren't planning to come yet."

She panted, gathering her control as he moved away slightly.

"He says that Kevin and some of the others are teaching him to play football."

"But he can't see!"

"Doesn't matter. Close your eyes, Eva." She obeyed, letting her head drop back into the support of the swing. His mouth returned to tormenting her, and she wiggled, trying to find more pressure, more penetration—anything to end it!

He swatted her on the ass. "Eager?" She heard him sliding his hand into his pocket. Her heart dropped. "The lube should be nice and warm."

"Harte—Master... What exactly are you planning?"

She got her answer when he began painting lube around her anus. Her body seized hard in a combination of dread and anticipation.

"Oh, this is perfect." She felt his slick finger pressing against her hole. "You know the drill, sweetie." She bit her lip and bore down, gasping as his finger slipped in. She tried to remember if he'd brought his toy bag outside. A quick glance told her that he hadn't.

She closed her eyes again and let the sensations run through her body. If she could free her hands, she'd play with her nipples; he loved watching her do that. Of course, he loved seeing her trussed and helpless even more. Damn wolf had an unlimited imagination!

"What are you thinking of? You seem so far away." He rose to his feet, but his finger remained in her ass, pumping steadily. He circled her clit with his thumb, and she felt fluid slip from her pussy and trickle back to her bottom.

"England. I'm thinking of England."

"Brat!" His laugh was husky. She peeked through one eye and saw that his eyes were the gold of the wolf. They didn't always shift during sex; they went gold only when he was entering that altered state where the need to dominate captured his libido.

Damn. This could really take some time. He was in his happy place.

She was too; the breeze caressed her bare skin, and she was absolutely, completely helpless. She had no choice but to give all her needs over to Harte's capable hands. She heard the rustle of fabric. He'd unzipped his pants, leaving the waistband fastened. She remembered the young couple in the club; he'd been fucking her in a swing similar to this one.

Eva chuckled. "Be sure to leave your belt on, or your pants might fall off."

"Quiet." His voice rumbled, and her wolf took a submissive posture. She was immobile. She couldn't wiggle or arch her pelvis to draw him in. She couldn't wrap her legs around his lean hips or draw her nails down the smooth skin of his back. All she could do was wait for Harte to bring her to ecstasy. She had complete faith that was exactly what he planned to do.

She felt the blunt end of his cock sliding through her labia as he slicked himself in her fluids. A finger slipped back to her ass, teasing and pressing in even as he invaded her pussy. She felt tight and full, and it was a bit of a relief when he finally needed both hands on her hips to steer the swing.

He remained perfectly still as he brought Eva to his body. Her hands were secured to the bar above her head; her ankles were bound into stirrups. All she could do was feel, so she closed her eyes and focused on the sensations that tore through her body.

Her nipples were tight from the cool breeze and from her arousal. He paused for a moment and reached up to cup her breasts and pinch the nipples into taut arousal. His hips thrust forward as he then held her steady by the shoulders. He paused again and fished into his pockets to bring out a delicate pair of nipple clamps. She hissed as he attached them, one at a time.

"What else do you have in your pockets?"

He grinned, pulling her back onto his cock. “Who knows? Maybe something for here...” He settled the pad of his thumb over her clit and circled through the slick lubrication. Her hips tried to buck up against his hand. “Or maybe something for here...” He reached behind, and the tip of his finger thrust into the slick rosette of her anus. Eva dropped her head back and groaned. Pressure and heaviness began to gather in her belly. Every thrust, every movement made the beads in the nipple clamps swing heavily. Every time he pumped into her body, his finger buried deeper, and Eva gasped in shock. The world had shifted in color, just as it had that night in the alley.

Harte growled in arousal. “Your eyes—they've gone silvery blue.”

She couldn't respond. Eva was too busy beating back the climax. “I'm...close...”

“Not yet. Don't come, Eva.”

She panted and moaned. She fought to relax her muscles, to ignore the rushing tide of blood that flooded her pelvis.

“Please.”

“Soon.” He was moving faster and faster still. His hips pounded between hers; his balls slapped against her bottom. He'd grabbed her hips again and was fucking her in earnest, fast and shallow and then deep and hard. He pulled out so far that he nearly fell away, and then returned in a long, hard push. She felt that steady tempo go ragged and knew he was there.

“Now, Eva!” He came inside her with a flurry of frantic thrusts, and through the grip of her climax, Eva felt the rush of his seed into her body. He cried out; his shoulders bunched up, the muscles tight. Sweat beaded his skin. Tied up in the swing, Eva could only feel; she could only take what he had to give her and let the climax sweep through her body. And when it was finished, he leaned forward to slip off the nipple clamps. Her nipples stung and tingled, the sensation rushing straight to her throbbing cunt, giving her one final, twisting spasm.

"Oh damn."

It sounded more like a prayer than a curse. Harte slipped to the ground, flat on his back in the sun-warmed grass. He looked like a big, sated wolf with a goofy grin on his face. Eva went loose and limp, still suspended in the chair. In the distance, she heard the phone ring.

"You aren't leaving me here to take that call."

"No. Can't move yet."

"Come on, Harte. I've got to use the bathroom. Honest."

He grinned, looked up at her, and lifted his brows.

"Please?"

"Oh, she's using the magic words."

Eva sighed. "Obviously they aren't the right ones for this situation." She dropped her head back and looked up at the huge white clouds scudding through the blue, blue sky.

"I've never had a home before. Did you know that?" He nodded, listening to what she had to say. "I've only had hiding spots, even when Mom was with me. Never a home." She inhaled. On the breeze, she caught the scent of wolves. The pack was gathering for a barbecue. After a couple of trips up to the Truckee compound, Harte and Eva had decided they needed to tighten the ties within their own pack.

"I love this place. I love the house and the very ground it sits on. But it's not my home, Harte." He sat up, looking at her with a very serious expression on his face.

"Eva, what's mine is yours. I thought you knew that."

She gave him a smile and then looked down the road. They'd be here in five minutes, maybe less. He'd timed it well.

"It's not my home, because to me, home is not a place to stay, Harte. It's the person you share it with. You're my home. And I couldn't love you more." He rose to his knees and looked up at her.

"Now if you'd take me out of this damned swing, I'll prove it to you."

The smile spread across his face as slow and sweet as honey. His hazel eyes glistened in the sun, and he lifted one dark brow. Eva sighed in frustration.

"Please, Master."

He unfastened the cuffs on her ankles and wrists, and as he did so, Eva wondered how he was going to explain the odd leather swing suspended from the big oak tree. When voices echoed from the front of the house, she wondered if they'd be able to make it to the bedroom before their visitors caught them in the buff.

When Harte pulled her into his arms and kissed her, she really didn't care anymore.

"Race me to the house?" He was grinning in challenge. In a heartbeat, two wolves raced up the lawn to the big white house. The little black and pink wolf won by a nose.

~ * ~

Belinda McBride

While Belinda's upbringing seemed pretty normal to her, she was surrounded by a fascinating array of friends and family, including a polyamorous grandmother, a grandfather who is a Native American icon, and various cowboys, hippies, scoundrels, and saints.

She has a degree in history and cultural anthropology, but in 2006 made the life-changing decision to quit her job as a public health paraprofessional and stay at home fulltime to care for her severely disabled, autistic niece. This difficult decision gave Belinda the gift of time, which allowed her to return to writing fiction, which she'd abandoned years before.

She has two daughters, six Siberian Huskies, and an array of wild birds that visit the feeders in the front yard. She supports no-kill animal shelters, and donates platelets twice monthly at her local blood center.

As an author, Belinda loves crossing genres, kicking taboos to the curb, and pulling from world mythology and folklore for inspiration. She is committed to taking her readers on an emotional journey and never forgets that at the end of the day, she's writing about love.

Loose Id® Titles by Belinda McBride

Available in digital format at www.loose-id.com and other retailers

Belle Starr
Blacque/Bleu

* * * * *

The UNCOMMON WHORE Series
An Uncommon Whore
When I Fall

* * * * *

"Educating Evangeline"
Part of the anthology *Doms of Dark Haven*
With Sierra Cartwright and Cherise Sinclair

* * * * *

"Hunting Holly"
Part of the anthology *Doms of Dark Haven 2: Western Night*
With Belinda McBride and Cherise Sinclair

Available in print at your favorite bookseller

Belle Starr
Blacque/Bleu
An Uncommon Whore
Doms of Dark Haven
Doms of Dark Haven 2: Western Night

SIMON SAYS: MINE

Cherise Sinclair

Author's Note

To my readers,

This book is fiction, not reality and, as in most romantic fiction, the romance is compressed into a very, very short time period.

You, my darlings, live in the real world and I want you to take a little more time than the heroines you read about. Good Doms don't grow on trees and there's some strange people out there. So while you're looking for that special Dom, please, be careful.

When you find him, realize he can't read your mind. Yes, frightening as it might be, you're going to have to open up and talk to him. And you listen to him, in return. Share your hopes and fears, what you want from him, what scares you spitless. Okay, he may try to push your boundaries a little—he's a Dom, after all—but you have your safeword. You *will* have a safeword, am I clear? Use protection. Have a back-up person. Communicate.

Remember: *safe*, *sane* and *consensual*.

Know that I'm hoping you find that special, loving person who will understand your needs and hold you close. Let me know how you're doing. I worry, you know.

Meantime, come and hang out with the Doms of Dark Haven.

~ *Cherise*

Chapter One

Someone should lock me up in the psych unit. Rona McGregor sucked in a breath of cool night air. Visiting a BDSM club held third place on her fantasy list, but she'd decided to take it out of order. Just this once. With an eager smile and her heart pounding, she lifted her ankle-length skirt and shoved open the door to the notorious San Francisco club named Dark Haven.

She hadn't done anything remotely adventurous in the last twenty years, but her time for insanity had finally arrived. Her children were in college. No husband anymore—*thank you, God.* She'd lost weight—she glanced down at her very full bodice—well, *some* weight. But truly, she didn't look too bad for a woman on the downslide to forty.

Rather than the den of sin Rona had expected, the small entry was dismally bland. A handful of people, also dressed in nineteenth-century clothing, stood in line to give their entrance fees to the woman behind the desk. A few minutes later Rona reached the front.

The perky young woman beamed at her. "Hi. Welcome to Dark Haven's Victorian night. Members sign in here." The receptionist's purple gown matched the streaks in her spiked hair. She'd apparently ripped out the bodice, leaving only pink netting over her breasts.

Rona suppressed a snort of laughter. Maybe the place wasn't all that bland. After her years as a nurse, bare breasts didn't unsettle her, but she'd never seen any quite so vividly displayed before. "I'm not a member."

"No problem. Oh, hey, I love your outfit. Major authentic. Did you go to the Dickens Faire at the Cow Palace today?"

Rona nodded. "That's where I found out about this theme night." And it had seemed like a sign from heaven. There she'd been, already in the perfect attire. "Since I haven't been in a place like this before, is there anything I should know?"

"Nah. Here's a membership form and release. Fill it out and give me twenty bucks to get in and five more for the membership, and you're good to go." The receptionist pushed a clipboard of papers across the desk. "If you hurry, you'll catch Master Simon giving an erotic flogging demo."

"Master Simon?" A young woman in the line squealed. "Oh God, he's so hot!" She waved her hand in front of her face so vigorously that Rona almost offered the lace fan clipped to her waistband.

Rona filled out the forms and eyed the others signing in. Satisfaction eased her nerves at the sight of the costumes: an evening gown over wide hoops, a tea gown like hers, two maid outfits with aprons. Any other night she'd be clueless as to what to wear to a BDSM club, but tonight she fit right in. How could she have resisted?

Then she noticed one lady wearing only a chemise. Another woman removed her coat, revealing a pristine white apron—and nothing else. A small worm of unease squirmed in Rona's stomach. She gave the receptionist the paperwork and asked, "Am I a little overdressed?"

"Hell no." The girl put the money away and handed over a membership card. "Dommes wear that much, and lots of subs start off dressed. Makes it more interesting when you have to strip, right?"

Strip. In a bar? Me? She'd only planned on watching. The thought of actually participating sent a shiver of excitement up her spine. "Right."

Rona tucked the card into her reticule, smoothed her gown, then opened the door to the inner sanctum and stepped into the nineteenth century. Her startled breath of air was redolent with perfumes, leather, sweat, and sex. As the passionate sound of Grieg's Piano Concerto in A Minor surrounded her, she moved into the dimly lit room crowded with men in frock coats and women in bell-like gowns. *How fun.*

She walked forward slowly, trying not to gawk. Dark wood tables and chairs dotted the center of the long room. A small dance floor took up one corner in the far back; a shiny metal bar with two bartenders behind it occupied the other. All fairly normal. Where'd they hide the kinky stuff that her erotic romance novels had promised?

Then a man strolled past wearing nothing except a terrifying harness strapped to his cock and balls.

Rona's mouth dropped. *Crom*, but she could almost feel her nonexistent male equipment shrivel up in horror.

Shaking her head, she started toward the bar, then noticed the right and left wall each held a small stage.

One platform stood empty. On the other... Rona took an involuntary step back, bumped into someone, and muttered an apology without looking away from the stage where—*surely that's illegal*—a man was whipping a woman chained to a post.

BDSM. Remember, Rona? She'd read about whips and chains and stuff—but seeing it? *Whoa.*

She pressed a hand to her hammering heart and squashed the impulse to go and snatch the whip from him. As if she could anyway. He stood a good six feet tall with a mature man's solid build; she had a feeling that if someone were to punch him, he'd just absorb it. In keeping with the night's theme, he wore a green silk vest over an old-fashioned white shirt. The rolled-up sleeves displayed thickly muscled forearms.

In contrast, his victim was completely naked, her dusky skin glowing dark red from the effects of the whip—No, it was called a flogger, right? The multiple strands stroked up and down her back so evenly that Rona could time her breathing to the rhythm. Mesmerized, she moved closer—threading her way through the tables and chairs scattered around the stage—and chose a table near the front.

Flogging. The word sounded brutal, but this...this was almost beautiful. The man swung the flogger in a figure-eight pattern, hitting one side of the woman, then the other. Rona leaned forward, setting her elbows on the table. He never struck over the brunette's spine or flanks, obviously avoiding her kidneys with appallingly impressive skill.

He slowed and paused for a moment before whispering the strands across the woman's back and legs. The woman had her side to the audience, and Rona could see her flushed face and glazed eyes. She was panting from the pain or... The victim's bottom tilted outward, swaying in a way that implied arousal, not pain.

Arousal.

A grin flashed over the man's tanned face. He stroked the woman's inner thighs with the leather strands, up and down, each time moving closer to the V between her legs. She moaned and wiggled.

Rona inhaled slowly, trying to damp the excitement sizzling through her veins.

The man started the flogging again, down the woman's back, bottom, and thighs. Suddenly, he altered the pattern and flicked the lashes between her legs, right onto her pussy. The woman gasped.

So did Rona. She'd been so immersed, it felt as if the whip had hit her...there. Her insides melted into a puddle of liquid heat. The receptionist had had it right—this was an *erotic* flogging. *Whew.*

The music changed, beginning the dramatic conclusion of the movement, and even the murmured conversations died. Rona could almost smell the arousal in the room, and her hands clenched. *So violent...so exciting.*

He was flogging the woman's thighs now, the blows gradually moving upward, even harder than before. And again he slapped the strands lightly between her legs. The woman's squeak turned into a low moan. Then her back, down her thighs, and up slowly. The third time he hit her pussy, the woman shriek and climaxed, writhing in her chains.

A trickle of sweat ran down the hollow at the base of Rona's spine, and her ragged breathing fought against the tight corset. How could something like this—a whipping—make her so hot?

The crowd cheered as the man released his victim. Although *victim* couldn't be the right word, not with that satisfied expression on her face. Rona blinked in surprise when a younger man jumped onto the stage and took the woman into his arms. After a very tongue-laden kiss, the couple stopped long enough for the two men to shake hands and for the woman to kiss the back of the flogger's hand.

He'd whipped a woman who wasn't his?

Rona swallowed. Her fantasy of a lover tying her down, maybe even spanking her, seemed pallid next to the reality of what had just occurred.

Across the room, a man and woman began to set up equipment on the empty platform. As the music changed to Nine Inch Nails, the crowd divided: some to the other stage, some to the dance floor. Left alone, the man who'd done the flogging wiped down the post and packed his weapon into a leather bag. Hefting the bag over his shoulder, he strode toward the stage steps and halted at the edge, stopped by a small covey of—Rona snorted—groupies? Did BDSM have groupies?

Shaking her head in bemusement, she turned to look for a waitress. Maybe she should add “Try out a hot dom” to her list. She grinned. Her ex had always ridiculed her five-year goal plans—as if disorganization were better. He'd have had heart failure if he'd seen her fantasy list.

No waitress in sight. She returned her attention to the stage and sighed in disappointment. Empty, like many of the chairs around her. Most of the people had moved to the other side.

A *thump* drew her attention to the table next to hers, and she gaped like a moron. The man from the stage stood there with his leather bag at his feet. On the table lay a black frock coat and old-fashioned cuff links that he must have removed before starting his demonstration.

She watched as he rolled down the sleeves of his shirt. His dark eyes looked almost black, and his deeply tanned face was lean and hard. With the lines of pain and laughter around his mouth and eyes, and silver glinting in his neatly trimmed black hair, he must have been around forty. And yet when he moved, muscles rippled and strained the shoulders of his white shirt.

Not only a hunk, but older than her. Yet she didn't even consider flirting. Not with this one. He was too...too intimidating. Not like a young, buff underwear model, all gorgeous and everything, but in a far-more-dangerous way.

Of course he's dangerous—he has a flogger, and he knows how to use it.

All her minuscule experience with BDSM came from reading erotic romances. She'd always wanted to try a few things, but Mark had laughed at her and refused to do anything to liven up their sex life. Not that they'd even had a sex life the last few years.

Her horizons had definitely expanded since the divorce, but not enough for her to jump into seriously kinky stuff. She'd simply planned to watch and note some ideas to add to her fantasy list, but certainly not to make a pass at a really, really experienced BDSM practitioner.

No matter how gorgeous he looked.

Don't drool. She tried to casually lean back but slouching in a corset was impossible. Stymied, she turned her gaze to the other stage, where a woman costumed as a schoolmarm wrapped ropes around a young man wearing only breeches. Rona managed to keep her attention there for, oh, a good minute, before returning to the man.

She frowned. He was trying to get a cuff link into his shirt and failing miserably. For some reason, the fingers of his left hand didn't bend. His frustrated growl switched him in her mind from a hunk to someone who needed her.

She walked over, pushed his hand to one side, and fastened the heavy silver link. "There." With a smile, she patted his arm comfortingly. "Now—"

She looked up into intent, powerful eyes, and every cell in her body went into a meltdown. He kept her pinned with those dark eyes, studying her as if he could see through to her soul.

He moved closer, forcing her to tilt her head back to look up at him. When her breath stuck in her chest, his lips curved into a faint smile. "You didn't even think before coming to my rescue, did you?" he asked, and his voice was as dark and smooth as everything else about him.

She should apologize. “I-I'm—”

“Be silent.”

Her throat just plain shut down completely, and the laugh lines around his eyes crinkled slightly. “Submissive,” he murmured. “But no submissive would shove a master's hands away and take over. You're new?”

He didn't wait for an answer but ran a finger down her cheek, her neck, across the tops of her pushed-up breasts.

His touch burned through her, leaving an aching need. The trembling inside her stomach worked outward until her legs wobbled. “Please,” she whispered.

He tilted his head. “Please what, pet?”

“Please don't tease me.” Feeling like an idiot—a very confused, aroused idiot—she dropped her gaze and tried to take a step back.

His hand closed around her upper arm, firmly enough that she knew she'd go nowhere.

“Look at me.” A finger under her chin raised her face. His lips curved into a faint smile. “Very new, I see.”

“Yes.” Her next effort to move back met the same results—none.

“A submissive need not call any dom but her own 'Sir,' but if she approaches a dom on her own and then reacts like this”—his finger left her chin to stroke over her trembling lips—“then she had best address that dom as 'Sir.'”

Acutely aware of the warmth of his finger still on her lips, she felt as if she were drowning in molten air.

He paused, then prompted, “Say, 'Yes, Sir.'”

Oh. “Yes, Sir.” She'd used the phrase before, teasingly with the hospital doctors, sarcastically with idiots, but now it reverberated through her like the sound of a bass drum.

“Very good.”

A woman wearing only a corset, fishnet stockings, and high heels suddenly dropped to her knees beside the table. “Master Simon. Can I serve you in any way?”

He turned.

Freed from his gaze, Rona tried to retreat, but his hand, hard and ruthless, tightened. The feeling of being controlled swamped her senses.

Her heart raced as if she'd received an injection of Adrenalin, but with his attention diverted, she managed to pull in a steadying breath. *I'm a mature woman, an administrator, smart and professional. Why do I feel like a cornered mouse*? And it turned her on like someone had opened a hormone faucet.

She glanced down at the kneeling woman and winced. Not only willing to give Master Simon anything he wanted, but also blonde, slender, gorgeous. And young.

Rona was none of those. *Escape. Definitely time to escape.*

“THANK YOU, NO,” Simon told the kneeling sub, waving her off politely but firmly. Another youngster. He smothered a sigh. The enthusiastic, young ones seemed so very undeveloped. He preferred *women*, yet the interesting, older subs were usually involved, or they had emotional problems. He hadn't met a well-balanced submissive in quite some time.

I'm lonely. Divorced for several years, his son in college, his house empty, he'd recently grown aware of how much he'd like someone to embrace at night, to talk with in the evenings, to share everything from a new dessert to the day's victories and disasters. He could find a willing body all too easily, but not an open heart, an interesting mind, and an independent spirit.

But this one... Simon turned his attention to the submissive who'd dared to help him without asking. Not young, probably somewhere in her thirties. Her face had lines that said she'd seen sorrow. Had laughed. Her full breasts, pushed high and taut, displayed the silver striations that showed some baby had been held against her heart and nourished. The way she'd briskly brushed away his hands from the cuff told him she was used to being in charge. The melting look in her eyes when he'd touched her said she was submissive.

Very appealing. And oddly familiar. Had she visited the club before?

But she kept trying to retreat. *Why*? Of course, a dom might make an inexperienced sub nervous, but she'd shown definite interest before...before the interruption. His eyes narrowed. The kneeling sub had been young and pretty. Was this confident woman uncertain of her appeal?

She tugged at her arm again and actually frowned at him.

"I don't believe we finished our conversation," Simon said.

Her gaze lifted. In the dim bar, her eyes appeared blue or green. Her hair, a streaky color between blonde and brown, had been pulled back into an ugly Victorian bun. That would be the first thing he'd fix.

He held out his free hand. “My name is Simon.”

As wary as a treed cat, she still managed to say politely, “It's nice to meet you, Simon.”

That lovely, low voice would deepen after she came a few times. His fingers closed over hers, and he kept his other hand wrapped around her arm. Now he had her securely trapped, and the knowledge appeared in her eyes. Her breath quickened, her tongue flicked over her lips, and she swayed, almost imperceptibly, toward him. Yes, the feeling of being controlled aroused her.

Now, wouldn't she look lovely in ropes? “And you are...?” he prompted.

“Rona.”

“Scottish? Yes, it suits you.” He looked down into her eyes, enjoying the slight tremble of her fingers in his. “Is this your first time in a BDSM club, Rona?”

“Yes.”

“And how long have you been here?”

“Not even an hour.”

“*Not even.*” The phrasing implied she felt off balance. And he'd definitely pushed—was still pushing, which wasn't appropriate or honorable to do to a sweet newbie. When he opened his hands and released her, the sense of loss surprised him. *I want to keep this one.*

But the choices, always, belonged to the submissive—unless and until she freely gave over those choices to him. "Do you want a guide, or would you rather explore on your own?"

She hesitated. "Um. Well..."

She didn't want a guide. Despite her obvious attraction to him, she'd prefer to see the place on her own. He almost laughed at his annoyance. Getting too accustomed to adulation, was he? This woman might tremble, but she wouldn't throw herself at anyone's feet, and that only increased his interest.

"All right." He ran a finger down her cheek, marking her as his in the indefinable way of dominance. "I will see you later, then."

AS MASTER SIMON walked away with an easy, confident stride, Rona stared after him. He'd only touched her with a finger, and her pulse had increased to serious tachycardia.

She'd read BDSM books but hadn't really grasped the power a dominant could exert. That walking, talking model of intimidation had wielded his eyes and his...his sheer presence...as skillfully as he'd used that flogger. Lord help her.

After sucking in a breath, she shook her head, told her body to stop reacting, and headed for the bar. One bottled water coming right up.

The diversion and the icy water worked, and within a few minutes, her self-possession returned. Putting her back to the bar, she looked around.

Lots of people, but no Master Simon in sight. Disappointment washed through her, cooler than the ice water. And how stupid to be disappointed after having turned him down. But she'd done the right thing. He was just too, too much,—her bottle stopped halfway to her mouth—and she'd totally chickened out, hadn't she? Here she'd made all those resolutions to dump her Miss Propriety image, to let go of her I'm-a-mother-and-a-wife-and-not-a-sensual-woman thinking, yet when a stunning man showed his interest, she'd run for the proverbial hills.

Of course, her plan for an exciting life hadn't included hanging out with a guy who enjoyed multitailed whips, but still...

She'd do better next time. For now, she needed to scope out the place. Aside from the demonstrations on the stages, she hadn't spotted any of the "scenes" she'd read about. But people kept disappearing down stairs near the front, so maybe the fun stuff happened on the lower level. She picked up her bottle and eased past a group of people, including a black-haired woman wearing a cute pink and white corset. Rona noticed the bright pink streaks in the woman's hair and grinned, remembering the receptionist. Matching hair color to clothing—not exactly correct for the period.

At the bottom of the stairs, she stopped, feeling as if she'd descended into a literal hell. Holy crap, Batman, but some of these people needed a psych eval. Like the blonde letting a guy stick needles into her breasts. In pure reflex, Rona crossed her arms over her chest when the man shoved another needle in, right through the woman's nipple.

Now that was just wrong. Maybe she should go back to the car and get her first-aid kit.

Instead she walked farther into the room. The industrial Goth music from upstairs blended with the sounds of flesh being struck, moans, high cries, the *snap* of a whip, a long, shuddering groan. A series of cracking noises sounded way too close, and she jumped, looked around, and then snorted a laugh. She'd clenched her water bottle so hard that the plastic had crumpled. Noisily.

She rolled her eyes. Hopefully no one would yell *boo*! at her, or she'd go into cardiac arrest.

By the second scene area, she noticed guys scoping her out. Cool. She moved her hips and made her full skirts sway. *Sexy me.* Then a young woman walked past clad in only a G-string, all firm skin and high breasts. Right. *Sexy me as long as I'm wearing clothes.* She might have lost some weight and firmed things up a bit, but those things were still well over thirty years old.

An hour or so later she knew a heck of a lot more about what kinky people did for fun. Watching Simon's flogging demonstration hadn't prepared her for canes or black whips—although no one in the place came close to his skill—let alone hot wax, needles, gags, and masks. As one dominant applied a line of small suction cups up a woman's back, Rona wondered if the glass cups ever went on more...intimate spots. She mentally added it to the list of things to try—someday—and just the thought sent a zip of excitement right to her clit.

As if she weren't already excited. A few steps farther, she glanced through a large window into a very authentic-looking medieval dungeon. A black-haired woman was manacled to the stone wall, and a man in jeans slapped the poor woman between the legs, sending her right up onto her toes. A minute later he dropped to his knees, gripped her buttocks, and put his mouth on her pussy.

Rona swallowed and fanned her overheated face as she moved away. Shocking and erotic as heck.

By the time she'd toured the room, her corset bones felt like bony fingers digging into her ribs, and her clothes as if they weighed a good twenty pounds. Finding an empty couch, she collapsed onto it. *Oops.* Proper Victorian ladies didn't drop like rocks; they undoubtedly sank gracefully down to a seat and, of course, sat erect rather than leaning back.

She'd have made a lousy Victorian lady.

She'd probably make a lousy BDSM person too. In fact, she might not even like doing it, although watching stuff like the way that belt had hit the woman's round bottom made her really…warm.

Maybe, while here, she could try a little bit—just a taste, not a whole meal. Have someone tie her hands or something. A quiver trickled through her insides at the thought of actually acting out some of her fantasies.

Mouth suddenly dry, she sipped the last of her lukewarm water. First she'd have to meet a dom. She could watch another demonstration. But the shows—scenes—down here seemed more personal. More intimate. If Simon wanted to beat on her, she'd rather do it here than upstairs.

She choked on the water. What the heck had brought Simon back to mind?

Well, she knew the answer to that. Any woman would want him, with that devastating combination of easy manners and merciless authority. *And don't think about his voice*—as smooth and rich as Dove's dark chocolate. Goose bumps prickled up her arms, and she sighed.

Hopeless, she was just hopeless. And *Master* Simon was way out of her league. She needed someone less intimidating.

She looked around. *Hmmm.* Not the old guy over there or the fat one. She checked the other direction and spotted a tall blond, maybe in his late twenties. Rather cute. He stood with his hands behind his back, watching a nearby scene. When he looked around, his gaze met Rona's. She smiled at him. *You. Yeah, you. C'mere, honey.*

He blinked and headed over. “Hi. You're new here?”

“That's right.”

Chapter Two

There you are. Simon stopped at the sight of the woman he'd been hunting. Someone else had captured his quarry first and secured her arms to chains dangling from the low suspension beam. The dom, one of the younger men, had removed her gown and petticoats, leaving her in a corset, sleeveless chemise, and drawers.

What a nice picture. Lovely, soft curves and pale skin, big eyes and a stubborn chin.

However, for someone so thoroughly restrained, the submissive had taken control of the play.

"Pitiful," Xavier said, joining him. The owner of Dark Haven wore a frock coat like Simon's over a silver-and-blue paisley vest. Very dapper, especially with his black hair braided back almost to his ass.

Simon raised an eyebrow at his friend. "You know the sub?"

"No. She's not been here before."

Then why is she so familiar? Simon watched for a moment and winced when Rona laughed at the dom. True, she had an adorable, low laugh, but the dom had totally lost control of the scene. From the young man's unhappy expression, he didn't know how to get it back—if he'd ever had it. The term "*submissive*" didn't necessarily mean pushover.

"I told David to stick to the easy subs," Xavier said.

"Friend of yours?"

"He took one of my classes for dominants. He's not bad, just inexperienced." Xavier started toward the scene, but a barmaid stopped him, chattering about a problem. He held up his hand to pause her, then turned to Simon. "Do me a favor and rescue David, would you? I'll join you shortly."

Simon heard Rona order the dom to try something in his bag and grinned. "She's a bossy one."

Xavier's black brows rose. "Like her, do you? Perhaps I won't owe you a favor after all."

"No, my friend, I will owe you one. However, since she's new to the lifestyle and community, I'd appreciate a reference." Simon clapped his shoulder and moved to where he could be seen but not interfere if David chose to ignore him. Not that there was any scene dynamic to destroy here.

David looked confused when he saw Simon, but he walked over. Frustration had tensed his muscles and jawline. "It's Simon, right?"

"Xavier sent me in case you wanted out. I met the sub earlier, and I wouldn't mind working with her."

"Hell yes. Take her." The dom scowled. "Xavier warned me about getting in over my head. Now I know what he meant."

“Like anything else, it takes practice. Does she have any hard limits or requests?”

“No blood sports. No anal. She wanted to play the rest by ear and chose 'Houston' for a safe word.”

“As in 'Houston, we have a problem'?”

David grinned. “Yep.”

She definitely has a sense of humor. Simon nodded acknowledgment and turned his attention to Rona, his anticipation rising. He'd wanted this woman since the minute she touched him. Totally illogical, but in life, as in the martial arts, he'd learned his instincts were rarely wrong.

He heard David grab his toy bag and leave, but didn't take his focus from the sub. He'd caught her as handily as any of the animals he'd hunted in his youth.

She'd been amusing herself, twirling and swinging on the chains like a child, and he suppressed his grin.

Looking up, she saw her dom leaving. “Hey! David, where are you going? Hey!”

Simon paced forward. Slowly.

She saw him. Her eyes widened.

Perfect.

OH SWEET HEAVENS—Master Simon. As Rona stared at him, the laughter inside her fizzled out, and her heart began an annoyingly fast pace again.

His black gaze wandered over her, stroking her with heat. Her gown lay off to one side, but she hadn't felt particularly exposed—until now.

After setting down his big leather bag, Master Simon took off his coat and tossed it on a chair, leaving him in the white shirt and vest. His movements unhurried, he removed his cuff links. When they dropped onto the table with a metallic *clink*, Rona's breathing hitched.

He turned, rolling up his sleeves and exposing his muscular forearms.

Oh Crom. Wait, she started to say, but nothing came out of her frozen throat. She tried again. "Wait. You're not... I didn't... Where did David—the other guy—go?"

His dark eyes fixed on hers as he moved forward. "The other guy is a dom, but perhaps you got confused and thought him submissive." His level tone sent icy shivers down her spine. "I don't believe you'll make that mistake with me."

"I don't think—"

"Very good." He cut right through her sentence. The feel of his callous hand cupping her chin silenced her completely. "Thinking is my job, not yours. Your safe word is 'Houston.' Use it if something—mentally or physically—becomes too much for you."

She considered yelling it and took a breath.

His jaw tightened which dried up that notion instantly. "Don't toy with me, pet," he said softly.

She shook her head. *Not me. No, never.*

"I like that wide-eyed submissive look." His gaze ran over her. "In fact, I like seeing you in chains."

His words brought her attention to her restraints, and a quiver of fear joined the heat in her belly.

He cupped her cheek, his big hand disconcertingly gentle. “No, don't be frightened. We're just going to talk. First I want you to meet someone.”

Master Simon glanced at a man standing off to one side and motioned him forward. Also in formal Victorian attire, the other man had coloring slightly darker than Simon's.

And as their attention turned to her, she felt like a mouse trapped in a feline festival. “Um. Hello?”

Master Simon's lips quirked. “Rona, this is Master Xavier, the owner of Dark Haven. Submissives here call him 'my Liege.'”

Her initial reaction—*you've got to be kidding*—died at the lack of expression in Xavier's calm, dark eyes.

“It's a pleasure to make your acquaintance, Rona,” Master Xavier said, his voice quiet but easily heard over the myriad of noises.

“Pleased to meet you.” *I love meeting people while standing around in my underwear.*

“Since we're immersed in the nineteenth century tonight, let me formally introduce you to Master Simon.” A smile flickered on Xavier's lips. “He is well-known in the BDSM community, has an impeccable reputation as a dom. And I call him my friend.”

The measured addition of the last part told her that Xavier didn't offer friendship lightly.

“Um.” She glanced up at Simon. A crease appeared in his cheek as if he found her discomfiture amusing. Kicking him might be satisfying—if he didn't own a flogger. “Thank you, Xa—uh, my Liege. I appreciate the information.”

Xavier nodded and walked away. No frivolous conversation for him.

And that left her with Master Simon. The sinking feeling in her stomach hadn't improved.

"Did you enjoy your tour, lass?" he asked politely.

Lass. Her grandfather from Glasgow had called her that, but coming from this utterly confident man, it made her feel funny—young and uncertain. And pretty. "Yes. It's an interesting place." He wanted to have a normal conversation with her standing here in chains?

"Have you tried BDSM before? At home, perhaps?"

On second thought, let's go back to normal. Her hands gripped the chains. "No. Never."

He stroked a finger across the nape of her neck, just under her bun. "Then I will give you your first lesson."

"But…why? Why me?" Every woman who walked by this man cast longing looks his way. *I'm not young. Or thin. Or gorgeous.*

"You, lass, have a self-image problem."

Well, that might be a little true, but she also had a mirror. It wasn't that she was ugly; it was that the competition was far too beautiful. And young. "Simon, I—"

His eyes narrowed, and her insides melted like ice cream on a sunny day. "I don't think I want you calling me Simon. Not in the club or when you're restrained…or in my bed."

The surge of excitement at the thought of being in his bed went all the way to her fingertips. And he'd done that deliberately, hadn't he? She sucked in a breath. *Keep your head in the game.* "What would you prefer?"

"You may call me 'Sir' or 'Master Simon.'" He brushed his fingers down her cheek. "I believe, for you, I'd permit a simple 'Master.'"

Master? No, that sounded way over-the-top. She shook her head.

"Oh, I think you will," he murmured. "Now let's talk about what I see when I look at you."

Oh, let's not.

"First, you're not twenty...or even thirty." Almost absently, he removed one of the hairpins holding her bun in place, ignored her frown, and removed another. "But I like a woman with some life experience, one who isn't at the mercy of her emotions, and where a missed date or an argument doesn't constitute the ending of the world."

Remembering her son Eric's last meltdown when his new girlfriend had stood him up, Rona laughed.

"There, now. That's lovely," Simon said. Somehow the heat in his eyes slid right into her body. He ran a hand over her upper arm and squeezed gently. "I think muscles on a woman are beautiful, but I enjoy softness in my bed. And under me."

Everything he said sent more urgency curling through her body, and she lowered her gaze. "Well." Good grief, when had she become so inarticulate? She facilitated meetings full of prima donna doctors, for God's sake. She straightened her shoulders and gave him a level look. "I'm pleased that you—"

"Yes." He smiled at her. "Yes, that's exactly what I mean by experience. You don't crumple easily." Another pin slid out of her hair. "Rona, it is your choice, but I would be pleased to introduce you to whatever elements of BDSM interest you."

The man was smooth and dangerous, just like she'd thought. But oh so tempting. Her eyes dropped to his leather bag filled with...things, and a shiver ran through her. Let him do...something?

His lips curved. "Ah, now that was a yes." He pulled the last pin out, and her dark blonde hair fell down around her shoulders in a wavy mess. He tucked her pins into his vest pocket and raked his fingers through her hair. Each small tug sent tingles down her spine. "We will talk, and you can tell me what you like."

"Uh-huh." Tell him her fantasies? Not going to happen.

He stopped, and his finger under her chin lifted her gaze to his. "Rona, first rule of a Dom-sub relationship: you share your thoughts, openly and honestly, hiding nothing."

"I don't know you."

"True. But you've heard me vouched for. You're attracted to me. Can you trust me enough to share what you found interesting in the club so far? Is that asking too much?"

She hadn't felt so cornered since the OR nurses had stormed her office about an instrument-throwing surgeon. "No. I can do that."

"Excellent. Considering your current position, obviously you find bondage and public display acceptable." He set his hand on her nape, his thumb curving around the side of her neck. His keen eyes focused on her face. "BDSM includes other pleasures. Like flogging."

As he'd done to that woman?

The laugh lines beside his mouth deepened. "Your pulse sped up. Excellent."

"Whipping."

She flinched. Earlier, she'd seen a dom use a long whip to create horrible red stripes on his victim. "No."

"Plain, bare-assed, bare-handed spankings."

She swallowed at the thought of being over a man's—Master Simon's—knees. Her fantasy list definitely needed revision. "Um, maybe."

"So everything except the whip." He nodded. "Then there's hot wax." He paused. "Piercing."

Needles? For fun? Hell no. She tried to pull away, and his hand gripped the back of her neck firmly. "Gently, lass. I'd say the wax is a maybe, but any piercing is a hard no. Is that right?"

Did he read everyone this easily or just her? She nodded.

His eyes crinkled, and then he brushed her mouth with his. His lips lingered, firm and velvety, and without any thought on her part, she tilted her head back for more.

"You are a sweet one," he murmured and took her face between his hands, holding her as his mouth urged hers open. He kissed her slowly. Deeply. Thoroughly.

With her wrists restrained, she was at his mercy, and the knowledge sent anticipation humming through her system.

He lifted his head to look at her for a long moment, then smiled and kissed her again until every drop of blood pooled in her lower half. Her body throbbed for more.

He moved a fraction of an inch back and caressed her cheek. “Where did I leave off? Ah, there are a variety of toys for fun like...a dildo. A vibrator. An anal plug.”

Just the thought of someone using those on her made her squirm. “Maybe.”

One side of his mouth curved up in a slight smile. “That was more than a maybe, lass. Have you ever used an anal plug?”

Her backside tensed, but with her hands chained over her head, she couldn't cover...anything. “No.”

“I look forward to seeing your reaction. Did you happen to see the cupping earlier?”

Oh, she'd definitely seen that one. “Yes.” Her voice came out husky.

He raised an eyebrow. “Interesting. And where else do you think a master might apply those cups?”

The dom had put them on his sub's back, but she'd imagined them on her nipples or even...on her clit. A wave of heat rolled into her face, as inevitable as the sun in summer.

He chuckled. “I'll enjoy that almost as much as you will.”

“I didn't say yes.” She hadn't, dammit.

"You didn't have to." He grasped the ribbon at the top of her chemise and pulled it open. Her nipples puckered.

"How about electrical play?"

All too aware of the warmth of his hand just above her breasts, she tried to concentrate on what he'd asked. "Electrical play?" She shook her head, then remembered the TENS unit a chiropractor had used on her sore back. Could those electrodes be placed elsewhere? Her vagina clenched, making her aware of how wet she'd become.

"Oh yes." The glint in his eyes made her stomach twist uneasily.

She swallowed. "Why so many questions for just one time?"

"There's always another time, pet. One more question." He studied her face as he ran his knuckles down the cleavage her chemise now exposed, and the closer his hand came to her breasts, the more her nipples tightened. "How about sex?"

Sex? Her breath caught. Sex with him? Every cell in her body jumped to life, waving pom-poms, and cheering. Her gaze dropped to his waist, to... She looked back up hastily. What was she thinking? "Uh no. I don't think so."

"Then, for tonight, I'll use only my hands." He didn't make it a question.

"Uh..." She nodded. Hands seemed safe enough. The thought of him taking her, being inside her... She wasn't ready for that intimacy. She might not be ready for this either.

"All right," he said easily. "We will begin." He strolled around her, and she could actually feel his gaze stroke over her thinly clad body. "You look lovely in Victorian undergarments, pet, but they're in my way." Without asking permission, he undid her corset, tiny hook by tiny hook, and tossed it onto a nearby table, leaving her in her chemise and drawers.

To her surprise, he ran his strong hands over her ribs, then massaged the painful ridges from the corset. She groaned from the relief. "Thank you."

His grin flashed, a moment of sunshine in the stern face. "I've heard they're uncomfortable." Reaching up, he unclipped her right wrist and lowered her arm. When he gathered up her chemise, she realized he planned to pull it over her head, baring her breasts.

She had one arm still chained, and her instinctive recoil got nowhere.

He raised his eyebrows.

With the other dom, David, she'd felt in control. Not with Master Simon. Lord, he didn't even speak, just looked at her, and her defiance oozed away. A sigh whispered out.

"Good girl," he said, his voice as soothing as a caress. After she slid her arm out of her chemise, he held out his hand, palm up.

She couldn't move for a second. Did she want him to chain her wrist back up? Her stomach shook in an internal earthquake. And then she set her hand in his.

Approval warmed his eyes. "This is what submission is, Rona," he said as he clipped her cuff to the overhead chain. "I can overpower you easily enough, but that's abuse. In domination, the only power I wield is what you freely give me."

After repeating the process with the other arm, he pulled the chemise over her head, leaving her bare from the waist up.

As the coolness brushed over her breasts, she looked around. Oh Lord, two doms and their subs had stopped to observe. A hot flush rose into her face. What was she doing here, letting herself be stripped?

"Look at me, pet."

Her gaze returned to him, and he held it until everything else faded except his dark eyes. He studied her for a long moment until her muscles stiffened with anticipation. Then he cupped a breast in each hand.

Oh Crom. Pleasure rushed through her like a tidal wave. Her nipples had been hard already and now tightened until they ached.

"You have lovely breasts, Rona." He paused and then frowned. "The correct response to a compliment is 'thank you, Sir.'"

"Thank you, Sir," she whispered. His gentle pinches on both nipples made her want to pull away with embarrassment and yet push forward for more. And she'd grown wet below, very wet.

As if he'd heard her thought, he put his boot between her bare feet and nudged her legs open. "Are your drawers traditional?"

When he ran a finger over her exposed skin just above the waistband, her stomach muscles quivered. "Traditional?"

"Crotchless?" He put his hand between her legs, right on her exposed pussy.

She gasped.

His grin flashed white in his tanned face. "I do love historical accuracy." He unhurriedly ran a finger through her wet folds, back and forth, never touching the one place that throbbed like mad. As her head spun, she started to draw her knees together and got another of those looks she'd begun to recognize.

"Don't move, pet, or I'll restrain your legs too."

She froze.

Her thighs quivered uncontrollably as his fingers explored her even more intimately, tracing over her clit, around her entrance. When he pushed a finger gently inside, she raised on tiptoes, stifling the moan in her throat.

"Very nice," he murmured, and she heard the approval in his deep voice through the swishing of her pulse in her ears. His finger eased farther into her, and his other hand touched her breast, tugging lightly on the nipple.

Oh Crom. Sheer, insane need swept over her like a landslide. When his thumb pressed on her clit, everything receded except the feeling of his hands on her. Her eyes closed as her insides gathered.

"No, not yet, sweetheart," he said. His touch lifted. "I want you a little on edge when I teach you about pain."

Her eyes flashed open. *Pain?*

The flogger he took from his bag didn't look like the same one he'd used before, but still—leather-covered handle, multiple blunt lengths of suede.

"You're going to whip me?" Her voice shook.

The dark eyes glinted with amusement. "Oh, I think so, yes." He brushed the flogger up her legs, her stomach, and teased the soft, dangling strands over her breasts until the peaks ached. The scent of leather filled the air as he lightly ran it up her arms and down her back, continuing until her skin grew so sensitive that each small caress sent a pulsing thrill through her.

The flogger brushed against her butt, and then the strands flipped across her bottom in the first blow.

She jumped. But it didn't hurt, didn't even sting. Instead the ends thudded against her skin like tiny hammers. More flicking touches moved down her legs and around to the front. As the lashes tapped slowly up her thighs, her heart started to pound. She pulled her legs together.

"Stay in position, or I will chain your ankles, pet." No anger, just a statement.

She moved her legs out. A little. Caught the expression in his eyes and opened them all the way, leaving her pussy dangerously vulnerable to those strands. A shudder went through her. Why didn't she use that safe word he'd given her?

But his intent gaze held her in place. And so did the way she felt—incredibly aroused—every nerve alive and singing with excitement.

He tucked the handle of the flogger into his waistband and moved closer. "You're being a good girl."

His hands cupped her breasts, his thumbs circling the nipples until a stream of electricity flowed straight to her clit. Her exposed clit. The open-legged position just begged for his touch. Her hips tilted forward, and she bit her lip, embarrassed. She wasn't like that, had never begged for anything. Ever. And yet... *Please touch me.*

He moved a hand to her pussy, sliding through her wetness. When his finger traced over her clit, she gasped at the sheer rush. But his finger eased away, gathered moisture, and then circled her clit. Around and around.

Pressure built inside her, and everything tightened, begging for just a little more. She moaned.

"Lovely," he murmured and stepped away. Before she could whimper a protest, the flogger struck her again, up and down her legs, front and back, then over her bottom, and a sting joined the thudding sensations. Not hurting, not really. Over her shoulders lightly and her hips, the blows circled her, and each time, the strands landed a little harder.

Still it didn't hurt, exactly, but she'd rather have his hands on her.

His eyes narrowed. "There goes that mind of yours, thinking away. You definitely need a tad more."

She caught her breath, hoping he'd touch her. Amazing how her inhibitions had disappeared.

Smiling slightly, he laid the flogger down next to his bag and pulled out a leather collar, fully as wide as his hand.

A collar? What kind of "more" was that?

He fitted it around her neck, adjusted her chin to rest in a small notch, and buckled it. Then he stood in front of her, caressing her cheek. Waiting.

He hadn't fastened it too snugly, and yet when she tried to move, she realized it raised her chin and kept her from looking either around or down. A flash of panic went through her and died at the steady look in his eyes.

"I won't leave you, sweetheart. If anything bothers you too much, use your safe word. Do you understand?"

She tried to nod and couldn't.

His eyes crinkled. "Say, 'Yes, sir.'"

"Yes, Sir."

"Good. Now you just stay put while I enjoy myself."

What did that mean? Her hands curled into balls as he knelt. With her chin held up by the collar, she couldn't see him. *The bastard.* Yet the arousal in her body edged up a notch as she waited for his touch. She had to wait; couldn't do anything else.

She heard a rustle, felt his hands on her pussy, and damn, it felt so good, his firm hands doing whatever he wanted. He buckled some sort of harness around her thighs and waist. Okay, that wasn't so bad, but then something pushed up inside her. Something cool. Hard. Not his fingers.

"What are you doing?" Her voice shook.

"Whatever I want, sweetheart." Liquid drizzled down her pussy, wet and cold, and she jumped. She felt a pinch over her clit, one that didn't release. Not painful but…disconcerting. A few clipping sounds and then tugs on the harness. "I'm just adjusting everything so it stays in place."

So what stays in place? She throbbed from the pressure of whatever was inside and from whatever sat over her clit. What was he doing?

When he stood, he had a microphone on his collar and a box—*a control box?*—clipped to his waistband.

Before she figured out what that combination meant, he ran his firm hands over her, stroking her skin, cupping her breasts, sending the warmth rising in her again. His lips settled on hers, and he took a long kiss. God, he could kiss. Her body relaxed...and heated.

He pulled back, smiled into her eyes, and then flipped a switch on the box.

Something made tapping sensations her clit and up inside her. Like tiny hammers. She jerked, her eyes wide. "What is that?"

"I'll show you in a bit. Your only job is to let me know if anything becomes uncomfortable." He put a finger on her chin and gave her an uncompromising look. "Otherwise I do not want to hear you speak. Am I clear, pet?"

She stiffened yet melted inside at his low, resonant voice and the commanding look in his eyes. "Yes, Sir."

As the tapping increased—somehow different from a vibrator, more inside than out—her clit tightened until it felt as if it would burst. Everything down there coiled, aching for more, and it wasn't enough. She smothered a moan. And she realized he'd stepped away to study her reactions.

He nodded. "Perfect." And then his flogger struck her thighs. The added sensation shocked through her and zoomed straight to her clit. Her legs tensed, and she rocked. He didn't stop. The leather strands hit lightly up her back, and each blow made the burning need in her pussy worse, so much worse.

She closed her eyes, swamped by the sensations.

He lashed her bottom, the backs of her thighs. "Rona."

With his words, the tingling on her clit increased in force and speed, and she moaned uncontrollably.

A second later the tapping abated. The flogger didn't. "Rona. Look at me."

Again, the vibrations intensified for a few seconds. Not nearly long enough. And the flogger never stopped, weaving a sensory spell around her. Up her legs, almost touching her pussy.

Oh God, just a little more. Her hands closed into fists, and her neck arched.

"Look. At. Me."

Again, the tapping strengthened, quickened, and the searing wave of arousal inside her and across her clit almost got her off, but then the vibrations slowed. She forced her eyes open.

His smile flashed in that chiseled face. "That's a girl."

Her back arched as the jump in sensations blew through her again. As they decreased, she stared at the mike clipped to his shirt. *Oh, Crom.* He could change the intensity of vibrations with his voice—with sound control.

The flogger struck her harder, each blow a flashing pain that stung and shunted more urgency through her until every nerve seemed swallowed by need. But she couldn't, couldn't get off. She whimpered. "Oh please..."

He chuckled, and just that tiny amount of sound shot through her like he'd pinched her clit.

Her hands clenched as she hovered on the pinnacle, with pain and pleasure so securely wound together, she just might die.

"All right, sweetie," he murmured.

Oh God, the feeling with his words. Sweat rolled down her back as she strained toward the climax she couldn't reach.

And then he said loudly, oh so loudly, "Let's hear you scream, pet." The vibrations turned exquisitely powerful inside and across her clit, and his flogger lashed across her breasts.

She exploded, wave after wave of blazing pleasure pouring through every nerve in her body, shaking her like a rag doll. Her legs simply collapsed.

"Very nice," he said, and the sound kicked off more vibrations. As the intense spasms shocked through her, she couldn't move, couldn't do anything except feel each rippling wave. When they finally stopped, she hung limply from the chains, her mind hazed. Satisfied. Stunned.

She barely registered his removing everything, undoing the harness on her thighs, then the collar. Too heavy to stay upright, her head rested against her chained arm.

"Hang on another minute, lass." He unchained her wrists and caught her around the waist when she'd have folded right onto the floor. A second later her brain went into a roller-coaster swirl. She blinked in astonishment—*he's carrying me*?—and stared up at his corded neck and strong jaw. Rock-hard arms held her against his solid chest, and the scent of his subtly musky cologne surrounded her. The disconcerting sense of fragility blended with the wonderful feeling of being cherished.

Chapter Three

Now wasn't she the nicest armful he'd had in a long time? The way her body fit against his made Simon wonder if their personalities would match equally well. Logical or not, everything inside him said yes.

He took a seat in a nearby leather chair and settled her comfortably on his lap. Her soft ass pressed against his painfully rigid cock, and she obviously felt it. “What about you?” she murmured. “Can I—”

“No, sweetheart.” He kissed the top of her head, warmth seeping into him both from her body and from the knowledge that she wanted to give back as well as to receive. “This evening was for your pleasure.”

And for his, in a way. He'd enjoyed introducing her to BDSM more than anything he'd done in a long time. He smiled, remembering how the wariness in her eyes had warred with the arousal of her body. When she had set her hand in his, the trust she'd given him had squeezed his heart.

He rubbed his chin on her silky hair, pleased with her light fragrance of vanilla and citrus that created the feeling of a garden within the wilderness of the club. Her cheek rested against his chest, and she gripped the front placket of his old-fashioned shirt as if she feared he'd leave her. Not a chance.

But he shouldn't let her get too comfortable. This woman needed to be kept off balance, at least for now. So he contracted his grip and ran his free hand over her bare breasts, smiling when she startled.

"Don't move, pet," he cautioned her.

Sweetly submissive, she stilled, although her breathing increased.

He pleased himself with the feel of her round breasts. Despite her recent orgasm, her satiny nipples responded quickly, forming dark pink peaks. When he pinched one, she quivered and looked up at him.

Her turquoise-colored eyes were very vulnerable in the aftermath of the scene and roused all his protective instincts. Odd. He hadn't felt this intensely about anyone since the birth of his son. He kissed her lightly, reassuringly, and felt her muscles relax.

"Did you like your first experience with BDSM?" he asked. He knew one answer, considering how hard she'd come, but a woman's fears and worries couldn't be plumbed in just one evening.

"Well. I... Yes, I did."

No coy answers from this sub. Damn, she pleased him.

He stroked her cheek, holding her gaze. "What part did you like the most?"

She stiffened, obviously unused to intimate questions. She'd have to learn better. Not only did he require it as a dom, but also as a lover. And he wanted to know her all the way down to her soul. He tightened his grip and moved his hand back to her breasts, increasing their physical intimacy to match the emotional. “Answer me.”

Her body softened at his firm order. *Submissive.* But still silent.

“All right, I'll help. Did you like the flogging?” He ran his hand under her round ass to where he'd struck the hardest, and squeezed her undoubtedly sore flesh.

She jumped.

“Or the electrical play?” He touched her still-wet pussy, enjoying the drifting scent of her arousal.

Her body stiffened, and she tried to sit up, but his arm around her shoulders kept her in place. She was going nowhere. He ran his fingers up and down her swollen labia and grazed the vulnerable little clit.

She inhaled sharply.

Was she this responsive with everyone, or did her body also recognize the connection between them? “Do I need to show you the choices again?”

Two people walking past overheard and laughed.

Her cheeks flushed a lovely pink. She cleared her throat. “No. The electrical stuff. Only, if I'd known you wanted to do that, I—”

“You'd never have allowed an electrode anywhere near this pretty pussy?”

“Crom no.”

Crom. He'd heard that odd word used as a soft curse one time before. Where? Then he smiled slowly as he remembered. “The riot after the football game.”

“Excuse me?”

"Last year, you helped my son when he got hurt in the riot." While Simon had fought the surging crowd from trampling Danny, Rona had braced his son's broken arm and checked him for other injuries. Her low, soft voice had been compassionate, and her matter-of-fact tone, reassuring. She'd directed her two teenage boys to help Danny stand, so Simon could get him out of the mess. Then, trailed by her sons, she'd moved on to assist others. Danny still called her his football angel.

"Oh." She frowned at him. "I don't remember you."

"You concentrated on my son." He rubbed his chin against her wavy hair. A ball cap had hidden it that night, and she'd worn jeans and a high school letter jacket. No wonder he hadn't recognized her. "What is a Crom, anyway?"

When she gave a husky laugh, he grinned. He'd been right, her voice had indeed deepened after she'd come. "It's the god of Conan the Barbarian. My superhero-worshipping sons and I decided Crom wouldn't mind if we took his name in vain."

"Ah." Both practical and quirky. "Well, my son and I thank you for your help that night." He kissed her gently for thanks, then continued, teasing her mouth, savoring the softness, the willingness to enjoy, and the delightful skill with which she ran her tongue over his lips, alternating with gentle nibbles.

When he slid one finger over her clit, she gave the softest of moans. Perhaps they weren't finished after all, and now that he knew more about her, he was damned if he wanted to stop.

He gently pinched her clit between his fingers. When she gasped, he took possession of her mouth, hard and deep, even as he slipped a finger into her. After pulling his hand back, he thrust harder into her and felt the surging arousal of her body.

After ending the kiss, he smiled down at her. Her eyes had glazed with passion; her lips were red and wet. The hand she'd wrapped behind his neck resisted his movement away even as her pussy contracted around his finger. Passionate and responsive. Intelligent, brave, and submissive. Her appeal grabbed him by the guts and pulled. He took a slow, steady breath. "Let me clean up the scene area, and we'll find somewhere else to play." The Victorian Room would serve nicely, considering the theme tonight, and she'd look lovely bound to the four-poster.

Her eyes widened and then narrowed. He could almost hear her brain switch back on.

RONA PUSHED HERSELF to a sitting position, dismayed at her behavior. She'd wanted to explore, but jumping right in like this... What had she been thinking? She didn't really know this man, and he'd kept touching her as if she belonged to him. Crom, his finger still filled her, eroding her resistance. She grasped his thickly corded wrist and tried to push his hand away.

His arm didn't budge an inch. In fact, he deliberately pressed in farther until his palm brushed against her throbbing clit.

A spasm of delight sent heat soaring through her like she'd entered a sauna. She sucked in a lungful of air, wanting nothing so much as to say, *More.* "Stop, please."

His head tilted. His dark eyes had never left hers. He slid his finger from her, ever so slowly, his gaze studying her.

She felt the warmth of an embarrassed flush. He knew exactly how turned on he'd made her, dammit.

His lips quirked, but the arm around her loosened. He wasn't going to push her.

She breathed a sigh of relief until he lifted his hand and licked the finger that glistened with her wetness, sampling it like a fine vintage.

"You taste as hot and sweet as I thought you would." His eyes left her no doubt that he imagined his mouth replacing his hand.

Her vagina clenched, feeling only emptiness where he'd been. Everything in her burned for his touch. *Take me. No.* Her thoughts jiggled in her head like a heart in atrial fibrillation until she finally remembered why she needed to leave. The second item on her "I'm free to change" goals: for at least one year, she could only have sex with a man once before moving on to a new guy. She'd decided to take no chance of getting caught or stuck in a rut.

Not even with someone like this. *Especially with someone like this.* She firmed her lips and pushed off his lap and onto her feet.

He frowned but rose in instinctive courtesy. Unfortunately, that left her looking up at him. His shoulders broad and muscular. He could overpower her easily, and damn her for wanting him to. Damn him for being so devastating.

"I really must go," she said firmly, despite the flutters in her stomach. "Thank you for the sample of BDSM, Master Simon. I...learned a lot."

"You view this as a lesson only?" His eyes narrowed. "Was I mistaken in the impression that you enjoyed yourself?"

Considering how she'd screamed, he knew full well she'd gotten off. And yet his words still made her feel guilty, as if she was being rude. "I did enjoy myself. But..."

"Continue."

Authoritative jerk, she thought, and yet every time his voice took on that commanding tone, she wanted to roll over and go belly up like her neighbor's wimpy dachshund. "I won't do anything with anyone more than once."

"So, good or bad, each man gets only one shot?"

"That's right. That's my rule." Posted on the bulletin board at home, no less.

"I see." His hand curved around the nape of her neck as if she were a kitten being dragged by its mother. "Rona, I would like to see you again. If you prefer to avoid...intimate...surroundings, I'll take you to dinner."

"No. But thank you." She gave him a firm nod and held out her hand, pretending she still had on clothing. "I enjoyed meeting you."

His mouth thinned into a hard line...but it hadn't been hard at all when he kissed her. His fingers on her neck tightened, and then he released her.

"It was nice meeting you too, lass." He took her hand, turned it over, and grazed his lips over her palm, sending a rush straight to her pussy. Damn, he was potent. His gaze brushed over her blatantly peaked nipples, and a corner of his mouth tipped up. "We'll talk soon about this rule of yours."

She could see he expected her to argue over that statement, but she'd lived long enough to know the utility of a quick retreat. Especially since her body had started a raging argument with her head.

When she pulled her hand away, he let her go. He ran a finger down her cheek, the look in his eyes so intense, it felt as if he'd touched her soul. And yet gentle. Caring.

More shaken by that look even than her arousal, she slung her hoop over her shoulder and grabbed her clothing and shoes. Clutching everything to her bare chest, she marched through the place, up the stairs, and to the changing rooms near the front. Once there, she leaned her back against the cool metal of a locker and sighed.

Why did he have to be so...so overwhelming? Every time he gave her one of those commanding looks, she wanted to fall at his knees and say, *Take me. Please.* Was she that much of a weak-willed female?

Oh yes. When it came to him, definitely yes.

And that last look he'd given her... She'd better stick with easier men to date or the first item on her list—*not get involved with anyone for at least five years*—wouldn't last a month.

Chapter Four

The drenching morning rain had given way to clear skies, and now the late-afternoon sun warmed Rona's shoulders. She strolled down the center of the blocked-off avenue, dodging the others also enjoying this pre-Christmas street fair. The raunchy lyrics of Hollywood Undead blasted out from a boom box down the street. Sex toys, fet-wear, bondage equipment—this was the place to shop for a loved one whose tastes edged into kinky. Or if you wanted to indulge in buying for yourself.

She glanced at a man leading another by a leash and grinned. Who would have thought she'd find such things tempting? Her trip to Dark Haven two weeks ago had opened her eyes in many ways.

And complicated her life. She frowned. Hoping to get that overbearing, *commanding*, overmuscled, *gorgeous*, man, *dom*, out of her thoughts, she'd gone on a flurry of dates. And each evening had been as exciting as giving a patient a bed bath.

Had just one taste of BDSM spoiled her for normal guys? The memory of how Master Simon's dark eyes had studied her as he cuffed her wrists sent a blast of heat through her like she'd sniffed a vial of pheromones.

Of course, the sights and sounds around her didn't help. She dodged an extremely tall man in a cat suit and cat mask, then a cluster of men in chain harnesses and jeans. Shrugging her canvas shopping bag to a comfortable position on her shoulder, she checked out the booths displaying garter belts, vinyl and latex clothing, and costumes. She wanted something exotic so she could blend in next time she went to Dark Haven. Maybe a sexy bustier?

She paused by a stall that sold sex toys. So many times she'd considered getting a vibrator, but it had seemed a kind of betrayal of Mark, no matter how flat their love life had grown. But now...

Several women clustered around the stall, decreasing her feeling of being conspicuous. *Look, Rona's going to buy a vibrator*! Edging to the front, she studied the offerings. *Where to start*? Dildos ranged from tiny—*why would anyone use something the size of a finger?*—to a terrifying one that resembled a foot-long mushroom and made her vagina cringe, if such a thing were possible.

Then she noticed the vibrator section. Oh yes. Right off her fantasy list—which had grown remarkably after her club visit. Tiny balls to go inside. *Nah*. Some the size and shape of a real cock. Her finger tapped her lips. Too bland. She spotted one that could be used in both orifices. Her butt constricted at the thought, but... *Hmm*... Next to it lay a combination dildo-and-clit vibrator, and her bottom actually wiggled at the idea. She started to reach for it...

A hand pressed against her lower back, and a deep, smooth voice murmured in her ear, “I'm going to get the wrong impression of you if we keep meeting in these types of venues.”

She caught the scent of sensuously rich cologne before she jerked around and stared up into dark eyes that glinted with amusement. “Ma—Simon.”

“Ah. I haven't been forgotten completely.”

When he stroked a finger down her cheek, her insides quivered as if the fabled San Francisco quake had started. Nice trick, that. She doubted if even the fancy vibrators in the booth could achieve such an effect. “What are you doing here?”

“Some friends are giving a demonstration of suspension bondage.” He glanced at his watch. “I have fifteen minutes free. May I join you?”

Oh yes. Then her brain kicked in. *Oh no.*

He shook his head. “So divided.” Lifting a finger, he attracted the attention of the booth owner, picked up the combination vibrator, and handed her some money.

Rona eyed the device. A guy wouldn't use something like that, would he? No. So he'd bought it for a girlfriend or… “Are you married?”

When he cocked an eyebrow at her blunt question, she sighed. At work, she'd been described as confident and articulate, yet in his presence, she tripped over her tongue like a verbal spastic.

“No, I'm not married, lass. Or in any relationship whatsoever.”

Wasn't he going to ask her that question in return? Her mouth turned down. Didn't he want to know?

Smiling, he lifted her hand and tapped the fading mark on her ring finger where her wedding band had been. "I don't need to ask, lass. And you're too honest to scene with me if you were involved."

"Both telepathy and X-ray vision, huh?"

He chuckled. "I've been a dom for quite a while. Eventually you learn to use your eyes."

As the seller counted out his change, a shriek split through the noise of the crowd. Rona turned.

Near the center of the street, two brawling, red-faced men had knocked an older lady to her knees. As "fuck yous" filled the air, they tried to tear each other apart, heedless of their victim.

Worse than Saturday night in the ER. Growling in disgust, Rona dodged around the men to get to the woman. Slinging an arm around the frail waist, Rona pulled her up and out of the battle zone. Looking over her shoulder to make sure she'd gone far enough, Rona gaped.

Standing between the two men, Simon had stopped the fight. For a second. Then one swore and lunged around Simon to attack the other.

Shaking his head, Simon shoved up his sleeves, stepped forward, and...

Rona blinked. His fists had moved too fast to follow, but now one man lay moaning on the ground, arms wrapped around his stomach. Simon had the other on his knees, his hand clamped in the man's hair.

From the way the jerk's arm dangled, his shoulder was dislocated.

With a tiny quiver, Rona recognized the stern set to Simon's jaw as he talked to the brawler in a low voice. When he stepped back, the brawler scrambled to his feet and fled through the gathered crowd.

Simon dragged the other one to a sitting position. After saying a few words, he hauled the guy to his feet and shoved him on his way. Apparently oblivious to the scattered applause from the crowd, Simon rolled down his sleeves and retrieved his purchase.

When he joined Rona, his intent gaze scrutinized her, top to bottom, before he turned to the old woman. "Are you all right, ma'am?"

"I am now." The lady smiled at him. "You did a fine job there. Thank you."

"My pleasure."

"Well, I need to move along. I still have to get a present for Henry." The woman brushed the dirt from her lavender sweats and frowned at the rip in one knee. "Our fortieth anniversary is tomorrow, and we buy each other a treat every year." She nodded at Simon, patted Rona's shoulder in thanks, and walked toward the toy booth.

Rona stared. The treat for Henry was a sex toy? After forty years of marriage? *Damn.*

Simon huffed a laugh, then wrapped an arm around Rona's waist. "Come, lass."

"Where'd you learn to fight like that?"

He steered her down the street. "Military, then the martial-arts circuit for a time. I quit when my son arrived." He lifted his left hand, tried to curl the fingers, and smiled ruefully. “I fear I hit a few too many solid objects before then.”

Frowning, Rona took his hand. White scars from old surgeries traced over his skin; the bones underneath felt rough and uneven. “You must have broken every...” She looked up guiltily, let go, and put her hands behind her back. *Bad Rona.* Hadn't she already learned that grabbing a dom was a no-no? “Sorry.”

His flashing smile lightened his face. “True, a submissive doesn't touch without permission.” When he grasped her hand and ran his thumb over her knuckles, the suggestive caress sent a tingle through her. “But I enjoy having your hands on me too much to object. For now.”

“For now?”

He threaded his fingers into her hair and tugged her head back, forcing her to look up at him. “I think, eventually, I will enjoy reprimanding you just as much. Your ass turns such a pretty pink.”

Before she could speak, he gave her a hard kiss and released her.

She stared at him, the sheer heat his words had engendered burning away any sarcastic response.

Smiling, he took her hand and started walking again. “The stage is down this way.”

“Simon. We're not dating.”

“We will.” He ran his thumb over her lower lip, and the carnal look in his eyes dried up all the saliva in her mouth.

She looked away, concentrating on her walking. *I'm not attracted. Really.* And that's like claiming that

Lois Lane never really wanted Superman. Nonetheless, *remember rules one and two from the goals list.* "Simon. I appreciate the trouble you've taken, but I'm not interested in...in anything more."

She winced at the thoughtful look in his eyes. Despite the noisy crowd and the brightly colored booths, all his attention was now focused on her, nowhere else, with an unsettling concentration.

"You're attracted to me," he said so confidently that she glanced down to see if she wore a sign saying I WANT YOU. "And you're not involved a relationship. So...?"

Obstinate, wasn't he? "I was married for twenty years. The last few years, we just tolerated each other until our children left the nest, and when they did, we got a divorce. I promised myself I'd never get trapped like that again."

He raised an eyebrow.

"Being married..." It had been like wading through a dark swamp, unable to find a way out. "I have a new life. I'm free to explore and experience everything I missed. That includes a variety of men."

"Ah."

OBSTINATE, WASN'T SHE? Simon shook his head.

She lifted her stubborn chin and lengthened her stride, as if she could shake him so easily. She couldn't. Not after the way his body and heart had leaped when he'd seen her in the crowd. He stepped around a bare-chested gay couple dancing to Combichrist and rejoined her.

Unfortunately, he understood how escaping a cage might make a woman wary about being caught again. It would take some clever bread crumbs to lure her closer.

And he wanted her closer. Even if he disregarded that unexpected connection from before, she attracted him. She'd helped his son at the riot and rescued the old woman with no hysterics or screaming, just compassion and practicality. And she could have claimed involvement with someone but hadn't. She might not share her emotions freely, but what she shared would be honest. And that was as unusual as it was appealing.

He wanted her in his life, wanted to see if they matched as well as he believed.

No, he wouldn't let her run away, not if the need to explore proved to be her only objection. He smiled down at her, thinking of how she'd look cuffed to his bed while they...explored. But deeply held opinions rarely changed with logical arguments. So for now, his plan must be to keep her near, and he just happened to have the perfect way to do that.

As they neared the stage, he stopped. "Rona, this coming Saturday, I'm holding my annual Christmas party for those in the lifestyle." He touched her cheek and caught a trace of her citrus and vanilla scent—tangy and sweet, well suited to her. "I'd be pleased if you'd come. You will meet plenty of unattached doms."

"Really? Even though I said no to...seeing you?"

"Even though." He wanted to see what they had in common—and what they'd fight about. He already knew she'd be an interesting opponent, forthright and clever. He might deliberately lose an argument just to hear her husky laugh. Then again, considering her obvious intelligence, she'd probably win all by herself. He pulled an invitation from his wallet. "Since you're new, I'll make sure you don't get in over your head."

"Well. Thank you. I'll think about it." From the flare of excitement in her eyes, he knew she was hooked. He'd have time to convince her to give them both a chance at happiness. And those soft curves would feel wonderful under him.

Smiling at that thought, he handed her the bag containing the rabbit vibrator he'd bought. "I got this for you, lass."

"You what?"

"I would have enjoyed showing you how it works, but since you prefer otherwise, you may simply think of me when you use it. Tonight." Before she could recover from the shock, he kissed her lightly on her soft, soft lips and walked away.

* * * *

The lunch crowd in the hospital cafeteria had thinned quite a bit by the time Rona managed to cut free of her phone and e-mails. The scattered tables held a spattering of nurses in scrubs, med students, two surgeons between cases, and a few visitors. She set her tray on the small table and sat down across from her friend. "I hate hump day."

Brenda laughed and dipped a french fry in ketchup. "Me too. Speaking of humping, did you know that Charles Madigan got a divorce?"

"Really?" Rona dumped a sparing amount of ranch dressing on her healthy salad. Dieting was tiresome, but the anticipation of baring...everything...this weekend proved more than sufficient incentive.

"Makes good money, our age, single, gorgeous. Why aren't you looking interested?"

"He's all right, but I want...more."

Brenda frowned. "*More* like in that bar you went to?"

Rona laughed at the disapproving tone. "Uh-huh."

"And how the hell do you figure on finding...more? You got a plan mapped out, Ms. Obsessive-Compulsive."

"Thanks a lot. You know, if you don't write down what you want, you'll never know if you get there." Rona nudged aside the insipid-looking excuse for a tomato, then speared some romaine leaves. "Actually, a man invited me to a party." She snickered. "A *more* party."

"Oh...my." The brunette pointed with a french fry. "Did you meet him at that club?"

"Yes." The memory of Simon's implacable voice threatening to chain her legs apart sent heat through her body in a mighty wave. Knowing she'd turned red, Rona lowered her head and poked at her salad. "And again at a street fair." *Where he bought me a vibrator. And told me to think of him while using it...* Oh, she certainly had. The jerk had known she would.

"Twice? And now a party? Ooooh, this sounds good."

"No." When eagerness to see him roused, Rona stomped it flat. "I'm not going for him. I want to meet other guys. Getting involved isn't in my plans."

"So enjoy him without getting involved. Like Max does." Brenda jerked her chin toward the surgeon. He was notorious for his having affairs with several women simultaneously, although he'd discovered the dangers of dating two OR nurses at once.

Rona studied him with rising hope. That might just work. "Sex with Simon one night, then with someone else a day or so later, and so on. No way could anything get serious."

"That's the spirit."

Boy, it sounded a bit—*a lot*—slutty, but making up for lost years wasn't for sissies. And tonight she'd revise the rule list: *No sexy seconds unless dating additional men.*

Chapter Five

On Saturday evening, Rona walked through the open front door of Simon's three-story, stone-and-stucco house. A myriad of guests stood in small groups under a huge sparkling chandelier, and laughter and conversation filled the foyer. The party had definitely started.

"Merry Christmas!" A young woman in an elf costume with bright green fishnet stockings hurried across the gleaming dark wood floor.

At the high-pitched greeting, people glanced toward Rona. A second later a man disengaged from a small group and strode across the room. Master Simon.

Rona pulled in a breath as her nerves went on alert as if someone had called a code blue for a heart attack.

Arriving first, the elf beamed at Rona. "Come on. I'll take you around."

"Mandy, I'll show her to the dressing room," Master Simon said as he stopped behind the elf. He squeezed the young woman's shoulder. "Thank you, pet."

The elf gazed up at him in adoration, then scurried away, the white pom-pom on her red hat bouncing with each step.

Simon watched her for a second, and he murmured, “So much energy.” Then his black gaze turned toward Rona like a dark laser beam, the type that would cut a villain right in half.

Her heart gave a violent *thud*. The man had dressed simply, in black slacks and a white shirt that set off his dark tan, yet when a smile lightened his stern face, her blood fizzed in her veins like a shaken Coke.

“Rona. I'm pleased you came.” He held out his hand, waiting patiently until she gave him hers. His fingers closed, encasing her in warmth.

“Thank you for the invitation,” she said, falling back on proprieties. She caught sight of his guests and frowned. Although the dominants remained fully clothed in jeans or suits or leathers, all the submissives were in elf costumes. One wore only a Santa hat and red nipple clamps. *Oh Crom*. Rona's stomach sank as she glanced down at her slinky black dress.

Growing up, she couldn't afford the trendy clothing her friends wore, and had hated never fitting in. Shallow or not, her feelings hadn't changed. She stepped back. “I don't think that I—”

He chuckled. “Relax, pet. I took the liberty of selecting an outfit for you.”

An elf pranced by wearing only red high heels, a red thong, and a hat. Rona winced. *Do I even want to know what he got me?*

Ignoring her hesitation, he set a hand on her low back and steered her across the foyer to a powder room. "I left your costume on the counter in one of my company bags—look for a Demakis International Security logo."

"Well." All arranged. He'd obviously put some thought into making her comfortable. "Thank you."

"I think a more enthusiastic expression of gratitude is in order." With one finger, he tilted up her chin. Before she could protest, firm lips explored hers, teasing for a response. When she sighed and leaned toward him, he yanked her against his solid body and took the kiss from sweet to devastatingly possessive.

Crom. Her memories hadn't come close to how he really kissed or how easily he could control her. Heat pooled in her belly like molten lava.

When he pulled back and steadied her on her feet, she was breathing like an asthmatic having an acute attack.

"Now that was a very nice thank-you," he murmured. "Go change, lass. Then meet me in the living room. I'll explain the rules and introduce you around."

As he pushed her gently into the powder room, she frowned. *Rules?*

* * * *

In the living room, Simon did the rounds, greeting his guests, making introductions. Along with the local BDSMers, quite a few friends had arrived from out of town. Busy or not, he kept an eye on the arched doorway, his anticipation rising. He spotted Rona the minute she walked into the room.

She paused in the doorway. Her hands rubbed the white fur downward in a nervous gesture, although her face appeared serene and self-confident. To come to a party by herself, to try something so new... Brave lass.

And she looked beautiful. A fuzzy red Santa cap with a white puff ball at the end sat on her wavy blonde hair. The long-sleeved, red velvet coat trimmed with white fur reached only to the top of her creamy white thighs. Right where he wanted his hand. If she bent over, everyone would have an enticing glimpse of the ribbon-tied, peppermint-striped bra and thong set he'd bought.

Wanting her to feel comfortable, he'd chosen relatively conservative clothing. Of course, being a dom, he'd selected for his own pleasure also.

The wide sleeves would accommodate wrist cuffs, and only a securely fastened leather belt held the buttonless coat closed. Poor sub. Belt and ribbons could and would be removed over the course of the evening. He hardened at the thought of revealing those sweet curves.

When she spotted him, her eyes lit up in a way that made his chest compress. Her head might tell her not to get involved, but apparently her emotions matched his. He'd do his best to see that her emotions won.

He crooked a finger, then grinned as her passage across the room netted interested glances from the dominants.

One stepped away from her friends. Tara gave Rona a long look. "Oh, that's nice. Tell me she likes girls and not boys."

"No," Simon told the tall domme, not looking away from his sub. "She's straight."

Tara's eyebrows went up. "Well, well. I haven't seen that look in your eyes in a long time...if ever." She slapped his arm in approval before returning to her group.

Rona stopped in front of Simon.

"You look lovely," he said and enjoyed how her cheeks turned pink.

"Thank you. And thank you for...for giving me enough costume."

"You are very welcome." He tugged her silky hair lightly. "Do bear in mind that submissives usually wind up wearing less clothing by the end of a party."

The wary look she gave him included a fair amount of excitement. "I'm not sure I understand."

"These are the rules: as is normal for a submissive at a party, you will serve the doms food and drinks. Since you're not owned, a dom may touch any part of you that isn't covered." He grinned when her arms wrapped protectively around the coat. "Touch only, pet. Scenes and intimate play must be negotiated. The safe word in my house is 'red.' Some doms and subs have their own safe words, but if someone shouts 'red' in here, everyone shows up to enforce it."

"That's both scary and reassuring," she said.

Smart girl. Despite all the precautions, BDSM still hovered on the dangerous side. "Before playing, you will inform the dom of your inexperience. But as an additional precaution, I had this made for you." He pulled the gold necklace from his pocket and put it around her neck. It settled just below her throat.

She picked up the lettered part and tucked her chin down to read it. *Elf-in-training*. Her laugh was husky and open.

Would she laugh during sex? He'd given her intense; how about playful? He shoved the question aside. "Now, who would you like to meet?"

* * * *

Rona chatted with an older dom named Michael in the great room. During the past hour, she'd wandered around, just observing the interesting scenes going on. Master Simon had scattered BDSM equipment over the entire first floor for the party. Tables and spanking benches with various forms of restraints were in the living and dining rooms, a massive St. Andrew's cross stood in the center of his great room. The large granite-countered kitchen held a stockade, and chains dangled from the exposed beams. All set up to entice people to play.

So, dammit, why couldn't she find a dom who was half the man Master Simon was? Whenever he entered the room, she could feel his presence—a shimmering aura of power. His gaze would sweep the room and settle on her. He'd look her over so thoroughly, she'd feel the heat rise in her cheeks. And then he'd turn away.

Leaving her alone, as he'd promised.

That was what she wanted, right? She really did need to have a few more men on her string before indulging in hot, roaring sex with him. Just the thought made her mouth dry. *Bad sign, Rona.*

Time to jump into the party spirit and stop stalling. She smiled at the man beside her. Maybe she'd start with him.

“Doms.” Master Simon's voice filled the room, making her breath hitch. “If you are not occupied, I need assistance judging the first contest. Any uncollared elves who are not busy, please line up here.”

A contest? Great. Unless he planned something intellectual, she'd surely lose. She hesitated.

A hand closed on her arm, and she looked up at the gray-haired dom beside her.

Michael frowned at her. “Simon might have said 'please,' but it wasn't a request, sub; it was an order.” He pulled her across the room to Master Simon.

“She wanted to think it over before obeying,” Michael said and let her go.

“Really.” Master Simon's eyes darkened with displeasure.

Oh Crom. “I don't like contests. I lose,” she said hurriedly. Why did his disapproval make her chest tighten and her stomach sink? She looked down.

“I see.” He lifted her chin, forcing her to meet his gaze. “Unfortunately, your opinion doesn't count, does it.”

He hadn't really asked a question, but she answered anyway. “No.”

His fingers flexed on her chin just enough to remind her of her manners.

“No, Sir. I'm sorry, Sir.”

"Much better." He released her. "Join the others."

As she took her place at the end of the line, he said, "This submissive contest is for general friendliness and service." He grasped the first sub by her nape and asked the crowd, "If this pretty elf either gave you her name or served you in any way, please raise your hand."

Seven hands lifted, mostly dommes'.

Rona bit her lip as uneasiness twisted her insides. Concentrated on getting her bearings, she'd spoken casually with a few doms but hadn't introduced herself.

Soon she realized the other elves had stayed very busy, serving drinks and food, giving back rubs, foot rubs, or playing with a dom as requested. Very few hadn't done much; unfortunately, she was one of them.

Master Simon gripped the back of her neck firmly, pulling her a step closer to him. She shivered as his hard chest brushed against her shoulder and his warm, rich scent surrounded her. He asked the crowd, "And this sub?"

Only Michael lifted his hand.

"Ah. Well, she is just in training, after all. Please help her out and put her to work, gentlemen." His hand dropped away. "All elves who earned more than five raised hands, you've done well. You're dismissed. The rest of you slackers, remove one article of clothing and leave it on the table there."

When three-quarters of the subs dispersed, Rona sighed in relief. At least she wasn't the only slacker. *Remove something.* Well, she hated wearing hats anyway. Her hand had just touched the fuzzy cap when Master Simon added casually, “I should mention that if I find an elf without an elf cap, I will toss her out on the street...naked.”

Rona snatched her hand away and heard him chuckle. Crom, she didn't have much to choose from. Maybe she could remove her bra in the powder room?

“You have ten seconds, and then we'll all help.”

Maybe she didn't like Master Simon after all.

“Ten. Nine—”

Jaw clenched, Rona unbuckled and pulled her belt off.

“One.”

She tossed the belt on the table. Lacking buttons, her Santa coat fell open, displaying her very skimpy bra and thong. She'd have to hold it shut all night. *That jerk.*

Looking around, she saw one elf must have waited too long. Three doms had surrounded her and were stripping her of clothing. Rona bit her lip, trying to decide if she'd find that exciting or frightening. She rubbed her chilled hands on her coat.

“Rona,” Master Simon said.

“Sir?”

“Please take a filled tray from the kitchen and serve drinks until it's empty.”

Cool. Something active to do. “Yes, Sir. Thank you, Sir.”

He grinned.

In the kitchen, when she picked up the tray, she understood his amusement. Holding the tray required both hands, and now she couldn't hold her coat shut. "You bastard," she muttered.

"Excuse me?"

She whirled so suddenly that the drinks sloshed.

"Did I mention the rule about speaking without permission?" His eyes glinted with laughter.

"Yes, Sir."

He smiled slowly. "You're penalized one ribbon." Reaching over her tray of drinks, he tugged on the ribbon serving as the left strap for her bra. The bow came undone, and he pulled the ribbon out of the grommets.

Held up on only one side, her bra sagged, exposing her left breast.

Still holding the tray, she looked up at him.

"I like that helpless look," he murmured and ran his fingers down her neck to her bared breast.

Her attempt at retreat only backed her into the kitchen island. Trapped between it and him, she stared over his shoulder as he stroked her breast, circling the peak with one finger. She could feel her nipple pebbling under his confident touch. How it ached.

A gentle pinch made her jump; the glasses chimed on the tray. Her eyes jerked up, and he held her gaze as his fingers teased her nipple. When he squeezed the tip, a hot sizzle shot straight to her groin. Her fingers locked on the tray as he increased the pressure—as her excitement skyrocketed.

His eyes crinkled. "We need to get you into a scene before you explode," he said softly. He brushed his lips over hers and stepped back. "Go serve, lass. If you find someone you'd like to top you, I'll release you from your duty."

As she walked through the rooms, everyone greeted her politely. Some took a glass; some ignored the drinks and made themselves free with her body, running their hands over any exposed skin. The air around her grew increasingly warm.

In the living room, she spotted Michael talking to two tough-looking doms in black leathers. A redheaded sub knelt on the floor between their chairs.

"Rona." Michael waved her closer. "This is Logan"—he nodded toward the dom with steel blue eyes and dark brown hair—"his sub, Rebecca, and his brother, Jake."

Jake looked as hard and lean as his brother but had a nasty scar across his tanned forehead that his thick hair couldn't hide. He considered her for a long moment, then cocked a brow. "That's a nice elf costume, blondie."

Uncertain as to how she should address them, she said, "I'm pleased to meet you, Sirs."

"Your arrival is timely." Michael grinned. "We're arguing about where a woman's legs are the most sensitive. I think it's behind the knee. Jake says just below the ass."

Rona frowned. Did he expect her to offer her opinion?

Michael rose and set her tray on an empty chair, then pushed her to one end of the coffee table. "Bend over, sub. We're going to conduct an experiment."

No way. If she bent over, they'd—

All three doms frowned at her hesitation. *Oh Crom*. She obeyed and tried to reassure herself that Michael wouldn't do anything horrible. *I want Master Simon here.*

"Hands flat on the coffee table, Rona."

She did, all too aware of how her coat didn't cover her butt. But at least she stood sideways to the two men in the chairs; they wouldn't see it. She dropped her head and closed her eyes. Now what?

"Look at Logan and Jake," Michael said.

Okay. Both men watched her with that focused dom look.

"Now don't move, sub." Michael swept his hands up and down her legs. Then his fingers brushed behind her knees, tickling until she wiggled. He laughed and moved his hand up to the tender skin just below her bottom, caressing it. Not a tickle now. Her lips compressed as pleasure ran through her.

"Jake wins," Logan announced, and a grin flashed in his leathery face.

"My turn." Jake stood, tall and muscular. As Michael seated himself, the other dom walked behind her. God, looking right at her butt, dimples and—

His hand caressed the crease below her bottom, touching and grazing until she could feel her thong turn damp. When he slid his hand down to stroke behind her knee, she sighed in relief.

"Sorry, Michael. That's two for two," Logan said. "Looks like, on this sub at least, below the ass beats the knee area."

"In my opinion, that spot wins every time." Jake slapped her bare butt lightly, startling her, and took his seat again.

Were they done? Could she move now?

"There's one more theory to consider." The rich timbre of the voice from just behind Rona made every muscle in her body contract. *Master Simon.*

She turned her head, trying to see him, and got a stinging swat on her bottom. "Don't move, sub."

Her jaw clenched, and yet heat seemed to stream off her as if from a raging forest fire.

"And what's your theory, Simon?" Logan asked.

"That with the right dom, a touch anywhere is erotic."

The men grinned at each other. Michael said, "Perhaps you should demonstrate."

Rona strained her ears. Nothing.

"Now, lass." His voice seemed to caress her, despite the stern authority in it. "Don't move. Keep your eyes on the other doms.

A quiver ran through her, and she forced herself to stay still. A moment passed. Another. He stood right behind her. She could feel his warmth and his gaze on her exposed bottom.

His fingers grazed over her ankle. She pulled in a ragged breath at the sensation and the knowledge that this was *Simon's* touch. A moment later, his hard hand closed around her calf and squeezed, and somehow the warmth of his skin and the slight scrape of his callous fingers sent electricity sizzling straight to her clit so fast that she had to force down a moan.

The doms burst out laughing.

Jake shook his head. “Always some bastard screwing up a good experiment.”

A low chuckle sounded behind her, and Rona stiffened. What was he going to do?

“But I have to say, Jake,” Master Simon said, “I also prefer the just-below-the-ass spot.” A pause and then his hand traced the crease between her thigh and bottom with one…deliberate…stroke. Warm, rough, firm.

No longer under her control at all, her hips pressed back against his touch.

Master Simon's laugh was deep and masculine. “Up you come, lass. Experiment's over.” He gripped her arm and helped her stand. With a shock, she realized his other hand hadn't moved and now cupped her buttock. He squeezed slightly.

Her legs shook as she looked up at him, feeling the strength in the ruthless grip on her arm, keeping her right beside him so he could touch her as he pleased. His fingers stroked over her bottom, slowly, and each movement increased her arousal.

When he finally released her, satisfaction glimmered in his eyes. He touched her cheek gently. “Do you know how lovely you are when you're aroused, sweetheart?”

He tilted his head at the other doms. “Thank you, gentlemen, for allowing me to participate,” he said and strode away.

As Rona tried to get her breathing under control, the doms exchanged glances. “Well, that seemed clear enough," Jake drawled. "You ever see Simon get territorial before?"

"Should be an interesting evening." Logan pulled his fair-skinned sub between his knees, and the pretty sub's eyes closed in pleasure as he played with her hair. A wistful envy ran through Rona. What would it be like to sit at a man's feet, to feel his—Master Simon's—hands on her?

"Not for me, apparently," Michael grumbled.

Rona frowned. Had she missed something?

Michael handed over her tray of drinks and smiled at her. "Off you go, pet."

By the time she'd emptied the drink tray, she'd grown—almost—used to being on display. The excitement that Master Simon had roused hadn't dissipated at all. The sights and sounds of people making love, of floggers and groans and whimpers, kept her in a pure state of need. Three doms had asked her to play, all interesting and pleasant men, so why had she said no?

Because she'd gotten fixated on Master Simon. Just like now, each time she spotted him, her whole body seemed to jump up and down, screaming, *Him, him, him.*

She set the tray down and leaned against the living-room wall. After all the lectures she'd given herself, and the goals she'd posted on the bulletin board, she was still being stupid about a man.

Chapter Six

Ah, there she was. Simon spotted his little sub leaning against the wall just outside the kitchen. He'd kept an eye on her—she continued to refuse other doms. Good. Watching her with someone else would hurt like hell. He wanted to be the one to show her more, to bring her to orgasm. He wanted her trust...and more.

Gently, though. She'd take flight too easily.

First the bait. He set his bag beside the high recliner-style table, one of his favorites, with extra width and leather padding. One by one, he pulled the vacuum cups out of his bag and lined them up on a paper towel on a nearby coffee table.

The sub he'd commandeered in the kitchen set down a pan of bleach water. "Ooooh, Master Simon, you're going to do cupping?"

He nodded. When he turned, he saw Rona join the people gathering around the table. If she wanted variety and exploration, he'd be happy to fulfill that need. He captured her gaze. "Come here, lass."

A SHAKING STARTED in Rona's stomach at the smoky growl of Master Simon's voice. Then the words registered. "*Come here.*"

"Me?" Her voice squeaked.

"You." He rolled up one sleeve, looked over at her, and frowned. "Now."

Oh no. She needed to think, but her feet moved her forward. Her hands went numb, and yet desire sizzled through her with each step closer. Her skin felt sensitive, the brush of her Santa coat like sandpaper. When she met his intent, measuring eyes, her chest squeezed as if he had her ribs between his big hands.

She stopped in front of him.

"Good girl." He cupped her chin in one hard hand. "Such big eyes." He brushed his mouth across hers and released her.

"I-I..." What had she planned to say?

"Remember the rules about speaking, little sub." He patted the table. "I want you on here—without the coat."

The people. She didn't have anything on but that skimpy bra and thong. Her eyes met his.

"You've watched all night but haven't played...and you want to, Rona." He ran a finger down her cheek, his smile just for her. "I'll go slowly, little one."

A tremor ran through her. *I want to do this. And I want to do this with him.*

He waited patiently, but his confident posture said he already knew her answer. How could that feel so reassuring?

She pulled off her coat and handed it to him, shivering at the feeling of air—and eyes—against her skin.

"Good girl." The approval in his dark eyes warmed her. He grasped her around the waist and set her on the countertop-high table, then swung her legs up.

The slick leather chilled her bottom, and she clenched her hands in her lap.

"Now, tell me. Do you want to watch or just feel?"

She bit her lip and stared at the clear glass cups, which suddenly seemed a little ominous. "Watch."

"All right." He adjusted the table to lean her back in a reclining position. Before she could object, he tugged open the ribbons on her bra and pulled it off.

Great. Baby-chewed breasts with white stretch marks. She forced her hands to stay in her lap and not cover them.

To her surprise, his eyes held only appreciation as he looked at her for a long, long moment. When his callous hands finally cupped her breasts, her back arched. Somehow she felt as if she'd been waiting for his touch all night. His thumbs traced circles around her nipples, and heat pooled in her pelvis.

"I can see I won't have to warm you up very much," he murmured. He leaned down and took her mouth, even as his hands moved over her breasts, teasing and playing until the world rippled around her. He pulled back to smile at her. "I don't know when I've enjoyed kissing someone so much. You give everything you have, sweetheart."

And he kissed her again, a sweet kiss that turned forceful, his tongue taking complete possession.

When he stopped, she couldn't move, could only stare up into his intent gaze. Why did surrendering to this man feel so right?

After studying her, he nodded and said softly, “That's my sub.” And the utter assurance in his claim terrified her when she couldn't find any disagreement inside her.

He picked up a strap and buckled it just below her breasts. A softly lined cuff went on each wrist, and he secured them to the top of the table over her head. Then he walked to the foot of the table.

She eyed him nervously, again aware of the people watching. “What are—”

His stern glance strangled the words in her throat. *Silence. Don't talk. But…*

Her knees bent as he pushed her feet upward toward her butt. Then he restrained her ankles to the edges of the table, the position far too like the one her gynecologist used, only even more spread open—the width of Simon's table was twice that of a medical one.

She pulled on her arms and legs, suddenly feeling frighteningly helpless.

“Ah, lass.” He walked back and held her face between his hands. She looked into his eyes. Calm and confident.

“Nothing will happen that you won't enjoy, Rona. If you become too scared, you can use your safe word. Tell me what it is.”

She swallowed. His thumbs stroked her cheeks as he waited for her answer.

“Houston. It's Houston.”

“That's right, my lass.” He held her head between his hands as he enjoyed her mouth in a leisurely kiss, as if he had all night, as if people weren't waiting for him.

When he let her go, her resistance had melted away. The knowledge that right now she'd submit to anything he wanted chilled her a little. Master Simon knew exactly what he was doing, and she wasn't sure if she resented or admired his power.

He looked into her eyes and smiled. “Thinking again?”

She watched him walk toward the end of the table, and every one of those eased muscles started to tighten again. When he undid the laces of her thong and pulled it off, a sizzle of excitement shot through her system. Her moan almost sounded like a whimper.

His eyes crinkled. He didn't touch her, though, and she was glad—really—although everything down there throbbed in need.

“Let's start with your nipples,” he said. He picked up a small glass, bell-shaped cup and set it against her left breast. The coolness drew her nipple tighter. Shaking his head, he chose another size and fastened something that looked like a caulking gun with a gauge to the pointed end of the glass.

Unexpectedly, he skimmed his hand over her pussy, making her gasp. “Nice and wet,” he said. He ran his now-damp fingers around the glass rim before pressing it firmly to her breast. “Ready, lass?”

Her body burned with arousal even as anxiety shot through her. She gave him a nod and stared down at her chest.

"Tell me if it starts to hurt. For now, you are permitted to speak." He squeezed the handle.

One pump and her breast felt like someone was sucking on it really, really hard. Her nipple swelled into the bottom third of the clear cup. "Oh my God!"

He chuckled, his gaze intent on her face as he squeezed again. When the suction increased to near pain, she tried to push the cup away and rediscovered that she was restrained.

"That's obviously enough." He twisted the pump off, leaving her nipple fat and red inside the vacuum cup. "Next."

The other one went the same way.

"That looks so strange," she muttered, staring at the cups on her breasts. *Feels strange too. Like someone constantly sucking right there.*

He walked to the end of the table, and her hands clenched into fists. Her legs were splayed wide, her pussy on view for everyone to see. And he was going to do...that to her. Her breathing sped up again, yet somehow the fear only increased her arousal.

He ran his finger over her folds, smiling as her hips jerked. "You're very wet."

After being aroused all evening, she felt swollen and almost too sensitive when he slid a finger into her. *Oh God.* Her legs quivered, but the ankle cuffs kept her from moving. Watching her face, he thrust in and out with excruciating slowness, ramping up her burning need. Her hips strained upward. *More, more, more.*

A corner of his mouth curved upward in a smile. “I believe you're ready for the next step.”

He picked up a cup, twisted on the pump, and then seated the cold glass firmly around her clit, wiggling to get an adequate seal.

Oh God, she was really going to let him do this. The restraints, his hard hands, his control, the strange cups... She bit her lip, feeling more aroused than she'd ever been in her whole life.

His fingers flexed on the trigger.

Sucking and pressure and tightness. “Oooh.” Her hips strained upward, and her eyes closed as the shocking sensation blasted through her. The vacuum increased until her swollen tissue throbbed in time with her pulse.

“Look, Rona.” He twisted off the pump, leaving the cup on her clit.

She stared down. Pink flesh half filled the cup, pressing up against the sides. “That's me?”

“Oh yes.” He tapped the cup with a finger, and she jumped at the zing of pleasure. “It will remain that size for quite a while after I remove the cup.” His eyes glinted at her. She tried not to imagine his fingers on her clit afterward.

“How long do the cups stay on?” She should have asked more questions before starting this maybe.

“Oh, awhile yet.”

And she'd just sit here and stare at them?

“Don't worry; I'm not going to let you get bored.”

The crowd around rippled in laughter.

SIMON SMILE AS Rona's blue-green eyes showed her arousal—and her anxiety. With her body open and exposed, bound for whatever he wanted to do to it, she displayed her trust in him—trust he hadn't yet earned, but that she'd given him freely, without logic or reason.

Yet he wanted more than her arousal, more than her trust.

"What are you—"

He interrupted her. "Unless you're answering a question, I want you silent now, pet."

She bit her lip, and a tremor ran through her as her worry and arousal both increased. Lovely. How would she deal with additional stimulation? With pain? He picked up a thin cane from his toy bag. "Remember your safe word?"

"Yes." When he lifted an eyebrow, she hastily added, "Sir."

"Excellent." He brushed the thin wood across her ankle, up her calf. He glided the tip over her pussy beneath the cup, up her torso to spiral around the cups on her breasts, and then back down.

Her stomach muscles quivered under the teasing strokes. Her gaze was fixed on the stick.

He lifted it and tapped her thigh lightly. She startled, and the movement wiggled the cups. He could almost see the sensation break through her like a wave. *Very nice.* He struck softly then, up and down one thigh, moved to the other, continuing until the skin pinkened and her hips strained upward.

Her eyes slowly took on the glazed look of a submissive overwhelmed by sensation and endorphins.

He removed a glass dildo from his bag, wet it in her juices, and slid it in.

AHHH! RONA JERKED back to awareness as every nerve in her pussy shocked to life. She tried to move, couldn't, and her breathing sped up. She'd been drifting as the rhythmic sensations of pain from the cane somehow merged with the aching feeling from the cups and sent her somewhere else.

But now the dildo tightened the skin around her clit, her vagina throbbed, and each beat of her pulse pushed her closer to coming. Her eyes closed as she shivered.

"Look at me, Rona." His darkly masculine voice caressed her as surely as his warm hand on her face.

She opened her eyes. God, he was so gorgeous, like a blade, but not a bland kitchen knife—more like a medieval dagger. Elegant and deadly, but the look in his eyes was so caring. Almost loving. She smiled.

"There, that's better." He patted her cheek. "Keep your eyes on me, lass. And by the way, you do not have permission to come."

It took a minute for the meaning of his words to percolate through the molasses in her brain. *Not come*? "But—"

"No. No coming." His grin flashed. He stepped back and brushed that wicked, thin cane across her breast and then struck the side.

Unh! The sting echoed through her breast. He slapped the cane harder, circling around the cups on her breasts. Each sharp pain knifed through her, and yet all she could process was the thick intrusion in her vagina and the squeezing of her clit. She tried to wiggle, but the straps over her ribs held her implacably in place. And each erotically painful blow increased the coiling inferno inside her, brought her closer to coming.

"Oh pleeeeease." The moan broke from her. "I need—"*Need to come, need just a little more.*

He stopped.

Panting, she stared up at him, trying to order her thoughts.

He closed his warm hand over her restrained ones. "Now, sweetheart, you have two choices. I can bring you off here and now…or you can join me upstairs, and we can make love."

"Have sex?"

His eyes darkened, and he repeated, "We can make love."

The phrasing didn't sound right, but oh God, just the thought of his hands on her… She shivered and whispered, "You."

His gaze lingered on her face. Then he brushed a kiss over her lips. "You please me more than I can say, Rona." He released the vacuum on the cups and popped them off, one by one. The dildo slid out, leaving her empty and aching. He tossed everything in a nearby pan of water.

Rona stared at her body, shocked at her red, hugely swollen nipples. And her clit… Tripled in size, it blatantly pushed out from between her labia. Aching. Tight. Needy.

He undid the restraints and set her in a chair while he swiped down the table with a paper towel and spray. "Feel free to use the cupping toys," he told the people still gathered. "Logan, Jake, can you monitor the place for a bit?"

"Abandoning his own party," Jake said to his brother in mock disapproval. "Sure, Simon. We'll babysit for you."

After tucking her into her Santa coat, Master Simon took Rona upstairs and down a hallway to the master bedroom. A gas fireplace flickered to life, sending shadows dancing on the walls. The rich blue carpet under her feet was thick enough to wade through; dark wood furniture gleamed in the dim light.

"I've had visions of you in my bed," he murmured, stripping the coat off her. "And of making love with you."

He lifted her and put her in the center of his bed, forcing her onto her back with a merciless strength that made her mind whirl. When he pulled her arms over her head, she remembered he hadn't removed her wrist or ankle cuffs. A sharp *click* and he'd hooked her wrist cuffs to a single chain attached to the headboard. She yanked at the chain, a tremor running through her. Alone with a man she barely knew. And she'd let him restrain her. Was she insane?

"Relax, pet," he murmured, brushing her lips with his. "We will both enjoy this, or we won't continue. Say, 'Yes, Master.'"

Why did just the sound of his low voice make her muscles loosen? Why did she trust him like this? She inhaled, then frowned. Say what? "Master?"

A satisfied smile lightened his chiseled features. “That's the word. Say it again.”

She hesitated. When his strong hands cupped her breasts and pressed them together, the devastating sensation turned her willpower to mush. “Master.” But as she said the word, everything inside her tightened in denial...and yet the oddest sense of contentment filled her, as if the last piece of a jigsaw puzzle had snapped into place.

“That's right.” Still standing beside the bed, he kissed her slowly, his tongue possessing her mouth as thoroughly as his hands took her breasts. He drew back. As she tried to recover her swirling senses, he pushed a pillow under her bottom.

He stripped easily and unself-consciously, but the sight of him stole her air. His muscular forearms had hinted at his build but hadn't prepared her for the wideness of his chest, solid with muscle. Black hair dusted over his pectorals and spiraled to his groin as if to showcase his cock.

Her breath turned ragged. He was maybe a little longer than normal, yes, but the width... As if to tantalize, dark veins twisted around the incredibly thick shaft. He followed her gaze and chuckled. “Yes, I've been erect since you walked in this evening, and I look forward to taking you,” he said softly. “But I intend to play with you first. To love you.”

His hands kneaded her breasts gently. “Have I mentioned how beautiful these are?” He smiled into her eyes before lowering his head. His mouth closed over her nipple, and the sensation of heat and wetness around the still-puffy tissue made her head spin. He swirled his tongue across the peak, then pushed her breasts upward, tightening the skin, increasing the pleasure as he suckled hard. When his lips closed on her other nipple, the sensation ripped straight to her clit so intensely, it verged on the edge of painful. Her nipples contracted to fat, aching points.

And then he moved onto the bed, parting her legs. He settled between her thighs and...looked at her down there.

The excitement of being on display warred with embarrassment, and she jerked at her arms. She couldn't move. She tried to put her legs together, but he was in the way. He gripped her knees and ruthlessly pushed them back out—even farther than before. Cool air brushed over her wet pussy as her folds opened.

"Rona, either keep your legs apart—just like this—or I will restrain them. Which?"

Right now, the thought of added bondage seemed more scary than exciting. "I'll behave. Sir."

"Good. I enjoy watching you struggle to obey." His hands grazed up her inner thighs to the very edge of her pussy, and his thumbs pulled her outer labia more open, exposing her fully. He bent, and his tongue slid through her folds, dancing up and down, tracing patterns around her entrance, before finally moving up to the aching center of nerves.

That huge clit. She was so aroused that the throbbing there felt like torture. She barely had time to wonder how being licked would feel when he took it completely into his mouth. Devastating pleasure blasted through her. "Oh Lord!"

Her hips lifted uncontrollably. His hands pressed her flat, giving her no chance to move, and then he blew lightly on her clit.

The coolness tensed it further, and her legs shook. A whine escaped her.

His tongue circled the puffy ball of flesh, and her stomach clutched at the electrifying feeling.

"Your clit is here"—he touched it, and the startling sensation made her jump—"and the hood is all the way back here." Another light touch.

She moaned. He spread her moisture around and over the nub, each leisurely stroke an exquisite torment.

"It's so far out that I can tug on it." His thumb and fingers closed, and each tiny pull just intensified the sensation. *More, oh, please, more.* She bent her knees and pushed her hips up.

He slapped her thigh. The stinging pain shocked through her, and yet her clit pulsed even more fiercely.

"You will stay in place, sub." The low growl set her heart to pounding. "And you will take everything I give you."

His mouth replaced his fingers. Oh God, so hot. His tongue swirled around her clit, rubbing one side and the other, ruthlessly driving her up. Her head tipped back as every muscle in her body tightened...and held.

And then he sucked.

A blinding explosion ripped into her, great, shuddering spasms. She screamed. He didn't stop. Instead he mercilessly teased her nub with light flicks of his tongue, sending waves of pleasure reverberating through her system.

When he finally granted her mercy, she groaned. Her heart pounded so violently, her chest felt bruised from the inside, and a fine sweat covered her body. Nothing had ever felt like this before. She opened her eyes and stared at him.

His cheek creased as he smiled at her. "You come beautifully, but a little too fast." He nipped the inside of her thigh, and her vagina clenched. "I'll make you work for the next one, lass."

Next one? She wasn't the insane one; he was.

With strong hands, he flipped her over and onto her bent knees. When she tried to rise, he dragged her down the bed until her arms straightened, stretched toward the headboard.

She dropped her head to rest on her upper arm. "Simon?"

"Who?"

Her insides quaked at his icy voice. Just as he'd exposed her most intimate parts, this demand seemed to open hidden caverns inside her, spilling her secrets of need. Of desire. But he'd already known...known that she wanted this, wanted him to do whatever he desired. She'd been the one in denial. But that word he wanted her to say demanded even more of her than just exposure. No. "Sir, what are you doing?"

His hands ran over her body, firm and possessive, placing her for his pleasure. "Rona, I'm going to take you now."

She heard the crinkling of a condom wrapper, and her muscles stiffened in anticipation.

His cock pressed against her, and he stroked the head in her wetness, sending a shiver of hunger through her. Then he entered her with a steady, unyielding push.

She was very wet, and despite that, her body tried to resist as her vagina stretched around the unaccustomedly large intrusion. But oh sweet heavens, he felt good, filling the emptiness inside her.

Of course, she'd not get off this time, but how cool that she'd climaxed even once this first time together. She'd enjoy it when he got off.

He chuckled and squeezed her bottom. "Thinking again, lass?" Only halfway in, now he pulled back, and the friction stroking through her folds sent tension riding up her spine. He pushed in faster, then in and out, farther with each thrust, until his hips rubbed against her bottom. The startling fullness squeezed her swollen clit, and it throbbed with building desire.

She wiggled her hips, moving him inside her, and he laughed. "Still too much mobility, I see. Next time, I'll hog-tie you." The image sent a thrill through her.

"But for now, we'll do it this way." He pushed her lower legs apart, until she balanced precariously on her widespread knees. As he massaged her bottom, the movements made him slide inside her and sent zings of fire through her. Her inability to resist upped the intensity in a frightening way.

"Good," he murmured in satisfaction, and his hands secured her hips, anchoring her completely as he started to move. Out, in. Gently, then harder, pulling her back on her haunches to meet his hard thrusts. She struggled in his grip as her excitement steadily rose, and his merciless possession fueled the fire until each thrust sent flares of pleasure through her. Her mind hazed as need built to the explosion point. She clenched around him, nerves screaming, hovering on the precipice.

And then he leaned forward, his chest hot against her back, as he supported himself on one arm. His free hand slid around to her front, and she felt his fingers slide through her folds, finding her sensitive, swollen clit. He rubbed one side as his thick cock thrust into her, rubbed the other side with another thrust. He didn't stop, even as uncontrollable tremors shook her.

Her puffy flesh engorged, becoming so taut and sensitive that she moaned with each touch of his fingers. One more...harder... Something...to make her come. Her trembling legs strained to lift her to his cock...or lower her to his hand—she didn't know what she wanted.

More. “Please,” she whimpered.

“Please what, love?” His voice, intense, unbending. His rough jaw scraped her shoulder. His touch and thrusts never slowed.

Please do more, please... Not the words he demanded. “Master,” she whispered. “Please.”

“Nothing would please me more than to fulfill your request.” He leaned back, balanced on his knees. His palm compressed her mound as his fingers opened her folds widely, increasing the pressure on her clit. As he rammed into her, hard and fast, the slickened fingers of his other hand slid up and down her clit, plucking it gently. Up and down, thrust, up and down, thrust. Everything inside her coiled tighter and tighter, her hips tried to move, to get... He gripped her mercilessly, forcing her to take only what he wanted to give her. *Up and down.* Suddenly his cock angled and hit something incredibly sensitive inside her.

Her neck arched back, and then her climax surged upward from her pelvis, a volcanic eruption of heat and pleasure, one explosion after another until even her fingertips tingled. "*Oh, oh, oh*!"

She bucked against his strong arms, and he held her in place, forcing her to take more as he stroked her gently, inside and out.

Her head dropped onto her arm as she gasped for breath, the tremors easing. She'd never...never come like that, been so lost to everything. Tears burned her eyes as he kissed her neck, murmuring how beautiful she was, how much she pleased him. Her breathing slowed as he soothed her like a nervous filly.

When she slumped, his arms flexed, keeping her up. "Not quite yet, pet."

His hands moved to clasp her hips. He pumped into her in short, powerful strokes and then thrust deep. She had only a second to feel his cock jerking inside her with his release, and then he squeezed her swollen clit. She screamed as another explosion shook her very foundation.

HER PUSSY MILKED the last spasm out of his cock like a hot fist, even as the little sub's shoulders flattened onto the bed. Her hair spilled over her arms, and her skin was a creamy white against the royal blue of the bed quilt. She was utterly beautiful in her surrender. He remained in place for a moment, savoring the tiny shudders that rippled through her body at intervals, before pulling out. He quietly used the bathroom to remove the condom.

She hadn't moved when he returned. After unclipping the chain—she looked so pretty in cuffs that he left them on—he lay down beside her and gathered her against his side, settling her head in the hollow of his shoulder. With a soft sigh, she snuggled into him like a well-fed kitten, draping an arm across his chest and a leg over his thigh.

Cuddly and responsive, smart and submissive. He'd known her such a short time, and yet she filled the emptiness inside him. He wanted to keep her. Right here. In his bed.

In his home.

He rubbed a hand up and down her back. A few seconds later she patted his chest and stroked him in return. As thoroughly as he'd used her and as she'd come, her body must be as exhausted as her mind—yet she still tried to give something back. The woman warmed his heart, and his arm pulled her closer. Damned if he'd let her go.

Unlike a relationship that moved gradually from friendship into love, his feelings for Rona had bloomed suddenly, like the mountain wildflowers of his birthplace. Even at first, Rona hadn't seemed like a stranger. He'd known her. Much like when he'd arrived in San Francisco and something inside him had said, *This place. I belong here.*

He felt the same with Rona. *She belongs here. With me.*

As she snuggled against him, he touched one breast, smiling at the still-puffy, reddened nipple.

When he plucked the velvety peak, he felt the sensation jolt through her. Yes, the way she responded to him, to his voice and his body, said that part of her acknowledged the tie. But her practical brain wouldn't accept something so illogical.

She was a stubborn woman. He admired that. *Dammit.* She'd set her course and wasn't the type to lightly turn aside. Made a dom want to bring out the flogger.

Chapter Seven

Rona's head rested on Simon's shoulder, and under her hand on his chest, his heart beat with slow thuds. The room smelled of sex and his subtle cologne. When he pulled her closer, she let him, needing that comfort as a barrier against the lost feeling creeping through her. The knowledge of how alone she'd be in a few minutes. When he let her go.

That just didn't make any sense. She'd just had good—no, fantastic—sex, but now... She blinked back the tears stinging her eyes.

His arm around her tightened, and his free hand caressed her cheek. "Lass—"

"We need to get up," she interrupted quickly, her voice husky. He knew. And she didn't want to talk about it. About anything.

His hand paused, and his chest rose and fell in a silent sigh. "All right. I am the host, I suppose." He stroked her hair back behind her ear. "But we will talk of what is troubling you later."

The gentleness and yet the determination in his voice made her eyes burn again. Why did he have to be so...so perfect? Damn him. He'd already sucked her into wanting him, despite her vow to find other men first. She'd never felt like this before. *I belong here.* The thought sparked her to moving—she'd been comfortable with her husband too, and look how that had turned out.

So maybe she hadn't found Mark as totally hot or been taken so thoroughly or come so hard—twice—or... *Crom, can I get more illogical*? She pushed herself up and off the bed. “Well, um, thank you for a great time.”

Still sprawled on the bed, Simon put his arms behind his head and watched her with a quiet, steady gaze. “You are quite welcome.”

“I'm going back downstairs now.” She needed to find someone to help her get her mind off this...overwhelming man. She pulled on the Santa coat, wishing for the damned belt to hold it shut. Hopefully her bra and thong were still in the living room.

“For speaking and trying to leave without permission, you are fined your underwear,” Simon said, his voice level, without a hint of humor. “You may continue to wear the coat.”

“But—”

“Do you desire to forfeit the coat also?”

She shook her head. But no underwear? She looked down. Oh heavens. Her nipples remained a vivid red, and almost fluorescent in color, her clit still poked out from between her labia. She yanked the coat shut.

Simon rose to his feet. Without speaking, he peeled her coat open and cupped her breasts in his hands. She grabbed his wrists, then dropped her arms when his jaw turned stern. Mercilessly, he teased her nipples into rigid points, continuing until her toes curled into the rug.

"Now you may return downstairs. And, Rona?" He tipped her chin up, forcing her to look at him. "I enjoy seeing your breasts and pussy, and for tonight, I will permit my guests to also share in the sight. So if I see you holding the coat closed, I'll take it from you."

Her throat shut at the look in his eyes. Dark, possessive...heady.

"What do you say to me, sub?"

"Yes, Mas—"*No no no. He isn't.* "Yes, Sir."

His mouth compressed, and she saw the muscle in his jaw flex. "That isn't correct, but I'll let it pass for now. I think you will change your mind, Rona," he said softly, running his finger over her lips.

"No. I won't." She backed away from him and out of the bedroom. *I mustn't.* She remembered the long, boring years of inane conversation, of lying beside her husband, wondering where even the tiny passion they'd shared had gone; the times when they did make love in the missionary position, and if Mark felt greatly daring—or had had a few drinks—from behind.

Yet she couldn't erase the memory of the last hour, Simon's ruthless grip, his fingers teasing her swollen clit. Would sex with him ever be boring?

Maybe, maybe not. She couldn't—wouldn't—take the chance. She owed it to herself to sample everything a single life had to offer.

* * * *

The noise of the party burst over her as she reached the bottom of the stairs. Hauling in a breath, she let her coat flap open—*damn the man*—and went to have some more fun.

An hour later she couldn't figure out what had happened with her. The men were wonderful and nice, and she kept saying no to them. Because of *Simon*. She needed to leave. Being near him affected her judgment, no doubt about it.

On the way to the changing room, she walked past a scene in a nook under the stairs. She glanced in and stopped.

Chained to a post, a ball-gagged woman sobbed violently, tears streaming down her face, as a big dom struck her over and over with a thick cane. Angry crimson welts covered the sub's body.

The woman saw Rona, and despite the gag, the word she spoke—"red"—came through clearly enough. *The safe word.*

The dom ignored her. Rona didn't, and she raised her voice so everyone in the area could hear. "Red! She's saying 'red.' Stop right now."

The dom glared over his shoulder. "Get the hell out of my scene, slut." And he turned back, prepared to strike his sub.

Rona took a step forward—damned if she'd stand by—when a steely arm around her waist swung her to one side.

"My job, lass. Thank you for the alert." Master Simon caught the cane on the downswing and wrenched it from the dom. Rona flinched as she realized that the dom was younger, taller than Simon, and outweighed him by at least fifty pounds.

He swung. Simon slapped the beefy arm to one side, stepped in, and buried his fist in the man's gut. The man made a horrible sound and folded forward, clenching his abdomen. Turning slightly, Simon slammed the guy's face into his raised knee. The *crack* of a nose breaking twisted Rona's stomach.

Simon let the moaning man drop to the ground and glanced at the gathered guests. "Logan, would you pack up his bag, please. Jake, drag him out?"

Jake nodded, his face rigid.

"Nice work, buddy," Logan said.

Ignoring the others, Rona headed for the sub. She unstrapped the ball gag and started on the restraints. A second later Simon joined her, working on the other arm.

Once unbound, the sub collapsed, saved from a nasty fall only by Simon's arm around her waist. She had welts all over her body, and she shook so hard her teeth chattered.

Rona scowled at the chilled skin under her hand. She pointed at a sub in the crowd. "Get me a couple of blankets."

She targeted another elf. "I need a hot drink. Coffee, tea, hot chocolate—anything."

"Yes, ma'am." That sub ran for the kitchen even as the other returned with a soft afghan. Rona wrapped the sub in the blanket and followed as Simon carried her out to the living room. Still holding her, he looked around and said, "Jake, she needs a warm body."

One of the rugged brothers had returned. He took the sub and settled onto the couch, cuddling her against him and murmuring in a rumbling voice.

Nice. Rona accepted the hot tea from the sub she'd sent and tested the liquid with a finger. Nice and warm. After sitting beside Jake, she held the cup to the sub's mouth. "Drink, honey."

The sub didn't even seem to hear her.

Jake's big hand closed around the cup, and his voice deepened, darkened. "Little sub."

The sub stiffened in his arms.

"Drink this now."

Rona almost found herself reaching for the cup to obey the forceful command. Instead she shook off the effect, rose, and watched the sub drink the tea obediently. As the young woman's shivers diminished, her head drooped against Jake's shoulder, and he simply snuggled her closer.

Simon draped an additional blanket around the girl, his face still set in hard lines. "I'll speak with her later about safety and choices in doms."

"I'll take care of it, Simon," Jake said. "I saw the asshole earlier, and I didn't like him then. I should have watched him more carefully."

"And I should have checked my guest list more carefully. Let me know if either of you need anything."

Realizing she was gawking and there was nothing else for her to do, Rona started away. Her insides still quivered at the violence, more from the brutality of the dom than Simon's swift and incredibly graceful attack. She shook her head, remembering the effortless punch. Too tall and dark and smooth to be Chuck Norris, but he surely had the same moves. And that unfailing attitude of protectiveness. Crom, that drew her like a magnet.

Dammit, she just kept getting in deeper.

"Rona." Simon's resonant baritone, despite all her self-warnings, still sent a thrill through her, as if her body was tuned to its music.

She turned. "Yes, Sir?"

He walked up to her, stopping close enough she could smell his aftershave and tangy soap. Feel his warmth. She stiffened her spine and looked up.

Dark, dark eyes still holding a trace of anger. Then he smiled, and everything in her stilled as if she'd gotten the first whiff of spring after a long winter. "Lass, you did well. Not only recognizing that the girl needed help, but getting it. And helping her."

She shrugged. "Anyone would have done the same."

"No, sweetheart. You care, *and* you act. Effectively. That's a rare combination."

Dammit, his approval shouldn't please her so. She ignored the warmth glowing in her stomach and changed the subject. "Why didn't you sit with her instead of giving her to Jake? You're…" Comforting. No one could be as comforting and safe as Master Simon.

"Jake is uninvolved."

"But so are you."

His eyes crinkled, and he ran a finger down her cheek, his gaze intent. "I am rapidly becoming involved."

"No!" The loud response burst from her. "I am not getting involved. Not with you or anyone. I will experiment, play, and enjoy all kinds of men. I'm not going to confine myself with just one. Never, ever again."

She turned quickly to escape his reaction and hurried away.

SIMON STARED AFTER her, half inclined to put his fist through something. Maybe a wall. Maybe he'd see if that asshole dom was still outside.

"Well, she made that clear enough." A few feet away, Logan had his arm around his pretty, curvy sub, Rebecca.

"She certainly has no problem with expressing her thoughts," Simon growled.

Rebecca laughed, started to speak, and caught herself. She glanced up at her dom.

"Go ahead, little rebel."

"I don't think she'd be so upset if she didn't want you," Rebecca said. "She reminds me of...well, me. Professional, a little stunned by the BDSM stuff, but liking it." She grinned. "I've seen how she looks for you and watches you and hates that, but she can't help herself."

Logan nodded. "She definitely wants you."

"I know." Simon frowned at the doorway through which his sub had fled. "But she's liable to disappear rather than face it." Her ex was an incompetent bastard who had screwed up his marriage with her and kept her there until she saw involvement as a trap. How to get around that?

“She might insist she's looking for other men, but she hasn't accepted any offers all night,” Logan said. “Even Jake struck out. She's yours, my friend. She just won't admit it.”

She thinks she wants a ton of men. Simon rubbed his hand on his jaw.

As Rebecca leaned against her dom, she idly stroked her collar. Simon had been at the club the night Logan collared her. Rebecca had arrived first, wanting to see if other doms had the same effect on her as Logan.

When Simon had touched her, he'd known she responded to the dominant in him, but not the man—because her heart belonged to Logan.

Could he tolerate what it would take to show Rona the same? To watch another man dominate her? And if he set this up, he'd have to watch. Maybe see her leave with another man. The muscles of his stomach contracted as if anticipating a full-contact blow.

Logan frowned. “Whatever you're thinking looks ugly.”

“Painful as hell,” Simon muttered. “Probably not ugly.”

He nodded at Logan and his sub and went to secure the St. Andrew's cross. This needed to be as public as possible.

* * * *

Needing a moment to recover, Rona visited the kitchen and downed a glass of wine. On the way out, she spotted Master Simon wiping down the St.

Andrew's cross. Obviously he planned to do a scene with one of the subs, and...why that mattered to her... Well, it didn't.

A place deep in her chest started to ache. Probably not a heart attack. Unfortunately. *I really need to go home now.*

Once in the powder room, Rona started getting out her street clothes.

The door opened behind her, and Logan's collared sub walked in. The redhead grinned and said, “There you are. I've been looking for you.”

“Is something wrong?”

“Well.” The sub's brows drew together. “Not exactly, but... Come on. I'll show you.” Without waiting for Rona's answer, she shoved Rona's clothing back in the bag and led the way out. For a submissive, she seemed awfully assertive.

“Is it about that poor girl?” Rona hurried to catch up. The redhead moved amazingly fast, through the foyer and into the great room.

At the sight of Master Simon standing by the cross—with no other sub there—Rona halted and spun to retreat.

“Rona,” Master Simon snapped out.

Her feet stopped dead, her hands grew damp, and her heart did that annoying jump-up-and-down-it's-Master-Simon dance. She turned.

He crooked a finger at her. *Come here.*

A wave of longing ran through her, but she shook her head. “I'm not going to do a scene with you.”

"Not with me. Come *here*." His chin lifted just that infinitesimal amount that melted every bone and ounce of resistance in her body. How did he do that?

Feeling like a condemned prisoner heading for the gallows, she walked forward.

"Good." He smiled at her, but the look in his eyes was...different. No smile lurked in the depths.

"What's wrong?" she whispered.

Hands on her shoulders, he pushed her back against the wooden frame and lifted her arm over her head.

Snap.

"Hey!" She yanked at the wrist he'd just restrained to the upper arm of the X. Damn, she'd forgotten she still wore cuffs. Ignoring her struggles, he secured her other arm. "What are you doing?"

"Rona, you insist you want an assortment of men, not just one, but you haven't followed through. I'm going to let you experience the variety you wanted."

The floor seemed to drop out from under her. *Men? Other men?*

Before she could react, he pulled her left leg outward and clipped the ankle cuff to the X-frame's lower leg. The feel of his callous hands sent heat rushing through her.

"Master Simon... No." Her voice came out weak. Totally ineffective, considering he didn't stop.

Without speaking, he anchored her other leg, then tightened the restraints until she couldn't move anything, couldn't do anything except wiggle her hips. He didn't notice as he turned and raised his voice loud enough to echo through the house. "Unattached doms.

I've placed a sub on the cross for your pleasure. Her safe word is 'Houston.' Each dom will have three minutes to get an interested response from her, using hands or mouth—no toys. Whoever succeeds may remove her restraints and take her. After that, she goes back on the cross."

"Simon," she hissed. "You can't—"

"Is this not what you said you wanted?" The uncompromising look he gave her said *put up or shut up*.

But...

He touched her cheek with his fingertips. "Remain calm, pet. I'll be off to one side to ensure nothing gets out of hand. You're perfectly safe to enjoy your variety of men."

But...

And he walked away.

Rona's breath hitched inside her throat until it felt as if she'd choke. The room had gone silent, leaving only the harsh swishing of her heartbeat in her ears. She couldn't help but yank on the cuffs, but he'd done a fine job of stringing her up. Of course he would. Master Hotshot Simon. She glared at his broad back and realized his sleeves were rolled down. He wouldn't participate.

Disappointment had a bitter taste.

She looked away from him, and her eyes widened. Every single man at the party must have crowded into the living room, all eyeing her with that assessing, dominant stare. She shut down her first inclination—to yell *Houston* and *get me out of here*—and tried to stay rational.

Only what was rational about sex?

But this was her goal and exactly why she had come to the party. She'd wanted to mess around, but instead she'd focused so hard on damn-him-to-hell *Simon* that she hadn't noticed anyone else. Pretty stupid of her, really, especially since Mr. I'm Getting Involved obviously didn't have a problem handing her off to other men. Her throat tightened, and she swallowed and swallowed again, forcing the ache away.

Get over it, Rona. This is right off your goal list; stick to the plan, girl. She raised her chin. She'd show him how much she'd enjoy every single one of these guys.

And thank him for the treat afterward.

The doms cut cards to pick who went first. One tossed down his winning card and headed for her. Medium height, late twenties maybe. The solid blond looked just fine in his leather pants and black T-shirt.

"Uh. Hi," she offered.

Ice blue eyes met hers. "Be quiet. When I want you to speak, I'll let you know."

Pfft. She frowned. Why did his order tempt her to call him an idiot, but that same command from Simon would have sent funny little chills through her?

He went straight for the kill, one hand settling on her pussy, the other on her breast. She was still sensitive from Simon's attentions and the cupping, and it hurt when this idiot pulled at her nipple. When he massaged her clit, she cringed at the dry discomfort.

When Master Simon announced, "Time," she let her head tip back in relief.

The dom gave her a cold look and stalked away.

The next one was even younger, midtwenties, and serious eye candy.

He had a wide smile as he said, "Mmm, I like what that vacuum pump does." He kissed her softly, and his hand brushed over her breast. *Very nice.* Not painful at all.

He bent and sucked on her nipple. She leaned back, only there was no retreat against the wrongness of the sensation. His hand touched her pussy and—

"Time."

"Hell. That's just not long enough." He licked his fingers and groaned. "Find me later, sweetie, and we'll go at it."

She smiled back at him, not promising anything. His touch had been pleasant, but where was the zing?

"Look at me." The next dom's voice sliced into her thoughts like a scalpel through Kleenex.

Her gaze shot up and into intense blue eyes. The dom named Jake.

"Where's the girl?" Rona asked and winced. *Don't talk.*

When his eyes crinkled, he reminded her of Simon, only her heart stayed put rather than doing somersaults. "A friend of hers took her home. We'll make sure she's all right."

"Oh good."

His big hand cupped her cheek, and he tilted her head up. "You're a pretty sub, sugar. I like you."

"I like you too," she said. He'd cared for that poor sub so sweetly and—

“Look at me. Right at me, girl.” Dom voice—rougher. Her eyes met his, were captured. His hand grazed over her breast, slid down her stomach, and inched slowly toward her mound. And she realized, with each man who touched her, she liked it less and less.

His mouth curved. “That's what I thought,” he murmured and leaned forward to say quietly into her ear, “I'd have enjoyed teasing that pretty clit, but it appears you're not going to enjoy anyone's touch except a certain dom's.”

She stared at him in dismay. “No.”

“Oh yes.” His hand slid down over her pussy, and she had to force herself not to pull away. She'd make herself like this.

“Some little subs enjoy a variety; some enjoy just a few special men. And some want only one. Just one master of their own.” His fingers stroked her pussy gently as he leaned an arm on one of the uprights and talked to her.

One master. Just one. Master.

“I must say,” he said softly, as if he spoke only to himself, “I used to think that way too. Want only one. But I've done that, and it's... If it doesn't work...” He shrugged, and she saw pain smoldering in his eyes.

Oh, honey. Her heart squeezed. To give up on love... “No, Jake, just because once didn't work, you mustn't stop trying.”

“Time.”

His hand pressed against her clit, still not arousing, as he brushed a kiss over her lips. “Rona, just because once didn't work," he repeated back to her, "you mustn't stop trying."

The look he gave her sliced through her defenses like a surgeon's scalpel.

SIMON CLOSED HIS eyes and exhaled. If he'd had to watch Jake's hands on Rona for one second longer, he'd have broken something. With good control, the something might have been the table; otherwise, the bastard's jaw.

His sub had smiled at Jake. She'd talked to him and hadn't pulled away. Jaw tense enough to ache, Simon reset the small kitchen timer and nodded to the next dom. How much of this could he take?

But if she really desired variety, then he'd see she got it, even if his guts twisted into painful knots. She wanted him; he knew that, but either she'd realize it...or she wouldn't. And if she found someone who turned her on—Simon closed his eyes at the sheer stab of pain—then that would be that. No one ever said life had to be fair or that if you fell hard for a woman, that she must return the favor.

He inhaled and set himself to endure some more.

Chapter Eight

Rona set her teeth and endured the next dom's touch on her nipples. He wasn't handsome, but older and very polite. She felt nothing.

"Time."

She got a break as more of the doms cut cards, and Jake's words—her own words—kept circling her mind like one of those tunes that wouldn't leave. "*Just because once didn't work...*"

She'd been married—involved—once. Just once in her life. It hadn't worked. And based on that single instance, she'd decided against risking involvement again. Decided she needed to experience everything she'd missed. But after this assortment of men—and face it, any woman would want a man like Jake—she had to admit she felt nothing from them.

Yet one word from Master Simon sent zings and whistles through her like her body'd turned into an old-fashioned pinball machine. And it was more than just excitement, he *felt* right to her. Like she belonged with him. So why did she stubbornly insist on wanting more men?

How long would she continue to ignore her own feelings?

When the next man approached, she looked him in the eye and said, “Houston.”

“What?” He gaped at her.

“I'm finished. Houston. Let me down.”

Master Simon walked up with that prowling, always balanced gait of his.

The strange dom told him, “She said Houston.”

“I heard.” The look Simon gave her held no expression whatsoever.

Was he disappointed in her? She bit her lip and looked away as doubt crawled into her stomach and sent cold tentacles through her chest. Maybe he'd decided this was a good way to find her another guy.

“Scene's over, lads,” Simon told the waiting doms. “The sub thanks you for your interest.”

Rona nodded and tried to smile at the men, feeling her lips quiver. Her eyes stung. She'd thought Simon wanted her, but the cold way he looked at her now…

“I want down.” Her voice shook. *I want my clothes, and I want to leave. First he wants me, and then he doesn't, and—*

Firm fingers grasped her chin, lifting it. “Look at me, Rona.”

She looked past him, over his big shoulder. *I will not cry, not for this cold dom who flip-flops like a fish on dry land.*

A soft snort of laugher, then his voice lowered. “Look. At. Me.”

Her eyes flashed to his and were caught and pinned in his intent gaze.

“That's better,” he murmured. “What is going through that clever brain of yours, lass?” The warm, caressing tone wrapped her in warmth.

She tried to shake her head, and his fingers tightened.

“Answer me.”

“You looked so angry.”

“And you thought I was angry with you?” One corner of his mouth turned up. “Sweetheart, do you know how difficult it was to watch other men touching you?” His thumb stroked over her lips. “I haven't been possessive of a woman in a very long time, but you do bring that out.”

Oh. Relief welled up in her like a bubbling spring. “I didn't like being touched by them.”

His lips curved. “I noticed that,” he said agreeably. In the same move as Jake's, he leaned an arm next to hers on the upright, obviously prepared to listen as long as she wanted to talk.

“They bored me.” She took a breath. “I was bored with my husband too. I blamed it on being with just one man.”

He tilted his head. *Go on.*

“Apparently having more men isn't the answer.” She smiled at him. The banked heat in his eyes showed he was patiently waiting for her to finish, and then he'd take her. The knowledge set everything inside her to a boil. "You don't bore me, Simon."

His expression chilled, sending both anxiety and arousal sizzling through her. "Who?"

Jake's word—"Master"—slid into her mind and trembled across her heart, but she still couldn't bring herself to say it. "Sir," she offered hastily.

"That's better." His fingers threaded through her hair. "For that, you deserve a reward."

Currents of excitement hummed through her system. Her breasts tingled. He hadn't even touched them, and they tingled. This man—the dom—was definitely the man for her. "Oh?"

"You're in an excellent position for a flogging," he murmured. He wet one finger and circled her nipple. As the dampness cooled, the areola bunched into an aching peak. "How would the tips of a flogger feel against all this tender tissue?"

Even as her eyes widened, she felt the wetness between her legs. Lightning raced up her spine.

"Yes, look at those cheeks turn pink," he said, this dom who saw everything. His hand slid down the same path that Jake's had, and with his black eyes watching her so intently, just his touch made her shudder. He stroked past her mound, through the growing wetness, and up to slide over her sensitive clit. He touched her firmly, then gently, until she whimpered. Her hips tilted forward. *More.*

"No, you will not come yet. Or even very soon," he whispered, biting her earlobe. "First I'm going to tease you with the flogger and with my mouth and then take you, right here on the cross, until you scream so loudly that no man in the place will doubt whose sub you are. And neither will you."

Her breath caught.

The grin that flashed over his face set her heart to thumping before he took her lips in a devastating kiss. He cupped her breast, still puffy from his attentions earlier, and the muscles in his jaw set. "I realize you don't want to jump into any commitments, but it's too late, my practical lass."

"But—" When his eyes hardened, she felt every drop of resistance drain right out of her.

"And as long as we are involved, you will not be sampling a variety pack of men." His grin flashed. "However, I guarantee I will not allow you to be bored, whether we are together a year…or fifty."

Even as she shook her head in a reflexive refusal, she remembered the old woman buying the fortieth-anniversary toy for Henry. Obviously a relationship didn't have to be a trap. Rona could experience the world with just one man.

When Simon started to roll up his sleeves, her mouth went dry. He stepped back, inspecting her body slowly. "Say, 'Yes, Master.'"

Did she want to give him more? Give him everything? Just because he could dominate her? But she wanted him. Just him. Her eyes misted, blurring everything except his face…and his dark eyes, where the tenderness was as obvious as his controlled power. He cared for her. Oh, he really did.

Her heart somersaulted inside her chest, then settled, a solid weight of acceptance.

It was time to write a new five-year plan.

He ran a finger down her chin. "Well, lass?"

"Yes." She smiled and tipped her cheek into his palm. "Yes, my Master."

THE END

Cherise Sinclair

I met my dearheart when vacationing in the Caribbean. Now I won't say it was love at first sight. Actually since he was standing over me, enjoying the view down my swimsuit top, I might even have been a tad peeved—as well as attracted. But although our time together there was less than two days, and although we lived in opposite sides of the country, love can't be corralled by time or space.

We've now been married for many, many years. (And he still looks down my swimsuit tops.)

Nowadays, I live in the west with this obnoxious, beloved husband, two children, and various animals, including three cats who rule the household. I'm a gardener, and I love nurturing small plants until they're big and healthy and productive...and ripping defenseless weeds out by the roots when I'm angry. I enjoy thunderstorms, playing Scrabble and Risk and being a soccer mom. My favorite way to spend an evening is curled up on a couch next to the master of my heart, watching the fire, reading, and...well...if you're reading this book, you obviously know what else happens in front of fires.

Find more about Cherise on her Web site at http://cherisesinclair.com.

Loose Id® Titles by Cherise Sinclair

Available in digital format and print from your favorite retailer

Master of the Abyss
Master of the Mountain
The Dom's Dungeon
The Starlight Rite

* * * * *

The MASTERS OF THE SHADOWLANDS Series
Club Shadowlands
Dark Citadel
Breaking Free
Lean on Me
Make Me, Sir

* * * * *

"Simon Says: Mine"
Part of the anthology *Doms of Dark Haven*
With Sierra Cartwright and Belinda McBride

* * * * *

"Welcome to the Dark Side"
Part of the anthology *Doms of Dark Haven 2: Western Night*
With Belinda McBride and Cherise Sinclair

Coming to print in 2012

To Command and Collar
Part of the *Masters of the Shadowlands* series
(currently available in ebook format)

CPSIA information can be obtained at www.ICGtesting.com
Printed in the USA
LVOW120423030413

327326LV00001B/185/P

9 781611 189186